# THE CAT, THE LADY AND THE LIAR

# THE CAT, THE LADY AND THE LIAR

## A CATS IN TROUBLE MYSTERY

# LEANN SWEENEY

AN OBSIDIAN MYSTERY

OBSIDIAN
Published by New American Library, a division of
Penguin Group (USA) Inc., 375 Hudson Street,
New York, New York 10014, USA
Penguin Group (Canada), 90 Eglinton Avenue East, Suite 700, Toronto,
Ontario M4P 2Y3, Canada (a division of Pearson Penguin Canada Inc.)
Penguin Books Ltd., 80 Strand, London WC2R 0RL, England
Penguin Ireland, 25 St. Stephen's Green, Dublin 2,
Ireland (a division of Penguin Books Ltd.)
Penguin Group (Australia), 250 Camberwell Road, Camberwell, Victoria 3124,
Australia (a division of Pearson Australia Group Pty. Ltd.)
Penguin Books India Pvt. Ltd., 11 Community Centre, Panchsheel Park,
New Delhi - 110 017, India
Penguin Group (NZ), 67 Apollo Drive, Rosedale, North Shore 0632,
New Zealand (a division of Pearson New Zealand Ltd.)
Penguin Books (South Africa) (Pty.) Ltd., 24 Sturdee Avenue,
Rosebank, Johannesburg 2196, South Africa

Penguin Books Ltd., Registered Offices:
80 Strand, London WC2R 0RL, England

First published by Obsidian, an imprint of New American Library,
a division of Penguin Group (USA) Inc.

ISBN 978-1-61129-563-4

*This book is for three dear friends whom I have come to love: Kay, Lorraine and Jennifer. Thanks for everything.*

# Acknowledgments

There are so many people who help bring a book to life. My family: Mike, Jillian, Jeffrey, Shawn, Allison and Maddison make my world so much better. Thank you. The Tuesday night critique group, which tells me where I've gone wrong and what I've done right, has done much to shape this story. Kay, Amy, Laura, Dean, Bob, Millie, Susie, Charlie and Isabella hold a special place in my heart. The "fur" friends who inspire me—Indigo, Agatha Christie, Archie Goodwin, Rosie, Curry and Enzo have all helped the animal characters in my books act like they should. The cozy writers who are always beside me in spirit—I am so grateful for your support. My agent, Carol, stands by me and encourages me. Thanks for that! Last of all, I thank the best editor any writer could hope for. Claire, you are forever the best of the best.

*In ancient Egypt, cats were worshipped as gods.*
*Cats have never forgotten this.*

—UNKNOWN

# One

I try not to lie. Honest. But as I drove my minivan down the curving treelined road on the Longworth Estate, I convinced myself no other tactic would work. Not with the rules that Shawn Cuddahee of the Mercy Animal Sanctuary had told me I must obey during my visit to the owner of this grand mansion.

The Greek Revival house loomed in the distance, a stunning home in Woodcrest, South Carolina, and only fifteen miles from my place in Mercy. From what little research I'd done before embarking on this mission, I learned that the property encompassed twelve acres and that the historic house—brilliant white with tall green shutters—was more than a century old and four stories high. Having never been in an honest-to-goodness antebellum mansion as anything but a tourist, I felt a flutter of excitement. If I could get over my guilt about the lies I was about to tell, I might enjoy my assignment.

Shawn rescued small animals, those that were brought to him, dumped on him or found. The cat in question, a lovely long-haired black cat named Isis (according to her tags) had been saved from near-certain death by Shawn himself. He'd found her wandering near a busy highway. The fact that he'd rescued Isis from such a dangerous situation had led me here today. Shawn had tried to meet the registered owner, a woman named Ritaestelle Longworth, but his phone calls had not been returned. He'd even made a trip to Woodcrest last week, but the person who answered the door told him that Ms. Longworth was not seeing visitors. She was "indisposed."

In the past, Shawn had returned "lost" pets to their owners, only to discover them "found" again. And again. And again. He considered such behavior abuse. He'd told me he didn't care if this "Longworth woman" had a bazillion dollars; her cat needed to be cared for properly and not put in danger by indifference or neglect.

Yes, Shawn does have anger management issues—the local animal control officer has a restraining order against him—and when his calls to Ritaestelle Longworth were not returned, Shawn became so upset that I swear all the hair under his collar was singed. That was when I stepped in and said that by hook or by crook Miss Longworth and I would meet, and I would try to find out why Isis had ended up in a shelter.

I do help out at the sanctuary whenever I can, and this assignment seemed right up my alley—a cat in trouble. Right up my alley except for the lying part. But I do take cats in trouble seriously, and I always do what I can to help them.

Since Shawn had already identified himself as a shelter owner in the messages he'd left, we decided I couldn't associate myself with him—at least at first. I would introduce myself as a journalist. I'd actually gotten a few tips for this role from my stepdaughter, Kara, who really *is* a journalist.

My goal today was to assess the living situation. Did this woman miss her cat? Since Isis had no front claws, why was she outdoors? Was this a simple mistake, or had she been abandoned? If I learned that Isis had been neglected in any way, then that would be the end of any contact with this woman. Shawn would find Isis a new home. He didn't consider it catnapping when he had difficulty contacting the owner to return a newly homeless pet.

I reached a circular drive with a lovely pond in the center and parked in front of the house. The late-afternoon summer sun shimmered on the water, and the carefully tended garden surrounding the pond took my breath away. The flowers were a wonderful mix of reds, purples and yellows. Though I knew the names of many of the local flowers, these blooms were like nothing I'd seen before.

I slid from behind the wheel, and the next thing that caught my eye was a restored and gleaming black carriage positioned near the side of the house. *What a stage setter,* I thought. Then I made my way between the majestic columns and up the broad steps toward double, lacquered black doors. I'd learned that this house had been built in 1844 and the Longworths sat atop the social crowd in Woodcrest, a class system typical in small Southern towns. And yet Ritaestelle, the seventy-year-old head of household, couldn't seem to take care of a cat.

That thought saddened me, and as I rang the doorbell, I used my other hand to take my phone from the pocket of my linen skirt. I pulled up the cat-cam feed and tapped a screen icon for my living room video. I saw my three cats, Syrah, Merlot and Chablis, fast asleep—two on the sofa and one on the overstuffed armchair. I realized that my heart rate had picked up—I was worried about telling tall tales—but the sight of these cats, my three best friends, calmed me instantly. I replaced my phone and waited for someone to answer the bell I'd heard chime inside.

When the door opened, a thin black man in what I could only call butler attire answered the door. I felt like I'd been transported back 150 years.

He said, "How may I help you, ma'am?"

His face was unreadable—no smile, no frown. I imagined he'd spoken those words a thousand times before. He had close-cropped silver hair, but I couldn't tell if he was sixty, seventy, perhaps even eighty? Definitely older than my forty-three years.

*Sound confident,* I told myself before I spoke. "My name is Jillian Hart. I'd like to speak with Miss Longworth, please."

"I'm sorry," he said. "Miss Longworth is indisposed. If you'd like to leave your phone number, her assistant will call you."

Since Shawn's calls had never been returned, the same thing would probably happen to me. But I smiled and said, "That doesn't exactly work for me. I'm a journalist, and I—"

"You're a reporter?" he said. "There's nothing much to report on here."

"I'm doing a piece for my magazine on the grand homes

of the South. I understand this house is seeking historical status. Is that true?" I *knew* this was true since I'd done my research, so I hoped it was my ticket inside.

He hesitated, and I quickly dug into my shoulder bag and pulled out my slim silver digital camera.

I smiled. "I've already gotten some lovely shots of this wonderful estate. May I take your picture?"

Kara had offered me this tip, and she'd been right. Cameras can truly open doors. The butler gentleman held up a hand. "Please, ma'am. Before you take any more pictures, why not step into the foyer? I'll talk to Miss Longworth's assistant. I'm sure Miss Ritaestelle would like to see her home in a magazine, but you don't want no pictures of me. She can help you better with that kinda thing."

"Thank you," I said, trying to hide my grin. One hurdle down. But how many more to go?

He stepped aside so I could enter, and the rich smell of polished wood met me at once. The foyer was smaller than I expected because a massive staircase took up most of the space. Rich honey-colored paneling graced the wall and followed the polished stairs upward. A ninety-degree left turn after the first few steps blocked my view of the rest of the stairs, but in a house with four stories, they probably made plenty of twists on the way up. Then my eyes widened in appreciation at probably the most stunning grandfather clock I'd ever seen. It stood directly in front of me and was made of black walnut burl wood with arches at the top and a large golden pendulum behind its leaded glass door.

I'd managed to keep my jaw from dropping at the sight of this foyer. On the wall to my left was a small, inlaid glass-covered table. An art deco–looking vase of clear red glass sat on the table, and an oil painting of a wagon and horse traveling on a country road hung on the wall above it.

A brocade-covered bench stood against the wall to my right, and the gentleman gestured for me to have a seat. "Let me check with Miss Preston."

I assumed she was the assistant. "Thank you so much, but I didn't get your name." I smiled.

"It's George. George Robertson.

"Thank you, Mr. Robertson."

He nodded, walked away down the splendid paneled hallway and disappeared.

What I hadn't noticed when I first arrived—perhaps because I kept marveling at this place—was that this house was seriously chilly. More than air-conditioned chilly, even for July. Maybe old-house chilly. Yes. That was what it was. Definitely drafty.

Thankful for the three-quarter-length sleeves of my jacket, I clutched my purse in my lap—the handbag that held the notebook I hoped I would be putting to good use soon. I'm not a fan of bags or dress-up, but this visit required both. Who knew that lies needed to be properly attired? But I was glad I'd taken Kara's advice when she'd emphasized that I couldn't wear capri pants and a T-shirt for this assignment. I'd been planning on a sundress, but she said that wouldn't do either. Still, I was uncomfortable in this linen suit, and the high heels were seriously tight and hurting something awful. But the outfit had probably helped get me in the door. And even if I didn't learn the information I came for, I felt privileged to simply be sitting in a house that reminded me of a museum.

I thought about kitty Isis and took out my phone to sneak a peek at the picture I'd taken of her. Since she'd had an encounter with a mud puddle after getting lost, she'd been bathed and groomed—probably by Allison, Shawn's wife. Allison is so sweet, she could convince a Bengal tiger to let her bathe him. And the tiger would enjoy every minute.

Isis's diamond-studded collar glittered, and her green eyes stared straight into the lens. My bet was that this cat had posed for plenty of pictures. I told Shawn the diamond collar was probably the best clue that Isis had not been abandoned and was simply lost. But he wasn't about to agree with me. There had to be a meet and greet with the owner. A face-to-face assessment. He'd been burned too many times.

"Miss Preston will see you now." It was Mr. Robertson. He stood at the edge of the foyer near the hallway, hands behind his back.

My heart skipped a beat at the sound of his voice. Thank goodness I was holding my phone at an angle so that he couldn't see what I was looking at. I stood and slipped the phone back into my pocket. What was I thinking pulling up that photo? I could have ruined everything, but I'd assumed I would be kept waiting as long as possible. I'd taken Mr. Robertson and Miss Preston by surprise, after all. But as my cop buddy Candace would say, never assume. *Never.*

"Follow me, please," Mr. Robertson said.

He led me down the hall past a series of closed doors—tall doors a shade darker than the paneling. We walked all the way to the end and into a two-story library that smelled of must beneath more lemon oil. No doubt the thousands of books were the source of the musty smell. But it was a nice and comforting odor—old leather and aging paper.

Behind the desk, a young woman rose. She had ginger hair a shade lighter than my own, and by her looks, I guessed she spent time in the gym. Her bare arms were toned and tan. The sleeveless coral dress she wore was belted low on her slim hips and probably cost as much as five kitty quilts—the ones I hand quilted and sold for a hundred dollars each.

Mr. Robertson said, "Miss Preston, this is Miss Jillian Hart."

The woman smiled, and in a thick Carolina accent said, "So very nice of you to call on us, Miss Hart." She looked at Mr. Robertson, her smile growing even warmer. "Thanks, George. Perhaps you could bring us iced tea? It's quite a warm day."

He nodded and backed away, closing the door after him.

Two gold velvet wing chairs faced the desk, and the woman made a sweeping gesture at them. "Please join me."

I crossed over an oval oriental rug toward her, cursing my high heels the entire way. The trip down the long hall had taken its toll, and my feet were screaming. I'd worn these shoes only once before, and I decided it had been a mistake to stuff my feet into them today.

The chair on the right offered a better view of the gardens beyond the floor-to-ceiling window, so that was where I sat. I'd been so awed by the house and now this room that I hadn't noticed the laptop computer to Miss Preston's right. Until now.

She pushed it away, folded her hands on the desk and

leaned toward me. "I don't seem to be able to find anything on the Internet about a journalist named Jillian Hart, but there is certainly a good deal about a woman by that name who takes a great interest in cats. Have you come about Isis?"

# Two

So much for lying. I attempted to feign surprise. "Isis?" I asked. But my mouth had gone dry and I realized I'd now earned the title Dumbest Fake Journalist Ever. What to do? I couldn't stick to the lie ... but perhaps I could dodge the question. "Is Miss Longworth here? I had hoped to talk to her."

"I'm sure you did." She smiled. "Have you seen Isis? Is she at that shelter where you volunteer, perhaps?"

"Seems you know a lot more about me than I do about you. What's your first name, Miss Preston?" I said. *Buy some time; hope for one brilliant idea to get out of this mess.*

"Evie. We can converse as Evie and Jillian if you'd like. I have no problem with that. Especially since you have a reputation as a kind and generous animal lover. But if you found Isis, she needs to come home."

Ah, a tiny opening to accomplish my goal. To find out if Isis *should* come home. "I don't have her." Technically not a lie. "Does Miss Longworth miss her cat?"

"Of course she does. Quit hedging. I don't imagine you want money. You're not the type. But—"

The sound of a scuffle accompanied by a muffled cry came from somewhere above us. Evie's gaze went to the ceiling, and her clasped hands clenched tighter.

"That didn't sound good," I said. "Is someone hurt ... or sick?"

"That is *none* of your business." Evie's tone had gone

frosty, and she looked as if she was hanging on to her composure by a quilting thread. She'd moved her hands to the arms of her desk chair and tilted her head, apparently trying to hear better.

"If you're needed upstairs, I can leave. We can—"

The thud that interrupted me made us both jump. We stood, but though I was frozen, Evie raced past me, muttering, "Oh no. Oh no."

Seemed I'd become invisible. But like my cats, I felt that mysterious and ominous noises must be investigated. So I gave her a few seconds and followed.

Once I was back in the foyer, I caught a glimpse of a coral blur at the top of the stairs. Before I tackled the steps, the shoes had to go. I might already have developed blisters on both heels anyway.

Cursed shoes in hand, I took the stairs two at time as quietly as possible, making that first ninety-degree turn and then climbing about ten more steps to the first landing. But when I saw several people, including Evie, at the end of the hall to my right, I stepped back onto the step so I wouldn't be spotted. Peeking past the wall, I saw a silver-haired woman in a blue chenille bathrobe sitting on the floor. Evie knelt by the woman's side, holding her hand, and an older lady in gray slacks and a white pleated shirt stood above them.

I heard the one with the slacks say, "She was trying to get downstairs."

Evie looked up at the speaker. "How did that happen, Augusta? You're supposed to stay with her."

"And when I am supposed to use the ladies'?" Augusta said.

But Evie didn't seem to be listening. She was murmuring something I couldn't make out to the woman on the floor—the woman I recognized from photos I'd seen on the Internet: Ritaestelle Longworth.

"I'm fine, Evie. But I'm not deaf. I heard the doorbell, heard George talking to someone in the foyer. I want to go downstairs and—" She turned her gaze from Evie and looked straight at me.

I ducked back behind the wall, but too late.

"There she is," I heard Miss Longworth say.

Should I run down the stairs? Get the heck out of here? But then I remembered that my handbag was sitting on the floor next to that yellow velvet chair. I stepped out from hiding. "Yes. I came to talk to you, Miss Longworth. But first, are you okay?"

She squinted and pointed at me. "I know you. Where do I know you from?"

"I don't think you know me. Can I help them get you on your feet?" I started down the hall toward them.

But Evie put up the traffic-cop signal for stop. "You need to turn around and go back downstairs."

Miss Longworth was struggling to rise, and Augusta and Evie turned their attention to her.

Bad decisions, I'm told, make for good stories. But I had the feeling this bad decision wouldn't sound like a good story to Shawn. I'd failed at this assignment and had been caught snooping around where I shouldn't have been. Time to leave while everyone was occupied. I hurried down the stairs and was met at the bottom by Mr. Robertson. A silver tray with two glasses of iced tea sat on a small telephone table in the hallway.

George was holding my handbag. "You need this, ma'am?"

"Yes, thanks." I was breathless from hurrying down the steep stairs.

"I suggest you go quick. I'm guessing Miss Preston isn't too pleased about now." He stepped aside and let me pass.

"Thanks, Mr. Robertson," I said.

He nodded solemnly, but I caught a twinkle in his eye as I left the house with my shoes in one hand and my purse in the other.

Minivans aren't exactly the fastest vehicles, so my get-away wasn't all that quick. Once I made it out of the long driveway and onto the county road, I hit fifty-five miles an hour, my max. My heart was still pounding, and I vowed never to do anything like that again. Shawn would have to deal with this problem himself. Maybe he'd be visiting Miss Longworth in the hospital. I mean, her hip or her leg could have been broken after that fall.

I heard the sound of a siren and checked the rearview mirror. Dark car with flashing lights on the dash. Not your regular squad car. Must be an unmarked. Up ahead I saw a speed limit sign: forty-five. *Wouldn't you know?* I had no reason to be speeding in the first place. It wasn't like anyone at the house would get in their car and chase me.

As I pulled over, I realized I'd been running from the lies I'd told. It was impossible to run from yourself, of course, and now my pocketbook would take a hit. Perhaps the officer would cut me a break.

I watched in the side mirror as a woman in a navy suit—definitely not your usual police uniform—got out of the police car. She was tall and broad shouldered, with steel gray hair curled tightly to her head. I noted she wasn't carrying the typical police "speeding ticket" pad. But I did see a gold badge glint on her lapel.

I rolled down my window and she offered me a thin smile. Her eyes said it all: *You are in trouble.*

But the first words out of her mouth weren't, "Do you know how fast you were going?" as I'd expected. Instead, she said, "Jillian Hart?"

"Uh, yes, ma'am." She was definitely a *ma'am.*

"I understand you were visiting the Longworth Estate. Is that correct?"

The word *ye-es* came out as two syllables, conveying my confusion. Was telling a small lie and sneaking up the stairs cause for an arrest in Woodcrest? But someone in that house—Evie Preston, no doubt—had wasted no time calling the police.

The woman said, "I don't know your business in coming to town, Ms. Hart, but I suggest you stay away from Miss Longworth." Her tone was stern, her pearl gray eyes filled with a lot more than a suggestion.

"Um, Officer— Sorry. I didn't get your name." Maybe I overstepped in coming here, but I hadn't done anything to be warned away, and in a manner that made it seem as if she was reading from an old *Bonanza* script.

"It's Chief. Police Chief Shelton. And they don't want you coming round to the house. Is that clear?" she said.

"Clear as can be. But who are *they*?" I said.

"I don't need to tell you that," she said tersely. "I advise you to keep away from the estate and out of Woodcrest."

"I'm not trying to cause trouble," I said, using my best

conciliatory tone. But this woman was definitely getting under my skin. All I cared about was a cat who either needed to go back home or needed to be sent to a place where she would be loved and protected. Seemed like such a simple task. But apparently not.

Chief Shelton's eyes softened. "I never said you were causing trouble. Miss Longworth is not strong enough to be bothered by strangers right now. Can you understand that?"

"Oh, you're her friend, then." That had to be the explanation for her pulling me over to give me this message in person. "I didn't intend to bother her. It's just that—"

"Good. Then we're clear." She started to walk away but stopped and looked at me again. "No ticket this time, but watch your speed, Ms. Hart."

She waited for me to pull out onto the highway and then followed me to the sign that stated, MERCY—3 MILES. I watched in my mirror as she made a U-turn and drove back the way she'd come—going a lot faster than the posted speed limit.

# Three

On my drive through town toward my house on Mercy Lake, I decided that Shawn wouldn't be thrilled with what had happened inside the Longworth house, or what had happened outside on the way home. I'd failed to fool anyone, I'd snuck around and got caught and I'd discovered that Ritaestelle Longworth wasn't well. Feeling a little down about all this, I decided I needed time with my three best friends before I talked to him.

As for the nature of Ritaestelle's problems, well ... that bothered me. She'd thought she recognized me, but I'd never laid eyes on the woman before. Was she confused? Did she have Alzheimer's? Those possibilities combined with the way the assistant reacted to me might lead Shawn to conclude that Ritaestelle wasn't equipped to care for her cat. But from what the assistant said, they clearly wanted Isis back.

And in my opinion, it wasn't clear that she shouldn't get her cat back. With plenty of hired help hanging around that mansion, how hard could it be to make sure one black cat got the attention she required? Added to that, Ritaestelle might be missing Isis this minute. A beloved pet can help the healing process.

The minute I disengaged the alarm at my back door and walked inside my house, I was reminded of this. Three gorgeous friends sat waiting, Syrah and Merlot on the floor, and Chablis stretched out on the granite countertop.

I knelt to give the two boys on the floor a scratch on the head, and Chablis jumped down for her share of affection a second later. I felt the tension in my shoulders ease almost immediately.

"What do I do, kids?" I said.

Merlot answered with a deep trill of a meow.

"Should I tell Shawn what happened or think of another way to see Miss Ritaestelle Longworth?"

Syrah cocked his head and twitched his ears, while Chablis lay at my feet and rolled onto her back for a tummy scratch. I obliged her.

The sight of them, plus the fact that Isis the cat had both a name tag and a microchip, convinced me that Ritaestelle cared about her cat and shouldn't suffer from missing her. Maybe I should try to talk to her again before I reported back to Shawn. Isis's safety had obviously been important at some point. But how could I get back inside that house? I'd burned several bridges today already. Perhaps I had no choice but to come clean to Shawn.

A familiar *rappity-rap-rap* on the back door that could belong only to my friend Deputy Candace Carson of the Mercy PD made me rise. Candace is in her twenties, while I am in my forties, but she's still my best friend. Maybe she could help.

She opened the door before I could get there and when she came inside said, "What have I said about keeping your door locked?"

I sighed. "I know. I get so anxious to greet my fur friends that—"

"And see what they've been up to?" She glanced past my left shoulder.

I turned and now saw what I had missed earlier. On the floor next to the breakfast bar that separates my kitchen and living room were buttons. Buttons everywhere. Just beyond lay my overturned button box.

I whirled, ready to confront my cats, but they had disappeared. Who said cats don't know when they've done something wrong?

"Darn," I said. "I'll be finding buttons for months. Under tables, stuffed in sofa cushions, behind the toilet. Sheesh."

I went over and picked up the small wooden box and saw teeth marks that had to belong to Merlot. He weighed twenty pounds, so his bite was definitely recognizable. But I was sure the other two had a paw in this mess, too.

Candace knelt next to me and helped retrieve buttons, saying, "What's with these, anyway?"

"I'm making an appliquéd Christmas quilt for Kara that incorporates all kinds of buttons in the design," I said.

"Christmas in July?" Candace held a square turquoise button and stared at it with what could only be interpreted as confusion. "And what's with this square one?"

"Cute, huh? You hardly ever see square buttons. Anyway, I always start early making gifts since orders for lots of cat quilts come in from now until a week before Christmas."

"Oh, I forgot. You plan ahead." She laughed. She wasn't wearing her uniform, and her ash blond hair hung loose on her shoulders. When Candace was on the job, she never wore her hair down. She usually braided it and wrapped the braid tightly at the nape of her neck.

"Day off?" I asked.

"I started my vacation today. One week without listening to Morris complain is like a trip to Disney World for me," she said.

Deputy Morris Ebeling, her sixtysomething partner, did need to put away his badge soon. He was a nice guy once you got beyond the grumpy facade.

After the last of the buttons we could find were back in the box, I stood, holding the box closer to again inspect the damage Merlot had done.

"You're smiling," Candace said. "Why?"

"This plain old box belonged to my grandmother, the woman who first taught me to quilt. But these teeth marks?" I looked at her. "I like them."

Candace's eyebrows came together in confusion. "Huh?"

"I have no idea where all the other dings and knicks on the box came from. Like this one." I traced one long scratch along the side with my finger. "But now it has a flaw from my little family, too."

"Okay, Miss Glass Half Full. And speaking of glasses, got any sweet tea?" She was already at the refrigerator and opened the door. "Ah, yes." She removed the pitcher and took two glasses from the cupboard above the dishwasher.

"You staying in town on your vacation?" I set the button box on the counter.

"Yes. I'm painting my mom's bedroom, among other things." She handed me my tea.

We both went into the living room and sat on the sofa.

"What fun," I said. "Or do you enjoy fumes and spills and drop cloths as much as you enjoy collecting evidence?"

Candace grinned. "I do. And she's got a leaky faucet that could use some attention, too."

"I know who to call next time I need help with home repairs. But now, maybe you can help me with something outside that realm. I've been volunteering more at the sanctuary and—"

"No. I cannot take a cat, or a litter of kittens or a rambunctious Lab that someone couldn't convince to even walk on a leash or—"

"It's not that. Shawn found this black cat named Isis." I went on to explain about the cat, her owner and what had transpired today.

I could tell Candace was becoming more and more interested as the story went on. When I was finished she said, "You were inside the Longworth house? Oh my god. Tell me what it was like. A palace, right? Like that palace the Queen of England lives in?"

"You knew about this estate?" I said.

Her eyes sparkled with interest, and she was leaning toward me. "Everyone knows about it. But hardly anyone from Mercy has been inside. Except for Ed. And you know Ed. He's not much for talking."

Ed Duffy owns Ed's Swap Shop—the business home of Mercy's biggest and kindest hoarder. His little house-turned-into-a-store is filled with Mercy's discards—afghans to xylophones. I filed Ed's connection to Miss Longworth for future reference.

I said, "What's Ed's connection to that house?"

"I heard he knew the woman—Miss Longworth," Candace said. "They were friends. But that's about all I know."

"Aside from this great tidbit about Ed—thanks for that—do you know anything else about Ritaestelle Longworth?"

"Just what goes around town, that's all," she said.

"That would be plenty, then. Tell me about her."

But I was distracted by Syrah's paw peeking out from behind the side of the sofa. Then his entire body swooped out, and he came around the couch, landing on his back. His paw was stabbing at something under the couch, and out popped a button. It slid across the hardwood, but before he could get to his prize, Chablis pounced from her hiding place behind my late husband's leather recliner. She batted the button, and Merlot joined in the game. This would be going on for days. Nope, I wouldn't get all my buttons back soon.

Meanwhile, Candace had been talking, and I hadn't heard a word. "Sorry. I missed what you said."

"I was saying that I thought the Longworth house would be like a palace inside because Miss Longworth is considered the queen of Woodcrest," she said.

"Shawn told me that she was socially prominent, but he in no way prepared me for what I saw. That estate is magnificent. But back to my problem. If I return after the police chief has warned me to stay away, could I be arrested for trespassing?"

"You wouldn't sneak in her window or break into her house if your cat's life depended on it, much less your own. I say, get yourself an invitation, and Chief Shelton can't do a thing about it. That police chief's something else, by the way. Got a reputation as hard-core. She doesn't put up with anything in her town. Bet she'd decide what time everyone could sneeze if the town council gave her the power."

"Uh-oh. Maybe I should leave this for Shawn to figure out," I said. "I don't want to make people angry."

"I'm not saying she's a bad person," Candace said. "From what I hear, she's a good cop. Just don't let her intimidate you. I know you want to reunite that lady with her cat."

"No matter what I think, Shawn will have to approve Isis's return to the Longworth Estate, and I haven't even talked to the woman—something Shawn insisted I should do. So how do I get that invitation to return? Miss Longworth's surrounded by all these staff people, and besides, I pretty much ran out the door with my tail between my legs."

"I'm sure you can get back inside. Someone as sweet and

nice as you just has to say the right words." She smiled—a knowing smile that I couldn't figure out.

"I give. What are those words?" I said.

"Ed Duffy sent me."

# Four

After Candace left for the paint store, I decided to call my friend Tom Stewart. He's a former cop and now a security expert and private investigator. Kara works for him and has gotten pretty darn good at installing alarms and surveillance cameras with his help, something that I'd never thought she'd do.

Cats jumped up to surround me on the sofa when I sat down and pulled my phone from my skirt pocket. I stroked Chablis, thinking about how much had changed in the last year, my relationship with Tom being one of those things. What does a forty-plus woman call the man she's romantically involved with? *Boyfriend* didn't sound right, and *significant other* was way too strong. We dated and shared lots of kisses and hugs. But I wasn't ready for more than that, and Tom respected my "let's take this slow" attitude.

My husband, John, who died of a heart attack two years ago, had been the love of my life, and I still missed him so much. But I cared about Tom and was beginning to feel comfortable with our daily talks on the phone and weekends spent at the movies or out to dinner.

This call, however, wasn't just to chat. See, Tom's mother, Karen, *was* a significant other to the very Ed Duffy I needed to talk to. I speed-dialed Tom's cell phone.

"Hey, Jilly," he said when he answered.

"Hi, there. I have a question."

"You want to marry me? Wow. But a proposal over the phone? Not how I dreamed this would happen," he said.

I laughed. "Me either. Actually, my question has to do with our friendly hoarder, Ed. Do you know anything about his relationship with a wealthy woman named Rita-estelle Longworth?"

He hesitated for a few seconds, then said, "That old lady from Woodcrest who lives in the big house? Ed *knows* her?"

"Guess that answers my question," I said.

"You don't expect to ask me about her and Ed and not tell me why. What's going on?"

I explained about my assignment to find out if Isis should be returned home and how I'd screwed things up this morning.

"You're way too hard on yourself. You had a setback, that's all. Want me to pick you up and we'll head to Ed's shop? See what we can pry out of him?" Tom said.

"Really? You'll help me with this?" I said.

"Sure. Talking with Ed at the shop is best because he's more likely to open up if my mom's not around. Could be he just collected junk from the Longworth basement once, but if Candace knew something was up between them, I'm betting there's more to learn."

"What time will you be here?" I said.

"Had lunch? 'Cause I haven't."

"Lunch will ready in five minutes," I said.

After we'd finished chicken-salad sandwiches, fruit and the iced lattes Tom had brought from Belle's Beans, we headed to the other side of town in Tom's work van. He had a consultation with a woman who wanted a security system installed, so after we talked to Ed, he planned to drop me off at home and head straight to her house.

Once we arrived at the shop, Tom held my hand as we maneuvered our way through the birdbaths, bicycles, lawn furniture, tires and other numerous items lying in the front yard of Ed's Swap Shop. A small bell tinkled when we entered, and Tom immediately called out Ed's name.

"Be right with ya," Ed called from one of the back rooms.

I spotted a washstand in a corner, and since I am a sucker for antiques, I made my away around a trunk of dolls and a basket full of old VCR tapes—all children's tapes as far as

I could tell. Times sure have changed in a hurry. How long had the VCR lasted? A decade? Fifteen years?

Tom was drawn to a table filled with tools, while I admired the washstand. We were both examining our favorite items when Ed appeared about two minutes later.

"Well, hey there. If it ain't my two favorite people—after your mother, that is, Tom." Ed wore his usual train conductor–type overalls, and his gray beard fell below his chin and was more scraggly than it had been when I'd last seen him.

He and Tom shook hands, both smiling broadly, and then Ed offered his favorite phrase. "What can I do ya? I saw you eyein' those tools. Nice, huh?"

"They are, but if I buy another tool from you, I might have to open Tom's Used Tool Shop. And that would be major competition for you."

"Oh, you got nothin' on me. Just try it and we'll see what happens." Ed laughed and looked at me. "Miss Jillian. I don't see enough of you."

I smiled. "Your shop is too tempting. I love that washstand, but I don't know where I'd put it."

"You love it? Then it's yours," he said. "Free, of course."

"Wait a minute," Tom said. "I pay for everything I get here."

"Well, you ain't pretty." Ed shared his wonderful broad grin, the charming one he often surprised me with.

"Thanks, Ed," I said. "But I need something from you that money can't buy."

"Uh-oh. You gettin' yourself into trouble again, Miss Jillian?" Ed said.

"Me? No," I said. "I'm helping Shawn with a little problem, and I heard you might have some info that could be useful. This concerns Ritaestelle Longworth."

Ed pursed his lips and looked at the floor. The silence that ensued made me want to look at the floor myself. How could simple body language create tension so quickly?

"You know her, right?" Tom said.

When Ed looked up and faced Tom, his eyes had gone stone-cold. "Yeah. What of it?"

"I—I tried to visit her." My stomach felt tight with apprehension. Ed was always affable and kind, but the look in his eyes was anything but. "They wouldn't let me talk to her. Her staff, I mean. Problem is, I sensed something was wrong with her."

"That's assumin' something was ever right with the woman," Ed said.

"What does that mean?" Tom asked.

Ed went behind the long counter, knelt down and came up holding a rifle.

I reached for Tom's hand, and he gripped my frigid fingers. But I let out the breath I'd been withholding when Ed placed the gun on the counter and started taking the rifle apart.

"Old guy brought this in this mornin', Tom. You need yourself a nice little deer rifle?" Ed's even tone had returned.

"You're changing the subject. I thought you liked Jillian and would want to help her out," Tom said.

He continued with his task and took several seconds before saying, "I like her just fine. But all's I got is advice." He leveled a stare at me. "Stay out of that town. Nothin' but trouble there."

Tom's direct questions didn't seem to be working too well, so maybe I could get Ed to talk with a gentler approach. "You seem upset, and I'm sorry if I've brought that on."

"You asked for my help, and that advice is all I got. Trouble's trouble, and that's what you'll find around every corner in Woodcrest," he said. "The Longworths were never a happy bunch, and I expect nothin's changed."

"I was so impressed by the grounds and the house. I take it you've been there?" I said.

"Been there. Yup." He had the rifle apart and was examining the barrel.

Tom said, "So what do—"

I squeezed his hand hard and interrupted with, "The house looks old, but it seems to be in fine shape. Ever collect anything from the place?"

Ed sighed. "You ain't gonna quit, are you, Miss Jillian?"

"No," I said. "I want to help a cat who needs a safe home—and you know how I am when it comes to cats."

"Then I think we should sit down and have some tea. But that don't mean I know anything that's gonna help you." He walked from behind the counter and into the hallway that led to the back of the house, gesturing for us to follow.

The tiny kitchen was as tidy and organized as Karen and Ed's cute little home, in stark contrast to the last time I'd seen this section of the shop. Just a few months ago the room had been overflowing with old microwaves, small appliances and kitchen utensils. But now there was even space for a little round table and two chairs in the far corner. This makeover had to have been Karen's doing.

The refrigerator was ancient—avocado green does give away an appliance's age—but I knew that Ed could fix just about anything and that it had probably been a project. Ed brought a bentwood chair from another room, and Tom set it so that he could sit on the chair and still face the entrance to the kitchen.

Soon we were all sitting around the table, iced tea in front of us.

"Some things a cop never lets go of, even after he's supposed to be done with the job," Tom said. "I don't like anyone sneaking up on me."

"You and your mother do fall a little short in the trust department." No smile. Ed's usual good humor had definitely not returned.

"What can you tell me about Miss Longworth?" I said.

"First off," Ed said, "you need to fill me in on Shawn's problem. Does this have to do with Ritaestelle's cats?"

I raised my eyebrows in surprise. "She has more than one?"

"Did way back when. You gonna tell me what's what?" he said.

"Sure." I explained for the third time today about my visit to the Longworth estate.

Ed shook his head, his lips twisted into one of those "I knew it" puckers. "I always told her she had too many folks hoverin' around. Did she listen? No. That's one hard-headed female."

"Is there something wrong with her . . . well . . . up here?" I tapped my temple.

Ed threw back his head and laughed, surprising me so much that I nearly fell off my rather unstable chair. The man could change moods quicker than my cats could trap a moth.

He said, "When I knew her, there wasn't much wrong with her except her *I* disease."

"She has something wrong with her eyes?" Tom asked.

"No, Tom." Ed poked his chest with his index finger. "*I* disease. As in *I want things to go like this* and *I am sure you'll listen since I am the one in charge.*"

"Oh," I said. "Money can do that to you, I guess."

"Don't get me wrong. She's a fine, upstandin' lady. Big-hearted, too. But I'm not comfortable around all that silver and polished wood." He swigged his tea and then set the glass down hard. "What else you wanna know about her?"

"Have you seen her recently?" I said. "I mean, she might have dementia or something, and maybe her cat would be better off in a new home."

"She calls me up regular every Christmas." Ed blinked several times, and his next words seemed forced. "Always says, 'How you doing, Ed? I miss you, Ed.' And that's what happened this past year. Nothin' wrong that I could tell."

I don't know what made me ask the next question. Just intuition, I suppose. "Were you in love with her?"

A flush rose from Ed's neck up to his face, producing two red circles on his cheeks right above his beard. "Fell head over heels for that woman, I did." He let out a *humph*. "Me and plenty of others."

# Five

Ed, still red-faced with embarrassment, turned to Tom. "But your mother's the only one for me now."

Tom held his hands out, palms facing Ed. "Hey. We all have stuff in our past. Some of it's good, some of it's bad and most of it's forgotten."

Ed nodded in agreement. "But Karen doesn't need to hear about this. See, I've never mentioned Rita. I always called her plain Rita. Made a very complicated woman seem simpler, I always said."

"I can safely say Ritaestelle has problems," I said. "Good example—you mentioned she loved her cats. And yet Shawn found her Isis wandering outside."

"That's pretty darn puzzlin'. And something else bothers me about what you told me. Rita always answered the door herself, so her not bein' right there to see why you came is strange. She wanted to know everything. Never had hired help screenin' folks at the door even though she could afford to. George was always there behind, mind you. But I mean, the kitchen in that house probably has five rooms and ten folks runnin' around cleaning the chicken for dinner. Yup, the Rita I knew would greet a guest herself."

Despite his love for Tom's mother, the concern in Ed's voice told me that Ritaestelle's predicament bothered him.

"Got any suggestions as to how I can reach her?" I said. "Even if she is beginning to suffer from Alzheimer's or is perhaps on a medication that makes her confused—"

"Why do you keep sayin' she's losin' it? Six months ago she was fine." I heard a tinge of anger in Ed's tone.

"Because she said she thought she knew who I was, I guess. Plus that wild look in her eyes," I said. *Just a feeling,* I added to myself. Maybe Ed was right and I was the one a little off about this.

"If there's anything wrong with Rita, the town surely knows," he said. "Sit around at one of them fancy-schmancy outdoor cafés on Broad Street. Or go to that park in the center of town. Strike up a conversation. You'll find out plenty."

"I would, but the chief of police pulled me over on the way out of Woodcrest." I recounted my interaction with Chief Shelton.

"Nancy Shelton is still bein' a sourpuss, huh?" Ed said.

"You know her, too?" I said.

He sighed heavily and rested both hands on the table. "Here's the deal. I'm *from* Woodcrest. Wrong side of the tracks, but I was born there. We, meaning me, Rita, Nancy, Rita's cousins and a bunch of others, all went to the same school. We all graduated within two or three years of each other. Rita went right through every grade with me, even though her parents kept tryin' to send her to a place for rich kids. She wanted to be with her friends, and she always got her way."

I said, "When did you move to Mercy?" Wrong question, I knew immediately.

Ed stared down at the floor, two fingers rubbing circles on the table. "Why do you need to know about me? I got nothin' to do with that place or that woman anymore."

His slumped shoulders and his downcast gaze made him seem so much older. What was distressing Ed so much? Whatever it was, I felt awful for making him feel so uncomfortable.

I leaned toward him and gently said, "I don't want to invade your privacy, Ed. This is about Ritaestelle, not you. But I—I think we need her story. Something is wrong in that house. I felt it. Here." I tapped my abdomen with my fist.

"Maybe so, but I'm about wore out with all this talkin'," he said. "I got things to do." His tight jaw and curt tone told me he was shutting down.

Tom saw this, too, because he stood abruptly. "We understand, don't we, Jilly?"

"Certainly." I reached across and placed my hand over Ed's. "I'm sorry if I upset you." The contented Ed I knew had disappeared before my eyes. This sadness and anger I'd stirred up made me feel guilty, but I couldn't help but be curious, too. What had happened between Ed and Rita-estelle? Bad breakup? Unrequited love?

Ed withdrew his hand. "Who says I'm upset?" He gathered our tea glasses and carried them to the small sink.

"Come on," Tom whispered through his teeth. He nodded toward the door.

"Guess we should go," I said.

Tom and I walked toward the kitchen entrance. Ed was rinsing the glasses in the sink and didn't turn as we were walking out. But he did say, "You want to avoid Nancy, I say go in disguise. That hall closet's full of stuff that could make you look like a different person."

"Okay," I said tentatively.

Tom held my elbow and led me out the kitchen door and toward the closet, whispering, "Let's do what he says."

He opened the closet door, and several shoe boxes fell from the top shelf, spilling their contents at our feet. Obviously Karen's touch was missing here.

I knelt and gathered up costume jewelry and fancy hair ornaments. Since Tom is over six feet tall, he made room on the shelf for the boxes.

I whispered, "Do I honestly have to play dress-up to talk to the people in that town?" I glanced up at the musty-smelling dresses and suits crammed in the closet.

"We'll take a few things to humor Ed, okay?" Tom said softly. "I've never seen him this bothered by anything, but apparently he not only has shoe boxes and trunks. He has a Pandora's box, too."

"You're right." I pulled out a cotton print dress hiding between two wool jackets. "How's this?" I held it up in front of me.

But Tom had started digging around in a plastic container on the closet floor. He whipped out a blond wig. "Or this?"

"It's July, if you haven't noticed. I'll end up with blisters on my scalp from the heat if I wear that."

"I'm sure Chief Shelton will remember your hair . . .

your face." He ran a finger along my jawline. "Hard not to notice you." He held the wig out.

I took it and held it to my nose. "Smells like a combination of my grandmother's Jean Naté and talcum powder." I sighed. "That's what I get for being a redhead. People remember the hair. We'll take the dress and the wig—but only to make Ed happy. A dye job might be easier than wearing this." I shook the wig, expecting a baby powder cloud to appear around the thing.

Tom fixed several strands of hair behind my ear. "Don't you dare think about changing anything." He pulled me to him and kissed me.

The wig—or Tom—had won.

After Tom dropped me off at home with my not-so-fancy dress and my ugly wig, three very interested cats followed on my heels as I took these prize items to my bedroom. Maybe if I left the fake hair within reach of prying paws, I'd have a good excuse to stick to sunglasses as my only disguise. I couldn't wear a wig that resembled something that looked like it had been run over by a lawnmower. That was what this fake hair would look like if my three felines had their way with it.

I went to the master bathroom and set the wig down. I tried to pull my too-short hair away from my face. I was hoping I could hide my hair under a giant sun hat. But a big hat on a stranger in a small town like Woodcrest was almost as memorable as red hair. And after several tries with bobby pins and clips, I couldn't make my hair obey anyway.

Tomorrow, Tom and I planned to visit Woodcrest and at least one of those "fancy-schmancy" cafés Ed had mentioned. I needed to see if I could tolerate this silly disguise.

But Syrah had jumped up on the marble vanity, and before I could stop him, he swiped the blond tresses down to his awaiting partners in crime, Merlot and Chablis. This wig was apparently the best thing I'd brought home in a long time.

I snatched up my future disguise and shook a finger at the cats. "You'll get your chance, but not right now, friends."

I stretched the wig onto my head and stared at myself in horror. I looked way too much like Lydia Monk, the deputy county coroner who is obsessed with Tom. And who definitely had it in for me now that she knew Tom and I were getting close. I ripped the wig off and shook my head at an attempt to restore my layered haircut. But I was still resigned to wearing it tomorrow. I tucked it away on the top shelf of my closet. I had just closed the door, much to the chagrin of my three amigos, when I heard the doorbell.

My kitties didn't follow me as I hurried to answer the door. The challenge of a closed closet door and what lay behind was far too important to be spoiled by a human visit.

Once I got to the foyer, I checked the peephole and saw Shawn's face. Despite the distortion, I could tell he was unhappy. I took a deep breath. Even though I wanted another chance to talk to Miss Longworth, I felt as if I had to tell him about my failure, and now was as good a time as any.

When I opened the door, I was surprised to see he wasn't alone. He came bearing a pet carrier. And from the wails emanating from that crate, I knew it held a cat.

After he came inside, he set the carrier down in the foyer and, hands on hips, said, "You gotta help me with this . . . this . . . *diva*."

I knelt and peeked through the crate's door. He'd brought Isis. I offered, "Hi, sweetie," and her reply was a wide-mouthed hiss.

I stood. "Sure. What can I do?"

"She can go back home, right? Your plan worked and you talked with the Longworth woman?"

"Um . . . why don't we go into the living room and chat? You look like you could use some sweet tea." Before he could protest—because Shawn likes to protest about anything—I started walking through the foyer. "Just leave her where she is. She'll be fine."

"But I don't have time—"

I turned and gestured for him to follow me. "Yes, you do. You look like you could use a break. Besides, we need to talk."

He reluctantly followed, saying, "I don't like the sound of this."

*And your instincts would be correct,* I thought.

Once we were settled in the living room with our tea—me on John's old leather recliner and Shawn on the sofa—I explained yet again what had happened today.

When I finished, Shawn closed his eyes and pressed two

freckled fingers and a thumb on his forehead and massaged the area between his sun-bleached eyebrows. We're both redheads, but he'd retained far more freckles than I, and his hair was almost the color of persimmons.

He said, "You've done enough."

"No," I said, so forcefully I surprised myself. "I don't want to give up. Not yet."

Shawn pointed in the direction of the foyer. "That is the most spoiled, arrogant cat I've ever had the displeasure to encounter. She won't eat regular cat kibble, she hisses and swats at everyone who tries to get near her and she's . . . she's . . . too full of herself. You should see her walk around my kennel like she owns the place. I've had her for a week, and she's wearing on my nerves."

I didn't speak for several seconds. "Shawn, are you feeling okay? Because I have never heard you talk that way about an animal before." Shawn was often impatient with humans, but never with the animals he rescued and cared for.

He looked at his scuffed-up tennis shoes. "Allison said the same thing. I can't keep her around anymore—the cat, not Allison. She just gets under my skin. And we can't let her roam around the sanctuary anymore. She nearly caught Snug."

Snug was Shawn and Allison's wonderful African gray parrot. "Isis is probably scared. And being aggressive is her way of showing it," I said.

Shawn pursed his lips, shook his head in disagreement. "She was scared the day I picked her up on the side of the highway. Scared for maybe a day or two after that, but now? Oh, she's not scared of anything. And poor Allison has the teeth marks on her arms to prove it. Me? I wear my leather gloves up to my elbows when I get near her."

"You expected me to take her back to the Longworth house, I assume," I said. "Because you know that putting her up for adoption might not be the best idea. She might be returned to you within a few days."

Shawn slumped back on the sofa, raised his eyes to the ceiling. "I was hoping to hear you say the cat was ready to go home. But from what you've told me, that Longworth woman isn't fit to care for her either."

He was always decisive, and yes, opinionated, so his waffling behavior was confusing at first. But then I decided I understood. "You have a set way of handling these situations, want to do right by your animals, but this particular cat is different. Am I right?"

Shawn sighed and picked up his tea, took a long drink. "Certain pets, particularly cats, need the right fit with a family. And you're right. Isis will be hard to place."

"Give me more time, then," I said. "If I can talk to Miss Longworth, get a feel for—"

The most god-awful screech came from the foyer. I stood and started in that direction, worried something was terribly wrong with Isis.

But Shawn grabbed my arm and stopped me before I could get by him. "Don't give her any attention for that outburst. There's nothing wrong with her."

"She sounds like she's mortally wounded." I craned my neck, trying to see into the foyer.

"Yeah. The drama queen has spoken. Your cats are probably out there sniffing around her crate, and she doesn't like it. She doesn't like much of anything."

I sat back down. "Maybe she simply wants to go home, Shawn. Give me more time? Please?"

"Oh, I'll give you as long as you want," he said. "If you keep her."

# Six

The minute I told Shawn that I'd gladly keep Isis for the time being, he left my house so fast I wondered if I'd dreamed the whole visit. But Isis promptly yowled and reminded me this was all quite real. My three cats sat around her crate, their ears twitching at the whines and growls coming from our new visitor.

I'd fostered cats before, and most of the time, my three are fairly easygoing with the meet and greet. Sometimes there's hissing and stalking, but since my cats were rescued from a shelter after Hurricane Katrina, that experience made them fairly gracious hosts to other animals. But I had the feeling that might not be the case this time.

The next step in what was becoming a very long day was spent settling Isis in her new basement home. I had a guest bedroom there. My three cats followed in excited anticipation when I carried her down. They seemed eager for me to allow this noisy feline out of her crate. But my gut told me I should wait. Neither Isis nor I needed any added stress today.

I set her up with a clean litter box, fresh water and the fanciest cat food I could find—a small can of grilled salmon. I didn't let her out of the carrier until I'd closed out my three curious friends. I heard Merlot mewing in protest after I shut the door, but this was how it had to be for now. I sat on the floor near the crate and set Isis free.

She sauntered out and slipped by, totally ignoring me. After an inspection of the room, the litter box and the food, she came back my way. Her tail twitched in irritation after she sat down in front of me. She stared up, emerald green eyes narrowed. Her gaze didn't waver from my face.

What did she expect from me? I was beginning to think that curtseying might be the answer. I returned her stare, and we sat like that for about twenty seconds.

Isis gave in first. I considered that a good sign. Maybe she realized I was top cat in this house. Then she stood and walked regally back to the corner she'd inspected earlier. I'd lined a cat bed with one of my little quilts. She stepped in, sat and began to groom herself. She was done with me.

I opened the door about a foot and slipped through, making sure not to allow Chablis and Merlot inside. Syrah, who I assumed was bored with this nonsense, was nowhere to be seen. I'd no sooner made it upstairs to the kitchen when my stepdaughter, Kara, used her key to come in through the back door.

"Hi, Jillian." She smiled and set down her purse on the small table by the door.

"Hey there," I said. "I'm so glad you showed up looking all young and peppy. I need some of what you've got going on." I gave her hug.

Her skin felt warm, and a bit of late-afternoon heat had sneaked in the door and still lingered. Her mahogany-colored hair was fastened with an elastic band, and the long ponytail hung over one shoulder. The recent addition of auburn highlights made her brown eyes seem more lively and inquisitive than ever. Or maybe she was simply happier these last few months. Her move from Houston to Mercy seemed to be agreeing with her. Small-town life, even for a dedicated city girl like Kara, was apparently helping her cope better with losing her dad. We both missed John, but he would have wanted to see her exactly like this: radiant and full of life.

Syrah came around the kitchen island and rubbed his head against Kara's calf. She reached down and scratched his head. He began to purr loudly enough to almost drown out the serious squalls coming from the basement.

Kara wrinkled her nose and glanced toward the basement door. "That doesn't sound like one of your cats. Or is somebody sick?"

"Maybe sick and tired of hearing that noise. Let's get farther away from the screeching and I'll explain."

She opened the refrigerator and took out the tea pitcher. "I need a fix first. This stuff is addicting, you know. Want some?"

I nodded and retrieved the glasses from the living room. I set Shawn's in the sink and placed mine on the counter so she could pour my tea.

She arched her eyebrows and nodded at the sink. "Someone else was loving your sweet tea today?"

"Shawn. He delivered the houseguest. One who thinks she's more special than your ordinary cat, I might add. She is the goddess Isis, and as you've heard, she's having a regular hissy fit—pun intended."

"Isis? The cat that started this whole cloak-and-dagger-pretend-Jillian's-a-journalist thing?" Kara finished pouring the tea, and with Syrah on my heels, we walked into the living room.

"That's the one. Seems there's no room at Shawn's inn for a spoiled-rotten rescue," I said. "And I'm betting that's a first for him. Though Shawn can be intolerant of humans, he usually has endless patience with animals. Until now."

John's recliner was Kara's favorite spot whenever she visited, and she sank into the aging leather cushions. She drew up her legs, her knees touching one arm of the chair. "My kittens are definitely spoiled rotten. Is that noise coming from your basement something I might have to contend with in the future?"

Kara's two kittens were four months old now. They'd been born to a rescue Shawn had me foster—a loving, sweet cat and the antithesis of Isis. Kara named her calico Mercedes and her orange tabby Ralph. Mercedes had been the name of her best friend in high school, but Kara claimed she'd never met a Ralph until I'd brought her the kittens. Some cats seem to name themselves.

"Ralph and Mercedes show no signs of the diva disease, as far as I can tell," I said. "Before Isis leaves here, whether to return home or to head to a new family, I hope my three can convince her she's a cat, not Egyptian royalty like her namesake."

"Tell me how your undercover operation went today. Did you come off as a decent reporter?" Kara asked.

"Major failure." I went on to explain what had gone

down, more embarrassed than ever about being spotted as a fraud so quickly.

"Ah, the Internet betrayed you," she said. "It's a curse and a blessing. But it sounds like you did learn a few things this morning."

"Not enough," I said. "I hope Tom and I can figure out what's happening in that house with a new ruse he and I devised—one I've decided I am very uncomfortable with, by the way." I told her about Ed's connection to Ritaestelle and what I'd brought home from his shop.

Kara laughed. "I can't see you as a spy. But Tom? Let him take the lead tomorrow. He's got the experience."

"I'm worried about this disguise business. Did you ever go undercover on an assignment when you worked for the newspaper?" I said.

"Print journalists aren't like the kind of investigative reporters you see on the TV news. We can't go in with hidden cameras. We have to be very upfront when pursuing a story, right down to our real name."

"That's tough," I said. "How did you get people to open up?"

"I tried to engage people, play straight with them, be honest. And in the end, I lost my job to the ever-shrinking hard-copy newspaper business."

"Do you miss it?" I said.

"I did at first. I mean, I played by the rules, wrote plenty of pieces I'm proud of, and when my position disappeared, I felt a little lost. But now that's all behind me," she said. "I'm closing in on buying the local paper, building my house and learning plenty from Tom about stuff I never even knew I'd like. Surveillance is so cool."

"What hints can you give me about getting people to open up?" I said.

"You've already been tagged as a troublemaker, and as we've both learned, word gets around in these small towns. You'll have to be careful."

"You think I do need the disguise, then?"

"To get as much information as you need, I'd say yes. Maybe I can help with the disguise. Show me what Ed gave you."

I led her to my bedroom, and minutes later, after I'd

donned the wig and showed Kara the dress, I could tell she was trying hard not to laugh. And I was more self-conscious than I could ever remember.

I shook my head, causing the stinky fake hair to offer up even more aroma. Syrah, who'd been observing me with intense curiosity, hissed and ran off when the hair on my head actually moved. I'd scared the poor guy.

"I cannot do this," I said, whipping off the wig.

Kara attempted not to laugh, but her eyes betrayed her. "Sure you can. But the floral dress from 1950? No way. I'd just wear a pair of sunglasses and the wig. You don't want to draw too much attention, and that dress would definitely make you look like an escapee from the funny farm."

I smiled. "Shawn's overly serious approach to anything remotely connected to animals has obviously rubbed off on me. I'm making this way too hard, aren't I?"

"Have fun with this. Get people to talk by becoming an engaging character," she said.

"Thanks for the great advice. And you know what? Since Shawn left Isis here, it's my call whether she goes home. After tomorrow, *I'll* decide what's best for her. No more going to ridiculous lengths just because Shawn has his rules."

"There you go." Kara raised her palm and gave me a high five.

"Thanks for putting things in perspective. I've got an entitled cat that needs a home—and soon. I'll chat up the folks in Woodcrest to please Shawn, but unless I discover that Ritaestelle Longworth is a serial killer, I know what I'll do with that prissy cat."

Kara said, "I was worried for a minute there. You love cats, but there is a limit to animal adoration. Wish I could go with you tomorrow because I'm betting you'll have a blast, despite all your anxiety over this."

"You want to go? I could tell Tom—"

She held up her hand. "I'm meeting with the architect."

"Already?" I said.

"Now that the old farmhouse on my property has been leveled, I'm ready to get started. Can you believe it?"

"Seeing a new home come to life is so exciting," I said. "Your dad and I enjoyed every minute of watching this house being built."

There had been a time when Mercy was the last place on earth I thought Kara would end up. But she was here for good now. When Tom first mentioned she should use part of her inheritance to buy the local newspaper, she'd completely rejected the idea. Though big-city newspapers were going out of business left and right, the *Mercy Messenger* was the first thing people picked up in the morning. But it needed help to stay in business. The police blotter surely didn't deserve an entire page. Especially when most of what was reported had to do with folks getting drunk and disorderly or smashing their cars into fire hydrants.

Kara said, "Do architects snicker when you come to a meeting bearing a stack of magazines with little Post-it notes marking hundreds of pages?"

"It might scare him. But why even worry about that? I mean, he's working for you, right?" I said.

She cocked her head and considered this for a second, and then smiled warmly. "Yeah. Why worry?"

"See, now I want to go with *you*," I said. "But . . . no. This house is your deal."

"I wouldn't mind, but we both have plans, and like I said, you'll have more fun than I will. I'm a little scared. This is a big deal," she said.

"We'll both be anxious. Come for dinner tomorrow and we'll talk about our day."

But after Kara left and Chablis sat on my lap, her eardrums no doubt stinging from Isis's noise, I pondered this situation I'd walked into voluntarily. Despite telling myself that tomorrow's visit to Woodcrest would resolve the problem, I understood that assuming something would be simple didn't mean it would be.

# Seven

Tom picked me up in his Prius about eleven the next morning. No way could we take my van. I was a marked woman in Woodcrest.

As I slid into the passenger seat, I still hadn't put the wig on. I still hated it as much as I had the day before. Shawn owed me big-time after this.

"You look tired," Tom said as we pulled out of my driveway.

"Did you know that goddesses are screeching, awful, spoiled creatures?" I said.

"What are you talking about?"

I explained about Isis on the way to Woodcrest. Tom was sympathetic about the hours of sleep I'd lost to the noise coming from my basement, but I had volunteered to help Shawn, and no good deed goes unpunished.

As we closed in on our destination, I put on the wig and a pair of large sunglasses with square rims, then took out a tube of lipstick. Good thing the sun was shining, or I'd look silly wearing the shades. Okay, I probably looked silly anyway. I pulled down the vanity mirror and applied the bright red lip color that Kara had given me before she left yesterday. And stared at the stranger in the mirror. "Nope," I said, whipping the wig off. "I can't wear this."

Tom glanced over at me and didn't say anything for a few seconds. But finally he removed his Atlanta Braves baseball cap and handed it to me. "Try this."

I tucked my hair behind my ears and adjusted the size of the hat after I put it on. This time I nodded when I looked in the mirror. "This will do. Even if a baseball cap doesn't go with this sundress." I'd taken Kara's advice and worn one of the few dresses I own—blue cotton with wide straps.

Tom smiled. "Works for me."

I realized I'd been holding my breath and now let out the air accompanied by a sigh. "Who knew I'm a wig-a-phobic?"

Tom laughed, and soon we were slowly driving down the main street in Woodcrest. The town bustled with activity—lots of folks sauntering on the sidewalks and window-shopping. Tourists? That wasn't what I had in mind. I wanted to rub elbows with the locals. Tom must have read my mind because he pulled into a parking spot in front of a small pharmacy. "I'll find out where the Woodcrest people have lunch. Be just a minute."

He was back in less than that. He opened the passenger door and said, "Come with me. Got the necessary info."

We walked hand in hand around the nearest corner, the summer sun hammering down on us, and soon arrived at an unassuming place called Fairchild's. The shades were rolled down on the two big front windows. Guess the black-and-white awning wasn't enough to protect customers inside from the sun's glare. Unlike the many cafés I'd noticed on the main street that offered outdoor tables, Fairchild's did not. The antiques store next to the restaurant had end tables and lamps and a small bookcase set outside. But the restaurant only had one of those chalkboard signs with the day's specials near its front door.

Once we were inside, the smell of fried chicken and what?—barbecue sauce?—made my stomach growl. I liked what I saw, even if my view of the restaurant's decor—or lack of decor—was dimmed by my sunglasses. Small tables were crammed within an arm's length of each other, and a glass counter lined the far wall. A board above the counter listed lunch specials, sandwiches, salads and soups. Beneath the glass was an array of tantalizing cookies, pies and cakes.

We walked up to where a young girl in a Fairchild's T-shirt and blue jean skirt was taking orders.

Tom looked at me. "Tell me what you want, and then grab us a table."

I chose the Southern Salad and iced peach tea. Two men were just leaving near the center of the crowded room.

While I waited for a teenager to bus the table, I exchanged the sunglasses for the half-lens reading glasses I sometimes use for hand quilting. I was already drawing stares. Just like in Mercy, the strangers are spotted immediately, and the Hollywoodesque sunglasses might have been part of the reason.

After I sat down, I licked my lips. The lipstick felt thick and . . . well . . . just wrong. Despite the warm day and the almost as warm restaurant, my hands were ice-cold. I was nervous and tried to conjure Kara's amused grin when she'd seen me in the wig. Maybe that would relax me.

*This is fun, Jillian. You're playing a part. Just go with the flow.*

By the time Tom arrived with our lunch, I'd already made eye contact with two patrons: a man in overalls at two o'clock right and a woman, maybe midsixties, next to our table on the left. Both these people stared at me like I'd stepped out of a spaceship.

Tom put my salad in front of me—a gigantic bowl with strips of fried chicken amid an array of romaine and spinach. Juicy hunks of fresh tomato and a scattering of corn kernels were almost hidden by a generous swirl of ranch dressing. *Calorie Salad* might have been a better name.

After Tom set down his pulled-pork barbecue sandwich, he said, "I forgot the silverware." He took the tray and walked back to the counter.

The woman next to me eyed my salad. "Since you're eating salad, I assume you're saving room for dessert. Have the lemon icebox pie. Best you'll ever eat."

What I'd ordered didn't land squarely in the *salad* category in my view, and Tom's mother made the best lemon icebox pie I'd ever eaten, but I smiled kindly and said, "Thanks for the tip."

I hadn't even noticed the gentleman with her until he said, "Don't mean she'll like that pie just 'cause you do, Dolly." He looked at me and grinned. "Chocolate cream is better."

"Is not." Dolly pouted and crossed her arms over her chest.

I smiled. "Guess you two eat here a lot. Been married a long time, haven't you?"

This seemed to bring Dolly out of her mini-depression at once. "Forty years."

"Wow," I said.

The man reached across the table and took Dolly's hand. "Forty years of bliss. Even if our taste in pie doesn't match up."

"Both pies are wonderful. That's why you and your gentleman friend need to pick both," the middle-aged man at two o'clock said.

I turned his way and smiled.

Dolly said, "Wayne over there should go into politics, don't you think, Miss . . . ?" She raised her eyebrows expectantly.

Uh-oh. Miss *What*? I didn't have to be as honest as Kara did on her assignments, so I could make up something or—

"Stewart," Tom said.

Thank goodness he'd arrived. Apparently I'm not all that quick on my feet.

He put out his hand to Dolly's husband. "Tom Stewart. We're looking to buy a place in a small town. City life isn't for us, we've decided." At least that last part was true.

"Then you've come to the right part of South Carolina. Peaceful here. And still as pretty as god made it," he answered. "I'm Herman, by the way. And this is my Dolly."

"I have to say, I'm impressed with this friendly town." Tom looked at me. "Just might be what we've been searching for, hon."

I cut a chicken strip in half and dabbed it in dressing. Before I took a bite of what looked and smelled delicious, I said, "We drove by this huge estate. What is that place?" I glanced at Dolly and then over at Wayne.

"The Longworth Estate," all three of our new acquaintances said in unison.

But it was Dolly who rolled her eyes. "Sad thing when someone so upstanding falls so far." She shook her head, looking genuinely glum—but with what? A hint of satisfaction, perhaps? She had such great facial expressions, she could have been an actress.

I chewed that glorious hunk of chicken and then said, "Oh my god. I don't think I've ever tasted anything this good." I didn't want to sound too interested in the town gossip. Not yet, anyway.

Wayne had pushed his empty plate away and was leaning back in his chair sipping coffee. "There's plenty more good choices at this here establishment. The chicken-fried-steak sandwich is my favorite." He looked over at Dolly. "Heard anything more about Ritaestelle? She get out of going to court?"

Herman said, "Woman's sick in the head. She's not going to no court. Chief Shelton's her friend from way back, so she'll fix it. No Longworth in their right mind needs to shoplift anything. Yup. Sick in the head."

This was good information. I had to keep them talking. "Does the poor woman have money trouble? I mean, that house . . . that beautiful acreage . . ."

Herman looked at me and tapped his temple. "Sick in the head."

Dolly looked about ready to burst. "You are too gullible, Herm. Always have been. I heard tell they found stuff from that new jewelry place in her purse. That man who owns that store where it came from needs that money. Disgraceful on Miss Ritaestelle's part, you ask me. Klepto-whatevers don't take precious things, and that man makes his own jewelry. Kleptos supposedly take silly items like . . . like ChapStick." For some reason Dolly thought Tom was her ally in this assumption, because she looked at him. "Isn't that right?"

Tom was in the middle of enjoying his sandwich but swallowed quickly and said, "You might be right about that."

Dolly nodded, looking pleased.

Wayne said, "Sorry, Dolly, but I'm with Herman. Something ain't right. Miss Ritaestelle's got to be sick. Think of all she's done for this town. Rather than saying—"

"Done right for this town in *your* minds, maybe." Dolly crossed her arms again, her cheeks flushed.

Herman stood. "I think we best be on our way. Old business isn't what potential homeowners in Woodcrest need to be hearing about. Come along, Dolly."

Dolly's lips were pressed together, and bright spots of color lingered high on her cheeks. She hoisted a large white vinyl purse over her arm and stood.

Wayne was staring into his coffee, and I saw a smile playing on his lips.

Herman shook Tom's hand and nodded at me. "Nice to meet you folks."

"Yes." Dolly mustered a smile. "Forgive me for my earlier remarks. The Longworth family has a long history of generosity. I sounded downright mean about Ritaestelle's difficulties. And that's not the kind of person I am."

She and Herman left the restaurant, and as soon as the door closed after them, Wayne leaned toward me. "Forty-two years ago Ritaestelle showed up at a local dance hall with Dolly's boyfriend. Or so Dolly says. But she says lots of things."

Tom said, "Women have amazing memories."

Wayne laughed. "Don't I know that."

"Hey," I said, "I resemble that remark."

We all had a laugh, and then Wayne left, too.

I said, "Seems there is something wrong with Miss Longworth—but shoplifting? The poor woman fell. How could she shoplift if she needs help walking down the hall?"

"Maybe Ritaestelle is having some sort of a breakdown. She could be on medication."

"True," I said. "Let's finish our lunch and head to the park. Hopefully we can find out something else."

Tom dug his fork into a gigantic heap of coleslaw while I continued the wonderful Southern Salad experience.

I felt guilty wearing Tom's hat as we sat on a white wrought-iron bench in the charming and well-manicured city park. He has this small bald spot on his crown that might become seriously sunburned. But I didn't dare take the hat off, and in fact I tucked telltale strands of hair back under the cap. I felt more comfortable with the sunglasses back on, but I had this sickening feeling that Chief Nancy Shelton might be just around the corner and would recognize me even if I'd worn the wig.

This acre of flowers and lush green trees smack in the center of town couldn't have been more lovely. The bench we'd chosen was one of four that made up a square surrounding a small fountain. The murmuring of spilling water helped to calm me as Tom and I sat in silence. Such a peaceful place.

A woman about my age—midforties, maybe—arrived

twenty minutes after we'd sat down. She was assisting an elderly lady who needed a cane to help her walk.

"There you go, Mama," the younger woman said. She handed her mother a brown paper lunch sack after they'd both sat down on the bench perpendicular to ours.

The birds and the squirrels began to arrive before the older woman tossed out the first bread crumbs. Her shriveled, arthritic hand trembled as she tossed the food to the anxious sparrows and blackbirds. Two squirrels sat up like little begging dogs, and I soon saw why. "Mama" reached into her skirt pocket and pulled out several peanuts. With a peanut in each palm, she bent toward the squirrels and held out her shaky hands. The squirrels approached quickly, grabbed their prizes and ran off behind the oak trees beyond.

"You've got them trained," I said with a smile.

The younger woman spoke. "She brought me here every day when I was a kid. Now it's my turn to make sure she gets as much joy as we shared back then." She placed an arm around her mother and squeezed her.

The cloudy-eyed and slightly confused look the old woman gave her daughter was one I knew well. In my grandfather's later years, he remembered only routine—and none of his family. We had become strangers.

Tears welled in my eyes at the memory, and the young woman saw this. "Ah, you understand." Her lips quivered, and she returned to their task, assisting her mother in getting a new handful of bread crumbs from the bag.

Tom took my hand in his and said, "You come here every day?"

"Yes," the woman said, not making eye contact. She remained focused on helping her mother. "I've never seen you here before. Tourists?"

"You could say that," he said. "But tourists on a mission."

She looked at Tom then. "What does that mean?"

"We need information about a local woman," I said. Looking for a house, pretending we were married, wouldn't cut it for me this time. I just couldn't lie to this woman. I couldn't play what suddenly seemed like a ridiculous game.

Tom turned sharply to look at me, but I avoided his gaze, removed my sunglasses and went on. "I'm Jillian, by the way."

"I—I'm Rebecca, and this is my mother, Gertrude." But her voice was hesitant, her look guarded.

The old woman turned to her daughter. "Gertrude, you say? That sounds so familiar."

Rebecca patted her mother's thigh. "That's your name, Mama. Gertrude Hill."

"Oh. That's nice, isn't it?" Gertrude went back to feeding the birds.

Rebecca took a deep breath and released it slowly.

"Do you know Miss Longworth?" I asked.

Tom sighed, and I felt his shoulder slump a little. He probably didn't think I was doing the right thing by taking this tack.

"Are you the FBI or something?" Rebecca said. "Has it gotten that bad?"

"Why would you think that?" Tom sounded as surprised as I felt.

"Are you?" Rebecca persisted. "Because I think you're supposed to show me a badge or something if that's the case."

I shook my head. "No. We're not police or FBI or anything like that. But we do know there's been trouble at the Longworth house. Have you heard about it?"

"Why is it any of your business?" She leaned against the hard bench's back, her hands clasped tightly in her lap. Her penetrating stare was on me.

My heart sped up. Was this another mistake? Had my gut feeling about this woman been wrong? I'd sensed she'd be honest and open, but now she was suspicious—and with good reason.

"I was in the Longworth house yesterday," I said. "I went there with some simple questions and soon discovered that Miss Longworth seems ill. Something isn't right, and I feel obligated to find out what's going on."

Gertrude looked at her daughter and said, "She's a good one, Becky." She raised a crooked finger to one eye. "It's right there in her eyes. What's your name again, sweetie?"

"Jillian," I said.

"Pretty name, just like you. And a sight better than Gertrude any day," she replied.

Rebecca smiled and took her mother's hand. "I should talk to her? Is that what you're saying, Mama?"

Gertrude nodded. "That's what I'm saying. Miss Ritaestelle made sure we got the mortgage for our first house.
Told the banker we'd always be good for the payments. Did
you know that, Becky?"

"No, I didn't," Rebecca said. The younger woman's face
had brightened; she was probably thrilled about these precious lucid moments.

"If Miss Ritaestelle is in trouble, then you need to help
Jillian. Now, I need more peanuts. Did you forget to bring
them again?" Gertrude said.

"They're in your pocket, remember?" Rebecca said.

Gertrude struggled to reach into the folds of her skirt
and came out with a handful of peanuts. "Well, slap me silly,
who put those there?" She tossed a few over her shoulder, and the four squirrels that had now gathered scurried
in that direction. Gertrude smiled broadly and turned to
watch.

"Who are you people?" Rebecca said.

"We live in Mercy. I volunteer at the animal sanctuary.
Shawn Cuddahee—"

"I know the place. I only briefly met Shawn, but his wife,
Allison, is so, so nice. I adopted my little dog Nick from
them about four years ago. But I interrupted. Go on."

"Shawn called and tried to speak with Miss Longworth
several times last week. No one returned his call. He
thought I might have better luck if I just went there," I said.

Rebecca shook her head. "I don't understand. Why
would Mr. Cuddahee be calling Miss Longworth?"

"He found her cat," I said. "But like I said, she never
called Shawn back and I never got to talk to her. I'm hoping to find out why."

"I heard she's not returning anyone's calls ever since
they found out about the shoplifting. It's a sad day when a
strong woman like that loses her way." Rebecca glanced at
her mother, who was engrossed in her bird feeding.

Tom said, "We heard about the shoplifting. But earlier
you seemed to indicate there's more than that going on."

"I'll say. Everyone's talking about it. Word is that Evie
Preston—that's Miss Longworth's personal assistant—has
made calls to big-time places like the Cleveland Clinic and
Johns Hopkins. Evie thinks she's sick or something."

If I still lived in Houston, I would have been amazed

that one person would know so much about what was going on, but this town was even smaller than Mercy. Everyone knew everything about what went on—and that was why we'd come to the park in the first place.

I glanced at Rebecca's mother and back to her. "Is Miss Longworth being treated by a doctor here for a possible . . . medical problem?"

"You mean Alzheimer's?" Rebecca said softly.

I nodded.

"Not that I know of, but we don't have many specialists. I have to take my mother to Charlotte to see a doctor there. I happen to have firsthand knowledge about Miss Longworth's recent problems. I took Mama to pick up a prescription a couple months ago. Evie was there with Miss Ritaestelle. Miss Longworth looked blank-faced, like she was almost sleepwalking. At the counter, when Miss Longworth opened her bag to pay, Evie spotted a handful of small-change items—nail polish, nail clippers, stuff like that. She took them all out and put them on the counter so she could pay for them. When Evie looked back at me, she seemed so embarrassed." Rebecca squeezed her mother close again. "Rumor is that not long after, Evie Preston told the police chief about that incident. See the chief and Miss Longworth are friends and Chief Shelton could help before things got out of hand. As many troubles as we've had, I never had that kind of problem."

Gertrude looked bewildered again. "You've got a problem, little lady? I know where the police officers can be found. Parked in their car outside the kolache shop on Briar Street."

I grinned. "Thanks for the tip, Mrs. Hill." That might prove to be useful information if word got around that I was asking questions. We would definitely avoid Briar Street.

"Mrs. Hill, you say?" Gertrude said. "Is she related to that handsome young lawyer, Peter Hill?"

Rebecca took her mother's elbow and said, "Time to move on, Mama. We have more birds to feed near our house."

Gertrude slowly rose with Rebecca's help, and as they passed by, I thanked Rebecca for her help.

"You take care," Tom offered.

Before they left, Rebecca leaned down and whispered, "Peter is my brother."

I managed to pat Rebecca's arm reassuringly and say, "You are so brave," before they slowly walked away.

"That police chief will hear about this conversation, you know," Tom said. "She'll make sure no one talks to you after this."

"Why? I'm only trying to help a cat and a woman who seems to be in trouble."

"I know," Tom said gently, "but you said yourself there's more to this. If Chief Shelton decides no one should talk to you, then I'm betting she'll get her way."

"I couldn't fool around with Rebecca and Gertrude. I can't help but wonder after meeting them if Kara will be so completely there for me one day. Make sure my cats are fed, their litter boxes are clean. And what about poor Rita-estelle? Does she have any family to—"

"What are you doing back in Woodcrest?" came a female voice I recognized. She was standing behind me.

I turned and looked up at Chief Nancy Shelton.

Tom rose and faced her. "I insisted she come back. Tom Stewart." He held out his hand.

The woman, once again wearing that navy blue jacket and skirt with the shiny police badge on her lapel, regarded Tom's hand as if it were a gerbil in a petting zoo. Would it be safe to touch?

But finally she shook his hand.

"You know your friend here"—the chief nodded at me—"well, she caused quite an upset at the Longworth house yesterday."

I so wanted to say that the "upset" had begun long before I arrived, but instead I said, "I meant no harm."

Nancy Shelton's stern look disappeared. "I understand. I'm not an unreasonable woman, despite what you think. I'm simply very protective of my citizens. I've had a day to think about my behavior yesterday, and I talked more with Miss Preston about your visit. I overreacted. You're concerned about Isis. Isn't that right? Mr. Cuddahee apparently found her and sent you here?"

I slouched in relief. "Yes. I want to bring Miss Longworth's cat back to her. She seems to need her friend more than ever right now," I said.

Chief Shelton closed her eyes, hung her head briefly. "You may want to rethink that."

"Why's that?" Tom said.

"Because I hate to tell you this, but the family told me that Ritaestelle tossed that cat out the door last week. I'd say Isis is lucky to be alive."

# Eight

Chief Shelton's words hung in the hot, sticky air. She was saying that Miss Longworth tossed her cat out the door like so much garbage. This was such unexpected information that I could hardly believe it. Neither Tom nor I spoke for several seconds.

Tom finally said, "You're sure the cat didn't sneak out? In others words, act . . . well, catlike?"

"That's not what I understand." The chief looked at me. "Is the cat okay?"

"Yes. She's with me." My voice sounded flat. I'd been so certain I would be returning Isis to her home. But now I wasn't so sure.

The chief said, "Do you think you can keep Isis for a while? Or . . . perhaps I can find someone to take her."

"It would be too stressful for her to end up at yet another place so soon," I said. "I'm just getting to know her, and I don't mind keeping her for a while." If I could get a good night's sleep, that is.

Shelton nodded. "All right. I'm not a cat person, so I trust your judgment. Where did you find her, by the way?"

"Shawn found her near the highway between here and Mercy," I said absently. Would Isis calm down? Would my own cats completely freak out by having such a spoiled animal in the same house with them for longer than I'd thought?

"If I can offer a suggestion?" Shelton said.

"Sure," Tom answered after a glance my way. He obviously could tell how stunned I was by this news. How dismayed.

"Please leave Ritaestelle alone for now. There have been problems. I won't betray her confidence, but plans are in the works to help her." Shelton looked at me. "When the family believes Ritaestelle is ready, they'll tell her that Isis is safe. In fact, I'll tell her myself. She and I go back a long way."

Just as Ed and Rebecca had said. They went way, way back. "I have no intention of bothering Miss Longworth. I've been trying to do the right thing by both her and her cat," I said.

"I understand," Shelton said with a sad smile.

Tom pulled a business card from his shirt pocket. "Why don't you call me when you think Miss Longworth is well enough to hear the news about Isis?"

She took the card and smiled. "Thank you for your concern. And again, forgive me for yesterday, Ms. Hart. Evie Preston was understandably upset when she saw you come upstairs and observe Ritaestelle at her worst. She called me right away, and I took off after you without thinking. Protecting our friends is important here in Woodcrest. Now, I have to get back to the station. But I do so appreciate your concern."

After she was gone, Tom said, "Protecting their secrets is what she meant."

"I—I— This is plain awful," I said, shaking my head. "Not what I expected. But I'm glad we came. After listening all night to that cat screech, I was ready to bring Isis with me today and drop her off at the Longworth place. Now I'm glad I didn't."

"A little information can make all the difference. Let's go." Tom put his arm around my shoulder. "You look completely wrung out. If you want, come to my place for a nap before you go home. Dashiell and I will make sure you're comfortable."

Dashiell was Tom's big, lovable cat. He purred as loud as a jet engine when he curled up in my lap. I leaned into Tom and we started walking.

He went on, saying, "By the way, the original Dashiell Hammett had a great quote that seems appropriate right now. He said, 'You got to look on the bright side, even if there ain't one.'"

I stopped and rested a hand on Tom's cheek. "Thanks for coming, and for stepping in when I was too taken aback to even speak."

"I'm glad I could help. You don't have to go it alone, Jilly. People care about you—and I'm one of them."

We hugged and I gave him a quick kiss. But as we continued on through the quiet little park to Tom's car, I only wanted to go home. After what I'd heard, I needed to love on my own kitties. And maybe, just maybe, I could make friends with Isis.

On the ride back to Mercy, I'd checked my phone and the video feeds from my cat cam, but I didn't see any of my three in the living room. Usually Merlot would be sleeping on the window seat about now, but he was nowhere to be seen.

Meanwhile, Tom got a call from a customer about a malfunction in a security camera he'd installed, and though he offered again to drop me off at his place for some peace and quiet, I refused. I arrived home about three o'clock, disengaged the alarm at the back door and walked into the kitchen. I heard the sounds of Animal Planet coming from the TV—Syrah especially enjoyed Animal Planet while I was gone—but when I called my three cats' names in succession, none of them came to greet me.

Strange. And even stranger, I heard no yowling coming from Isis's basement apartment. Suddenly I no longer felt tired. What went on while I was away?

I kept calling for my cats in a questioning tone as I descended the basement steps. The first thing I saw downstairs was the bedroom door ajar. A hint of panic tightened my gut. But when I reached the door, I saw scratch marks on the doorknob as well as all around the knob.

"Sy-rah?" I called, trying to keep the irritation I felt out of my voice. "What have you been up to, my friend?" This was his work, no doubt about it. Who knew cats could open doors? But he'd done it before, and now he'd done it again.

The bedroom was empty. No Isis, no other cats. Last autumn someone broke in and catnapped Syrah, so I still felt worried even though my home was now well-secured. That was how I'd met Tom, in fact. He'd set up the cameras and alarms and checked everything regularly. Since the alarm hadn't gone off, surely there hadn't been another break-in. But the question remained, where in this house were my cats and our less than friendly visitor, Isis? A quick look in the basement pantry, utility room and bathroom proved they were not down here.

I went back upstairs, and it didn't take long to find them—or at least I saw Syrah, Chablis and Merlot. They were in my quilting room and had my sewing machine cabinet surrounded. The scene reminded me of three ships on the ocean ready to attack a pirate vessel. Isis could be considered a pirate in this house—trying to steal attention and upset the norm. She must be in my Koala cabinet—a lovely piece of equipment that expands to provide a cutting table and plenty of room for machine piecing—not to mention plenty of places to hide.

Chablis was the first to break her intense stare on that cabinet. She turned and offered me a tiny mew in greeting. But Syrah and Merlot didn't take their eyes off the right-side cupboard. I didn't feel the least bit of sympathy for Isis. In fact, I was willing to bet she hadn't been grateful or sweet when Syrah opened that door downstairs and let her escape.

I walked over to the cabinet and squatted. Merlot was the next to acknowledge my presence. And when he looked at me, I saw his ear was bleeding a little at the tip. That would have to be thoroughly cleaned, and soon. But first, Isis needed to have another lesson as to who was boss in my house.

Syrah remained as still as a statue, his ears flat. He was one unhappy cat. I decided having three observers when I removed Isis from the cabinet might be a bad idea. I gathered up Merlot and Chablis, put them outside the room and shut them out. But I decided to allow Syrah to stay. He was top cat in the group, and I needed to help him maintain his status.

I got down on all fours, widened the cabinet door and peered inside the cabinet. Green slitted eyes stared back at me. Isis hissed when she saw my face. Syrah slowly moved in beside me and sat. He didn't spit; he didn't hiss; he just stared Isis down. She turned her head away briefly.

I quickly reached in and grabbed her by the scruff so she couldn't bite me as I pulled her out. To my surprise, she didn't try to scratch or bite. She allowed me to pick her up as Syrah watched intently.

I stood and looked down at Syrah. "Thanks, my friend. Good work."

Isis began to purr, probably more from fear than from anything else. Syrah can indeed be intimidating in his own quiet way. I carried Isis out to the living room with my three felines following close behind. When I sat on the couch and Chablis jumped up beside us, Isis hissed at her. I tapped the goddess's nose. She blinked and looked up at me. Bet that had never happened before. But she quit hissing, and soon all three of my cats were on the couch wanting a sniff of her. After about five minutes of this, Isis jumped down, her tail swishing. But a peace had been forged, and I was hoping against hope that I might actually get some sleep tonight.

I turned off Animal Planet, rested my head against the sofa cushions and the next thing I heard was my phone ringing. Seems I'd taken that nap after all. As I reached in my dress pocket for my phone, I realized that Isis had joined Chablis on the couch. Chablis likes it when I nap— she loves to snuggle close—and even though Isis was way at the other end of the sofa, I had to smile. My three cats had accomplished what I could never have done—tamed the entitled one.

The caller ID showed Candace's name and number. I answered with a "Hey there."

"How does iced coffee from Belle's Beans and a couple of chili dogs from the Main Street Café sound? I need a break from Mom and her painting instructions." I heard the strain in Candace's voice. She loved her mom dearly but didn't like to be "instructed" by anyone and certainly not by her mother.

"You're doing pickup and delivery?" I said.

"Absolutely. See you soon." She hung up.

I checked the clock on the DVR across the room. Past five o'clock. Wow. That was one nice snooze. But I needed to clean Merlot's scratch, splash some water on my face and change my clothes. I am not a fan of anything besides capris, jeans, T-shirts and shorts. And the nap had taken a toll on this dress. It was a wrinkled mess.

After I used soap and water on a less than happy Merlot's ear, I went to the bedroom, stripped off the dress in my bathroom and tossed it toward the closet and my hamper— and missed. I turned on the sink's faucet, and after dousing myself with cold water, I reached for a towel. And saw Isis already curled up on my discarded clothing. She blinked sleepily. Seemed she was making herself right at home. But whether we would become her family was another story. My cats may have put Isis in her place, but that didn't mean they wanted her around permanently.

I pulled on a pair of cutoffs and a T-shirt with a picture of a rather mean-looking Persian cat. The quote beneath the picture said, IF YOU WANT A FRIEND, GET A DOG. Of course, Persians are sweet cats and my felines are the best friends I could ever have, but the picture and quote made me smile.

Candace arrived thirty minutes later, but it wasn't until we were done with our decadent chili dogs and fries that Isis made her appearance. She promptly spit at Candace, her coat burgeoning to twice its size. Taking the straw from my drink, I drew up some coffee and used the straw like a blow dart to splatter the cold liquid in Isis's face. She blinked and sat down. But her glare didn't last as long as her previous attempts to intimidate me. She washed her face and then came over and rubbed against Candace's chair. What a little suck-up. But she made me laugh. Seems she was learning that this wasn't the Longworth Estate.

I'd been updating Candace on today's visit to Woodcrest while we ate. Now I told her how Isis had definitely begun to learn a few lessons.

After daring to pet Isis for a few seconds, Candace said, "Sounds to me like your work is done. Find this cat a home—and fast."

I sighed. "Not yet. Call it intuition, but something doesn't feel right about all this."

"There is nothing *right* about people changing drastically when they get older. It's difficult. Take my mother—please."

I laughed at the old Dangerfield joke.

"No, really," Candace went on. "Mom had certain traits when I was a kid that seemed a little controlling. But now? It's so much worse, and it drives me nuts."

"I understand," I said. "But as far as Ritaestelle Longworth? Don't you think it's odd to go from having money out the wazoo to stealing cheap stuff from the drugstore? That seems like such a major turnaround. My brain tells me to leave this alone, but my heart is telling me this is a woman who could use a friend."

Candace shook her head vigorously. "Don't, Jillian. Leave this alone. You've gone above and beyond. Just call it quits."

I sighed. "You're right."

Candace pulled a *Rear Window* DVD from the canvas tote she'd brought inside. "This is the special edition with the trailer narrated by Jimmy Stewart. Let's forget everything for a couple hours, okay?"

And so we did. Candace and I share a love of old movies, especially Hitchcock, and we enjoyed every minute. Isis even cozied up to Candace for a while, but then she and Chablis started chasing each other. I was amazed. Talk about turnarounds.

Once we both started yawning, Candace headed for home around ten p.m. I set the security alarm, poured myself a glass of water and went to my bedroom. The dress I probably wouldn't wear again for another year still lay on the floor. I tossed it into the closet, again missing the hamper. I shut the door and made a beeline for my bed.

But before I could climb beneath the covers, the doorbell rang.

*Huh?*

The only person besides Candace who would show up at my place this late without calling was Kara. My heart thumped against my chest. Was something wrong? And why didn't Kara call me if there was a problem?

I hurried to the kitchen, shut off the alarm and rushed to the foyer. But when I looked through the peephole, it wasn't Kara after all. The woman I recognized on my doorstep made me gasp in surprise.

Ritaestelle Longworth.

# Nine

The surprise must have still been evident on my face when I opened the door, because Ritaestelle Longworth said, "You weren't expecting me?" She smiled amiably.

Then I realized she wore a white chenille bathrobe with her initials in scrolled gold embroidery on the left pocket. She also had a red Velcro hair roller in her silver bangs and a honey-colored Coach handbag over her arm.

"I—I . . . Please come inside." I opened the door wider and then immediately thought about Isis. My three cats had raced after me to the foyer to see what was up, but not Isis. Had she gotten a whiff of her owner—a cat's sense of smell is hundreds of times more keen than a human's—and decided not to greet the person who'd thrown her out? Probably.

After Miss Longworth stepped inside, I shut the door after her, still too confused by her arrival to think of anything to say.

She erased the awkward silence by starting right in with, "Since you came to see me yesterday and we did not converse, I thought I would come your way and say hello. I looked up your address and that wonderful little GPS device in my car made the journey quite trouble-free. See, I knew I recognized you—from that article they ran in the newspaper a while back. How you solved that murder and helped all those poor cats find homes. You are such a hero, Ms. Hart."

Here she was, dressed in her nightclothes, a roller in her

hair, talking in her restrained, polite, Old South manner like she'd been invited for tea. Was this really happening?

"Um, thank you, Miss Longworth. What can I do for you?" I would have checked my watch had I been wearing one. Did she realize how late it was? Perhaps not. This woman was obviously troubled—and yet she was as smiley as a Cheshire cat.

"Please call me Ritaestelle. Now, I am most certain you are completely bewildered by my sudden appearance in your charming little town. Do you mind if we sit down? As you were witness to, I had a fall yesterday, and my hip is a smidgeon intolerant of me standing."

"Of course. Please come into the living room. Can I help you to the sofa?" I said.

"No, no, I can make it. Oh, and look at your lovely cats leading the way. How precious."

No mention of Isis. Did she even remember her own cat? This all seemed a little surreal.

We made our way to the living room, her limp obvious, and I wondered if she'd been seen by a doctor.

She eased herself into one of the overstuffed chairs and sighed as she sank into the cushions. "What a comfy, splendid chair." She glanced around. "And I do imagine you have a lovely view of the lake in the daytime, what with all your windows."

"I do. But, if I can ask again, why are you here and—" I couldn't seem to get the rest of the sentence out—the part about her being dressed for bed.

"Before we get into an explanation, my dear young woman—and you have every right to be inquiring—I could certainly use a drink of water. I left my house in rather a rush, as I am sure you have already determined." She smiled that odd and oh, so gracious smile again.

"Um, sure. Ice?"

"That would be wonderful." She reached down and patted Chablis on the head. My cat was sniffing at Ritaestelle's chenille slippers. Yes, the lady was even wearing slippers that matched her robe. Syrah had taken his regal sitting position at the foyer entrance, and Merlot paced in front of the windows. Moths and flies must be fluttering around out there.

I went to the kitchen, wondering if I should bring up

the subject of Isis, wait for Ritaestelle to say something or forget about her cat for the time being. Isis seemed to want the latter, considering she hadn't shown her face. Yes, that seemed the best option for now.

After I handed Ritaestelle her water, she thanked me profusely and then said, "Now, as to my attire. I do not normally leave the house dressed like this. But I had a chance to escape and I took it."

I blinked. *Escape?* Should I add paranoia to her list of recent problems? I tried to keep my voice even when I said, "You escaped? That sounds serious."

"It is seriously shameful when you are forced to leave your home in such an unpleasant fashion."

"It is." I nodded in agreement, feeling downright foolish. Perhaps I should have been a tad frightened by this visit, but it all seemed so innocent and, well, silly. Ritaestelle was probably in need of a doctor for more than her hip—and perhaps simply someone to talk to. I could do that much for her. "Can you tell me about what happened tonight?"

Ritaestelle sipped at her water and then carefully set her glass on a coaster on the end table beside her. "Certainly. I do owe you an explanation after you have so kindly invited me into your home. Let me begin by saying I know what you do—make those darling quilts for cats, help at the Mercy Animal Sanctuary. But you also assist with crime investigations. As I mentioned, that is how I recognized you—from your photograph in the newspaper. Your abilities in crime investigation are what interest me the most. You see, I think I have been a victim of sabotage."

"Sabotage? That's a strong word." Merlot loped across the room and leaped onto the sofa next to me. Then, strangely enough, all twenty pounds of him climbed into my lap. What was bothering him? He can be a big old fraidy cat, but this woman seemed harmless enough.

"That is the biggest, most handsome cat I have ever seen." She glanced down and then around the room. "But what happened to your other friends?"

Indeed, Syrah and Chablis had disappeared. And once again, though the focus was on cats, she still hadn't mentioned Isis. Maybe she had amnesia. Maybe that explained her other problems. "Merlot's a Maine coon, and this breed is often large. But forgive me if I'm a little confused about the mention of sabotage. What do you mean by that?"

"The sabotage. Yes, that is why I came. I am still a little unclear about certain events, probably because of the drugs someone has been spiking my tea with. I do so enjoy my tea. But perhaps sabotage is not quite the word I was searching for."

"You've been drugged?" This time I couldn't keep the surprise from my voice. That sure might clarify a few things.

"Yes, and I sincerely wish I knew why. And I wish I knew who was doing such a thing. I have two cousins living with me, along with my late brother's wife and her son. Then there's the staff: a cook, my assistant, my wonderful butler. We are a full house."

"That woman I saw you with—the one named Augusta. Who's she?"

"My cousin. But I cannot believe she would ever hurt me. After I heard the doorbell when you arrived, I so wanted to see who had come to call, as is my custom. But when I made it out to the hallway, I slipped and fell. What you witnessed was Augusta and Evie trying to help." Ritaestelle shook her head sadly and then met my gaze. "Why would someone want to harm me?"

"You mean drug you?" I asked, stroking Merlot. But he wasn't purring. He was in protection mode, I decided. So why wasn't I afraid? This visit simply seemed odd and somehow sad.

"Yes, why drug me? I am a very generous person in my community. I believed, perhaps wrongly, that I am well liked by the town folk and by the people in my home. And yet *this* happened. I even called my friend Nancy, who is now the chief of police. She came over, was quite concerned, and yet she seems to have doubts about whether I was even sedated. She said at times, as we age, we have to manage the world differently. We become forgetful and a tad clumsy."

"Did that upset you?" I said.

Ritaestelle said, "What bothered me most was that though Nancy can be quite abrupt, that day she was oversolicitous. She is never that kind, so I was, shall we say, confused—or more confused than those drugs were making me. She offered me the name of a doctor. I already have a doctor, and she knew as much."

Today, in the park, I had seen Nancy Shelton's concern for her friend firsthand. "Maybe she thought you weren't getting the best care," I said.

"I did not need a doctor visit or any more caretakers. I was feeling absolutely fine before someone put drugs in my tea." Ritaestelle glanced toward the ceiling briefly. "Is sabotage the correct word? Perhaps subversion is better."

I took a deep breath, making sure not to look at her outfit, but rather kept my gaze on the amazingly flawless skin on her face. The wealthy certainly can afford the best skin care. And like Scarlett O'Hara, she'd probably protected herself all her life from the damaging summer sun. "I hate to be forward," I said, "but *have* you been seen by your doctor, Miss Longworth?"

She smiled again. "Please call me Ritaestelle, remember? I see you have your doubts about me as well. Your lovely green eyes tell me as much. Are they green . . . or gray?"

"Depends on what I'm wearing," I said with a smile.

"To answer your question, yes. Burton, my personal physician for more than thirty years, came to the house about three weeks ago. He said he thought I might be suffering from a virus, wanted me to come to the office for laboratory tests and perhaps go to the hospital for an MRI of my brain. I was having none of that, let me tell you. I am as healthy as a horse."

"But you could have a medical problem," I said.

Her shoulders stiffened. "Nonsense. I am being drugged, and I want you to help me prove it."

That shut me up for a few seconds. Then I said, "Why me?"

"If an old friend who happens to be a police officer refuses to assist me, who am I to turn to? Besides, you, my dear, are trustworthy. A heroine. And I suspect you know where my cat is. You came to my house to talk about Isis, of that much I am sure. Her disappearance is a major concern—that and the sabotage. I do not understand where she has gone. She would never leave me willingly."

*No, not willingly,* I thought. Being shoved out the door

couldn't have been something Isis liked one bit. Until I learned more, I decided Ritaestelle shouldn't know that her cat was hiding somewhere in my house. Cats understand when they are in trouble. And they are smart enough to trust their instincts and hide from that trouble. The fact that Isis had not made an appearance told me a little something about Ritaestelle. Still, if the poor woman had been drugged as she claimed, that might explain why she'd thrown her cat outside; maybe she'd been in a state of confusion. But did it explain the shoplifting? Ritaestelle hadn't spoken about that.

I said, "I confess that I am aware your cat is missing. However—"

A loud and mournful meow echoed down the hall behind us.

"What was that?" Ritaestelle rose from her chair, groaning with the effort. She turned in the direction of the hallway. "Is she here? Is my Isis here? Because that most certainly sounded like her." She turned back to me, her calm facade gone. "Why did you keep this from me?"

There was no getting around Isis's presence now. Ritaestelle's Southern charm had evaporated like so much steam. She was angry—and I didn't blame her. Isis didn't come out to greet her mistress because she was probably trapped somewhere.

Was she stuck in the sewing cabinet again? Or had she gotten caught in a bureau drawer? These were unfamiliar surroundings, so she could definitely be trapped. "I'm sorry for not telling you about Isis right away. But I can explain," I said. "Can you wait here for a second while I find her?"

"You do have her, then? Oh, good gracious, thank the Lord." Her anger melted away, and all that I now saw in her body language was relief. "Show me where she is." She stepped toward the hallway and in the direction of the now insistent meows.

"Please. You're having trouble with your hip. Let me bring her to you."

"I respect the privacy of your home, so I will wait here, but do please bring her to me," she said.

I hurried past her toward the other part of the house. Ritaestelle may have been troubled, but she obviously loved her cat. Nothing heals a soul better than a furry friend. And she could definitely use some healing.

I stopped in the quilting room first, Merlot on my heels. No Isis. And no Chablis or Syrah either. I understood then that if I found my two cats, I'd find Isis.

Another pitiful meow came from my bedroom. Ah. That was where they were. I hurried down the hall and found Syrah and Chablis sitting outside my closet. I'd closed the door—and unknowingly closed in Isis. But the bawling had stopped, and when I opened the door, Isis didn't come streaking out as I'd expected.

I flipped on the light. My closet is a large walk-in, and L shaped. Now I heard a pitiful mewl coming from around the corner where I'd stored extra cat quilts and several boxes of John's things—photos and a few personal items I would never part with.

"Come here, Isis," I said softly. "I promise I won't tap you on the nose or squirt you with coffee." Oh, I was definitely feeling guilty now.

I walked slowly toward her soft meows. But when I found her, I had to cover my mouth to keep from breaking into laughter. The goddess was surely embarrassed by her predicament, and I didn't want to make her feel worse.

Isis had climbed into a basket—one that had come with a floral arrangement, I'm sure. It was dark-colored wicker with a handle—and much too small for her. And yet she'd managed to squeeze into it and now obviously couldn't get out.

I knelt and realized at once that she'd squirmed so much, she'd managed to wedge herself into that basket. I couldn't even get my hands around her body to get her out. This would require a dismantling of the basket.

"Wait right here, oh brilliant one." Like she was actually able to move anywhere. I do like to offer hope in these situations, however; this was the kind of problem my own cats had made me familiar with.

I hurried back down the hall to my quilting room, where there were plenty of tools to be found. I called out to Rita-estelle that I would be right with her, Isis in tow, and then gathered a small needle-nose pliers (excellent for pulling stuck needles through layers of a quilt), my large sheers and a seam ripper.

Taking my arsenal with me, I allowed myself a laugh and even picked up my phone from my nightstand. I had to get a picture of this first.

With all this going on, I'd have thought my own three cats would be following the action, but they must have decided Ritaestelle needed company. After I snapped a photo of Isis in all her glory, I worked away at one handle of the less than top quality basket. I used the pliers to pull away some of the wicker that attached the handle to the basket. I realized the sheers were too big for the job and ended up using the seam ripper to tear away the wicker strips. After maybe five minutes, I lifted one side of the handle toward Isis's back and then up and away.

Silly thing just sat there and looked up at me, as helpless as, well . . . a kitten. I gently reached under her and lifted her up and out of her tiny prison. How had she ever managed to get in there in the first place?

I held her close, which she didn't seem to mind at all. I left the basket and my tools on the floor, picked up my phone and off we went for the reunion. I was betting Isis would be more than ecstatic to see her "mom" after this latest experience.

But when I got to the living room, Isis purring away in my arms, the chair where Ritaestelle had been sitting was empty. Then my protector cat Merlot let out one of his loud, deep-throated meows—the ones I rarely hear. He was in the kitchen.

Had Ritaestelle gone for more water and fallen again? If so, I sure couldn't see her in there. I rushed around the counter, and the smell of the humid night air greeted me at once.

The back door was open.

Merlot and Syrah were sitting on the stoop, and Syrah's ears were twitching like crazy. That was always a sign that something was wrong.

"Ritaestelle?" I called, joining my two cats at the back door.

From somewhere down near the lake I heard her call, "Here. I am down here. We need help."

I heard the panic in her voice, but I couldn't see anything except the giant black silhouettes of the huge trees on my sloping back lawn.

I turned on the lights and saw her then.

What was she doing on the dock? What was she holding?

I got a taste of my own heart about then. Chablis wasn't here with the other cats. Had she gone down to the lake? And why was the back door open in the first place?

I had enough sense to shut the door before I set Isis down. I didn't want her racing off to find another highway. After making sure she and my two boys didn't get outside, I slipped out into the night.

I keep a pair of Crocs on the back deck and put them on before I ran down toward the water to the sound of Rita-estelle's pleas for me to hurry.

But I ran a little too fast. The pine needles were damp with dew, and I fell on my rear. I hadn't realized I was still clinging to my phone, but it went flying out of my hand somewhere to my right. I scrambled to my feet and made it to the dock. Ritaestelle's face was so pale in the moon-light, so fraught with terror, that I swallowed hard. Espe-cially when I realized she had Chablis under one arm. And it looked like she held a rock in her other hand.

"Help us. Help her," Ritaestelle said. She looked down into the water.

I followed her gaze.

The lake lapped against the riprap, a sound I'd always found soothing. But the sight of the woman facedown in the water, her lifeless body swaying with each small wave, was anything but soothing.

# Ten

I scrambled to the shore, climbed over the low metal corrugated retaining wall, and carefully stepped on the stones that led to the water. I squatted and reached out for the woman's outstretched arms. I could touch only her hands, but they were still warm.

She might be alive.

"Hurry, Jillian. Hurry," I muttered as my heart pounded wildly.

I waded into the tepid water, and as I fought to turn the woman over, I looked up at Ritaestelle. "My phone. I lost it up there somewhere. Please find it." I turned my head in the direction she should go.

"Oh, dear sweet Jesus. I will try my best." Ritaestelle must have dropped the rock she'd been holding because I heard something hit the dock and plunk into the water.

I struggled with the woman's slippery and surprisingly heavy body. She was such a small person, and yet turning her over seemed almost impossible. But I finally flipped her face up. Then I positioned myself at her head, grasped her beneath her armpits and began to drag her out of the water. I glimpsed at Ritaestelle, who was slowly making her way down from the dock and up onto the lawn.

I hauled the woman onto the riprap, worrying about tearing up her back on the rocks. Then I pressed two fingers to her neck and felt for a pulse. Nothing.

I smoothed sopping hair away from her face.

And stared into the wide eyes of Evie Preston.

Those eyes and her slack jaw confirmed what I feared. I was probably too late.

I fought back tears, thinking that I couldn't give up. I turned her head to the side and emptied her mouth of water. Then I did the CPR I'd learned in a class right after John died—was I even doing it right?—until my shoulders and arms burned. But she didn't suddenly gasp for breath like on television. Evie Preston, who couldn't be more than thirty years old, was dead.

I shook my head sadly and stood. How I wished I'd gotten to her sooner. She might have had a chance.

Her body was secure enough on the riprap that I decided I could leave her and find my phone. Still, it felt wrong to abandon her by the lake. No one should be alone in death.

Ritaestelle was limping in circles on the pine needles, Chablis clutched to her chest. She'd never find my phone. I had to do what needed to be done, even if fear and sadness wanted to take control.

As I closed in on Ritaestelle and Chablis, I saw that Ritaestelle was crying. Out of breath after the struggle to save poor Evie, I stood heaving, my hands on my hips. I was completely soaked, and my knees stung from kneeling on the rocks. I felt like I was in shock. But there was no time for that. I had to call the police.

Chablis made eye contact with me, and then her lids slowly closed and opened again. She seemed perfectly calm amid the swirling emotions brought on by this tragic death. It was as if Chablis knew she had a job to do—comfort a woman she didn't even know.

"Just hang on to the cat, and I'll find the phone," I said after I caught my breath enough to speak. I squinted in the dim light cast by my deck and back-door lights, searching for the spot where I'd fallen on the way down to the lake. Sure enough, the place where I'd skidded was evident in the pine needles just a few feet ahead. I got down on all fours and felt around where I thought the phone had probably landed. Seconds later, I picked up my cell and dialed 911.

I had to stay on the line until the police arrived, but in the meantime, I helped Ritaestelle up the slope while she protested the whole time that we had to help Evie, that Evie shouldn't be left alone. We stopped at the stairs that led up to my deck, and I told Ritaestelle to stay put. Then I dragged a lawn chair down from the deck and helped her sit.

Ritaestelle looked up at me, terror evident in her eyes. "Did I drown her?"

I pressed the phone against my chest so the dispatcher couldn't hear me. "Don't talk about what happened now. Wait for the police."

"But I—"

I put a finger to my lips. "Shh."

She squeezed her eyes shut and nodded. More tears escaped.

Seconds later the cavalry arrived.

Leading the charge was Candace, still dressed in the same shorts and cotton shirt she'd been wearing when she left my place not long ago. Two night-duty uniformed Mercy officers, a couple of paramedics carrying a stretcher, and Billy Cranor, a volunteer fireman, were right behind her.

I disconnected from the dispatcher and pointed toward the lake. "She's down there on the riprap, but—"

All of them took off before I could finish, with Candace yelling, "Stay left. Avoid that path you see down the center of those pine needles."

Candace, my wonderful evidence preserver.

Deputy Morris Ebeling, also in street clothes, came strolling around the corner of my house a few seconds later. Nothing short of the apocalypse would make Morris hurry.

"What the hell you been up to now, Jillian?" he said. "You look pretty messed up."

I was wet, and I glanced down at my scraped knees, which were plastered with wet pine needles. They didn't hurt. I felt numb.

He noticed Ritaestelle then, still weeping, still clinging to my cat. He sighed heavily and took a small notebook from his shirt pocket. "Who we got here? The owner of the Caddy or the owner of the Ford?"

*Must be like a parking lot out there now,* I thought. When

Ritaestelle said nothing, I decided to tell Morris what he wanted to know. But I only got out, "This is—" before he interrupted.

"What? She can't talk?" Morris eyed me like a stern father. He had to be twenty years older than me, so he was old enough to my father.

"Yes, sir, I can most certainly talk," Ritaestelle said quietly. She was hanging on to Chablis for dear life. "The Cadillac is mine, and I am Ritaestelle Longworth of Woodcrest. This tragedy, however, has nothing to do with this kind lady."

"Well, I'm Mercy police deputy Morris Ebeling. And seeing as how everyone's hoverin' over a body down by the water in Jillian Hart's backyard, I disagree that this here has nothin' to do with her. Are you that Ritaestelle Longworth from Woodcrest who lives in a house big enough to be a church?"

Ritaestelle nodded.

"I knew your brother before he passed on," Morris said. "He done right by me at a bad time in my life, so I guess I'll return the favor by doing right by you." Morris squatted so he was at eye level with Ritaestelle. In the gentlest voice—one I never knew he even could find—he said, "You want to tell me how you got that blood on your hands?"

My eyes widened when I saw what he had noticed and I had not. She *did* have blood on her hands, and Chablis had blood on her champagne fur. Guess fear and desperation blur such details. The smears of rusty red made my stomach turn over.

"B-but she drowned," I said. "I never saw any blood on—"

Morris glared at me, bushy eyebrows raised. I got the message.

"Sorry," I said. "I'll be quiet."

"Thank you, Jillian," Morris said through tight lips. "You'll get your turn, and I cannot *wait* to hear what you have to say."

He turned his attention back to Ritaestelle. "You want to tell me about the blood?"

Ritaestelle lifted her chin. "If you knew my brother,

then you know what Farley is whispering in my ear right now. He's telling me not to say a word."

"Yeah. Lawyers are like that." Morris offered up a small, genial laugh. "Don't say nothing to nobody. That's their deal. But see, Miss Longworth, that's not always best. You tell me what happened, and I promise, I'll help you."

Why did I want to scream at her not to say anything? A young woman was dead, Ritaestelle had blood on her hands and yet something put me squarely on Ritaestelle's side. Was that because she'd come to me for help? No . . . it was something about me I'd learned to respect in the last year: my intuition. I sensed that this lady had done nothing worse than leave her house in her bathrobe.

"I do appreciate your concern, Officer, and your sincere wish to assist me in this most difficult time, but I would appreciate a few moments to consider these events. A young woman who was in my employ has died in a most tragic fashion. I am very troubled, very saddened."

"Can you at least get over your grief long enough to tell me her name?" The old Morris was back and in familiar irritable form. He poised a small pencil over a notebook page.

"Evie Preston." Ritaestelle's lower lip began to tremble, and tears again slid down her cheeks. She turned to me. "What will I ever tell her mother?"

"I believe the police will notify her family," I said.

"But she worked for me. I am responsible for her," Ritaestelle said.

"Be responsible enough to tell me what happened if you care that much," Morris said, his tone downright nasty now. "And since you seem worried about talking without a lawyer, you don't have to tell me nothin' and you can have a mouthpiece sittin' next to you if that's what you want. I won't go into that crap about if you can't afford a lawyer, 'cause we know that ain't the case."

Wow. Was that an actual Miranda warning? One that would stand up in court? And why did Morris have to sound so cold, so mean?

"You are absolutely right, Officer," Ritaestelle said. "I need to quit sniffling like a crybaby and take responsibility here—so you can get on with the awful business of telling Evie's mother what happened. I am quite willing to enlighten you about what I know, and I do not require a lawyer."

I was a little confused by this turnaround on Rita-estelle's part but didn't have to time to consider it for long because Candace joined us.

"That's great you want to cooperate, but first of all, we need to collect evidence," Candace said. Everyone knew Candace was obsessed with evidence.

Morris stood. He closed his eyes and moved his head from side to side in disgust. "Aw, for crying out loud, Candy."

Candace looked at me. "Will you get my evidence kit from my car? We'll need photos before we take her robe. That is a robe you're wearing, right?"

Ritaestelle looked down toward her chest. "Why, yes. But I can explain. It is not as odd as you might think."

*Oh, yes, it is,* I wanted to say.

"By the way, I am Deputy Candace Carson, Mercy PD. Didn't have time to grab my badge when I heard about all this on the scanner, but believe me, I am a peace officer. I've spoken with my chief, and he's asked me to take the lead on this." Candace glanced at Morris briefly, and I'm sure she caught his unhappy expression before he looked at the ground.

Seemed like a good time for me to leave. I took off for Candace's car for the requested evidence kit. I'd calmed down enough that questions seemed to ricochet off the inside of my skull. Why had Ritaestelle come outside? And considering her condition, how had she made it down to the dock? What was Evie Preston doing here? And what exactly happened in the relatively short time it took me to release Isis from the mess she'd gotten herself into?

When I returned to the backyard, I handed Candace her evidence satchel. I saw that Morris was now down by the lake. Bet he was plenty miffed that Police Chief Mike Baca had handed this investigation over to Candace so quickly. But then I realized that once she'd discerned that Evie Preston had been the victim of foul play, she'd called up Mike and asked for the assignment—even though she was supposed to be on vacation.

Candace took her camera from the evidence kit first.

"Please hand the cat to Jillian and stand up, Miss Long-worth."

Ritaestelle blinked several times, as if processing these directions. Then she said, "Why, certainly."

I took Chablis from her arms. Ritaestelle struggled to get out of the lawn chair, and Candace finally had to help her stand.

Candace said, "Just put your arms out and let me photograph the bloodstains."

Again Ritaestelle looked down at her robe, her expression puzzled. But now her eyes widened in what sure seemed like horror. "On, my sweet Jesus. I cradled Evie's head and—"

"Miss Longworth," Candace interrupted. "Deputy Ebeling informed me before he left us that you invoked your right to counsel and then changed your mind. Let's be clear that you realize anything you say may be used against you in a court of law."

"I am completely aware. I simply mentioned that my late brother would have told me not to say anything. That does not mean I intend to follow any advice Farley might offer from the grave." Ritaestelle lifted her chin, her lips tight. "I will tell you anything to assist you in unearthing what happened to Evie. It is the least I can do for her now."

Candace said, "Then will you sign a document that you have waived your rights?"

"Certainly. Your name is Deputy Carson, correct?"

"Yes, ma'am."

"Maybe we could go inside for the pictures?" I suggested. "Better lighting . . . and better footing." I'd noticed that Ritaestelle's slippers were gone. She needed to get inside before the fire ants found her.

Candace said, "Good idea. The deputy coroner is on her way, and we don't want to be a *distraction*." Candace eyed me.

Her look was a heads-up that I would be the distraction. Deputy Coroner Lydia Monk dislikes me intensely—mostly because she is obsessed with Tom Stewart. For some reason she thinks he's her soul mate. Problem is, they've never even been on a date.

I helped Ritaestelle up the deck stairs and opened the

back door. I should have anticipated the three cats that would be waiting there. When Isis took off like a speed demon toward the lake, Merlot and Syrah followed.

I shoved Chablis back in Ritaestelle's arms and shot after them.

# Eleven

As I ran down the sloping lawn, I heard Candace shout, "Cats coming. Protect the evidence."

Like you could protect anything, especially evidence, from a cat.

I saw Billy Cranor race up from the shore toward the three escapees, his fireman suspenders flapping at his waist. Isis managed to elude him and headed for a pine tree. A declawed cat—not my favorite subject, the declawing—*can* climb trees. But Isis apparently never practiced her technique. She made it about six feet up the trunk but couldn't hang on. Billy grabbed her.

Meanwhile, after a futile attempt to avoid the path that Candace so desperately wanted us to stay away from, I reached the spot where my two had stopped to enjoy the outdoors before their inevitable capture. Syrah began furiously digging around in the pine needles, and I wondered if there was a mouse or chipmunk hiding under there. Merlot, knowing he was in trouble, decided to surrender by lying down and offering me his belly.

Billy said, "Can you handle those two while I take this one back to the house?"

"Indeed I can. Mine know better. The one you've got has never been taught the rules." I knelt by Merlot and scratched his head. "Lying on your back, huh? What a pathetic ploy." I scooped him up, and this got Syrah's attention. The jealousy factor is never completely obliterated when it comes to my three, even by an adventure like this. I said, "Come on. In the house where you belong."

Syrah raced ahead toward the back door—I swear he understands every word I say. Merlot began to purr. He's too big for me to carry around on any regular basis, so he was especially enjoying this trip up to the house. I again tried to avoid the more worn path, but Billy hadn't even bothered. This race and chase probably hadn't helped Candace's evidence collection efforts any either.

Before I made it back to the house, Morris Ebeling marched past me, his strides amazingly energetic. "Candy radioed for a Miranda waiver form and an evidence sack. Do I look like her errand boy?"

I knew better than to offer a reply, even a sympathetic one. I climbed the deck steps and opened the door carefully, in case Isis was free and decided to take off again. Syrah, who had been patiently waiting, slipped into the house first and scampered inside to who knows where. I'm sure he hoped to avoid the scolding I'd been giving Merlot.

Billy stood in the kitchen, still holding Isis. She was staring up at him with a look that I've seen on Candace's face before: complete adoration. Did almost every female—even the nonhuman kind—find this guy irresistible?

"Thanks, Billy," I said, setting my big cat down. Merlot decided to pretend nothing had happened and meandered over to his food dish.

"No problem. Better get back outside." Billy offered Isis to me, but I shook my head. I wanted nothing to do with that little troublemaker right now. He put her on the floor, and she dashed off in the direction Syrah had gone. Billy went back outside, anxious no doubt, to return to the action now that he was relieved of cat duty.

Ritaestelle and Candace were seated at the dining room table, and Isis's owner apparently didn't see that black blur race through my living room.

I wasn't sure if I should listen in on this interview, but with my open floor plan—the kitchen blending into the dining room and the dining room into the living room— how could I avoid hearing what they were saying? A gloved Candace solved my dilemma by waving me over.

She was clipping Ritaestelle's fingernails. A tiny rusty pile had accumulated on a white paper towel beneath the hand Candace held. Blood still stained Ritaestelle's hands.

"Do you have something Miss Longworth can wear?"

Candace said. "Deputy Ebeling is bringing me an evidence bag large enough to hold her robe."

"I'll find something," I said.

"You are such a kind person," Ritaestelle said. "Both of you are, and I am so grateful for your assistance. You, Jillian, seem to have saved my cat yet again. But where did she go? That handsome fireman was holding her, and now they both seem to be gone." Ritaestelle's voice cracked, and she reached up to her forehead with her free hand—and found the curler still in her hair. She yanked it from her bangs, muttering, "Oh, for heaven's sake. No wonder everyone believes I am as crazy as a loon."

"I don't think you're crazy at all," I said. "And Isis will come around soon. She's a little frisky tonight, that's all. If you'll excuse me, I'll be right back with something for you to wear."

I hurried toward the hall thinking that maybe I could corral Isis and bring her to Ritaestelle. But then I remembered that Candace would not want more cat hairs all over her evidence. Chablis had most certainly deposited a fair amount already. No, this reunion between Ritaestelle and Isis would have to wait.

I stopped at the entrance to the long hall that leads to my bedroom. Syrah and Isis were engaged in button hockey on the wood floor. The slippery surface made for a great game of paw and slide in pursuit.

Obviously the cats had no interest in murder, but I surely did. Doing CPR on a dead woman isn't exactly something you easily forget. I shuddered as I remembered Evie's eyes. No one deserved to die like that, and the thought of someone so young—about the same age as my stepdaughter—meeting such an end made my stomach clench.

Evie must have followed Ritaestelle here; otherwise, how had she found my house? Or was it the other way around? What if . . . ? No. I needed to put the questions aside for now.

I didn't have much clothing that I thought would fit Ritaestelle. She wasn't a large woman, but she definitely had more up top than me. I finally came back in the living room with one of John's Houston Astros T-shirts, a pair of khakis that hung a little loose on me and a pair of slippers.

Morris arrived with the evidence bag just as Ritaestelle finished signing the Miranda waiver.

I held up the clothes. "Best I could do."

Ritaestelle looked up, glanced at Morris and then at Candace. "Is there somewhere a little more private where I could offer you this awful bathrobe? And you may have it, dear. I never want to see it again."

Candace took the bag from Morris and helped Ritaestelle rise. They started slowly toward the hall and the powder room.

But I held up a hand before they could pass me. "Cats are in the hall. I'm sure you don't want hair all over that robe, so let me close them off first."

Ritaestelle turned a pleading gaze on Candace. "Can I hold my Isis after I change?"

"I suppose that would be all right." Candace looked at me. "Can you hurry? I feel like I'm moving in slow motion on this case. Before the deputy coroner shows up, I want to gather as much information as possible."

But as I herded what turned out to be all four cats into the closest room—my quilting room—I heard Lydia Monk's voice coming from the living room. "Oh boy," I muttered. I tossed the buttons they'd been playing with toward them and shut the door.

Candace must have heard the door close, because she and Ritaestelle were already heading my way. Ritaestelle's limp was even more pronounced, and she might not want to see a doctor, but she sure needed to.

"Could you keep the deputy coroner company while Miss Longworth changes?" Candace's tone was polite as she offered me an entreating stare.

I guessed that her words—to keep Lydia company—meant that Candace wanted me to make small talk until she and Ritaestelle returned. That wouldn't be easy. Hello and good-bye was about all I wanted to say to Lydia. Of course, she'd want to check the house to see if Tom was hiding somewhere before she got down to the business of solving a murder.

I took a deep breath and reentered my living room. Lydia was standing near the dining room table talking with Morris. The outfit was typical for Lydia: clingy low-cut pur-

ple shirt, black skinny jeans and feather earrings that reminded me of cat toys. She had a pair of tennis shoes in her
hand but still wore her black patent stiletto heels. Sheesh.
Could someone grab her and do a makeover?

I cleared my throat, and she and Morris turned my way.

"Good evening, Lydia," I said.

She smiled. Could she look any more smug? "Ah, Jillian.
Here we are again investigating a murder close to you. This
time in your own backyard. Sometimes I wonder about
you. You just seem to attract trouble."

"This has been a very difficult night," I said. "Have you
seen that poor young woman's body yet? I mean, that is
why you're here." I knew darn well she hadn't been down
to the lake yet because the tennis shoes were clean and dry.

"I know what my job is—thank you very much." Her
tone was scathing this time. "Tom around to help you wig-
gle out of your troubles tonight?"

There it was, as suspected. The reason she'd come inside.

"He's not here," I said, trying to keep my tone civil.
How I wanted to remind her to get busy with what was
important—investigating Evie Preston's murder, not questioning me about Tom.

Morris must have picked up on the tension because he
said, "They're waitin' for you down by the lake, Lydia."

She kicked off her shoes, sat and slid her feet into the
tennis shoes. "Like I said, I know why I'm here." She picked
up her high heels, tramped through the kitchen and out the
back door.

"Thanks, Morris," I said.

He nodded. "Got to keep that woman on task sometimes."

Candace and Ritaestelle returned. Candace held the evidence bag in one hand and Ritaestelle's elbow in the other.
It seemed to take forever for them to reach us at the dining
room table.

Once Ritaestelle was seated, Candace handed the
tagged paper sack containing the robe to Morris. "I took
pictures of the robe while she was wearing it when we first
came inside, so I think we're done with this piece of evidence for now. The nail clippings and her fingerprint card
are in the envelopes on the counter. I'll transport all this to
the station when we're done here, Deputy Ebeling."

Morris gestured toward the counter. "I'm keeping a log right over there. Got the names of everyone who responded, even the coroner." He began scratching at the mosquito bites on his neck. Bet the insects were having a feast down by the water.

"Great." Candace turned her attention to Ritaestelle. "Now, if you don't mind, please tell me, ma'am . . . why did you kill Evie Preston?"

# Twelve

"You believe I meant to harm Evie?" Ritaestelle sounded incredulous. "I—I tried to save her. She was lying there. She was bleeding. She needed my help, and I—" The tears began again.

I caught Candace's eye. "Um, do you want me to leave?"

"No. In fact, now that we've contacted the police in Woodcrest to talk with the victim's mother, we can get down to business. What time did Miss Longworth show up here?" Candace raised her eyebrows questioningly.

I glanced at Ritaestelle and then back at Candace. "I'm guessing ten fifteen. I was surprised to see her, but she was frightened. She believes someone has been drugging her. And by the way, when I let her inside, her robe was spotless."

"We'll get to that in a minute," Candace said. "Let's start with this claim that Miss Longworth was drugged." She pulled out a dining room chair and sat.

So did I.

The two-way radio Morris held at his side crackled, and then someone said, "Can you come down here to the lake? The deputy coroner is asking for you."

Morris raised his eyes to the ceiling and muttered something about the mosquitoes before he left.

The waiver Ritaestelle had signed was still on the table, and Candace pulled her notebook toward her—the one I'd seen in her evidence bag before. She picked up the pen that rested on the waiver, poised it over the notebook and looked at Ritaestelle. "Why did you come to see Jillian

Hart if you thought you were being drugged? Why not go to a hospital?"

"I have no fondness for hospitals or doctors. Besides, since I stopped drinking the tea—most of it went down the sink since yesterday—I have been feeling much better."

"Ah," Candace said. "You think someone drugged your tea. Did you report your suspicions to the local police?"

*Good question,* I thought. Except that I had a feeling Ritaestelle didn't want anyone in Woodcrest alerted to anything else that put her in a bad light.

Ritaestelle hesitated before saying, "I am sure you understand small-town life, Deputy Carson. I do not appreciate people learning about my private life if I am not the one telling the story. There would be talk. Besides, there is already talk around town that I am a shoplifter. Which I most certainly am not."

Candace began writing while saying, "So you decided to visit a stranger in another town? Can you see how that seems a little odd?"

"Oh, I do. But Jillian visited me first," Ritaestelle said. "She came to my house yesterday, and because of my condition, my *drugged* condition, I could not meet with her. But I know *of* her, and thus I know of her reputation for helping others. And my Isis had been missing for days, so once I had my wits, I realized that was why she called on me."

"Let me get this straight. You came here to reclaim your cat? And to get assistance from a stranger about these other problems?" Candace said.

"Yes. That sums it up quite well, Deputy Carson. I fear that I am being harmed—harmed by the removal of my dear Isis, harmed by these preposterous charges that I am a thief and harmed by someone who has been sedating me. Jillian Hart, from what I have read, is a kind and decent person. She will help me, so I do not regret coming here. I only regret what has happened to poor Evie."

"But you didn't bother to get dressed?" Candace said.

Ritaestelle raised her chin, her eyes still moist with tears. "I had to sneak out once Augusta fell asleep. She has been watching me like a hawk, and I have no idea why. I am telling you, Deputy Carson, there is something very strange going on in Woodcrest and more specifically inside my beloved home. And just so you know, I *have* spoken with the police chief about my situation—the shoplifting, that is. She happens to be a friend."

"I suspect we'll be speaking with Chief Shelton," Candace said. "Let's move along. Tell me everything that happened from the minute you got here."

Ritaestelle talked in her long, rambling style, relating the events that I already knew, but my interest picked up when she got to what happened after I left her alone in my living room.

She said, "I thought I heard something outside. Voices, perhaps? But then I began to wonder if the drugs were still playing tricks on me. Still, something made me get up and go to the back door. And then I foolishly opened it. Jillian's cat ran out into the night. I knew she would never forgive me if I was responsible for losing her cat, so I grabbed a broom to help me walk. I used it like a cane."

Candace looked perplexed, but she sounded as tough as nails when she said, "You can hardly walk, and yet you go down to the lake after a cat? You don't call for Jillian's help?"

"I did call for her, but she must not have heard me. As for the rest of it, I—I cannot explain my actions." Ritaestelle shook her head sadly. "You see, the cat ran right to poor Evie. She was lying there on the dock. She was not breathing. Her eyes were wide-open. She was . . . gone."

*Lying on the dock?* But I'd found her in the water. Obviously I'd missed something.

"How'd she get in the water? Because the victim is soaking wet," Candace said.

Candace and I were on the same wavelength, it would seem.

"The *victim*. What an awful word. But her being wet is my fault," Ritaestelle said. "I cradled my poor Evie's head and then realized what I was doing. I had assumed she was dead. But what if she could be brought back? So I tried to lay her flat on the dock so I could breathe for her. Rescue breathing, we used to call it back in the day. But it was dark, and she was so much closer to the edge than I realized. Instead of putting her on the dock, I rolled her off my lap right into the water." New tears sprang to her eyes. "If that poor girl drowned because of me, I will never forgive myself."

"You're saying you shoved her body into the water?" Candace was writing this down and didn't look at Ritaestelle, but I heard the suspicion in her voice.

"Pushed. Accidentally," Ritaestelle said. "And then Jillian came rushing out. I grabbed up her cat, and then I am afraid I do not recall much else aside from looking for a cellular phone. Yes. I remember that part."

Candace looked at me. "You found Miss Preston in the water?"

"Yes. I pulled her up on the rocks to do CPR, but . . . well, you know the rest." I hung my head. I felt that sting of failure again. Maybe Evie could have been saved if I'd known what I was doing or came out of the house sooner.

"And *you* didn't hear Miss Longworth call for you or hear this noise she talked about coming from the backyard?" Candace asked me.

"I was in my bedroom closet, so I couldn't hear anything." The adrenaline was definitely wearing off. My knees stung, and my wet clothes were making me shiver. I like to keep the house cool in the summer, so the air-conditioning was set at around seventy-two. And my body temperature felt like it was seventy-two.

Candace looked back over her notes and then said, "Miss Longworth stated that you went to look for Isis, right?"

"Yes. But there was a problem." I explained about Isis's predicament. And I wondered then that if I hadn't spent so much time helping her out of the basket, just brought Isis and the basket out into the living room instead, perhaps I would have been able to save Evie.

Candace rose. "You know, after hearing all this, I'm thinking we need to get a formal statement down at the police station, Miss Longworth. You know, with video running and everything?"

Ritaestelle seemed confused for a second or two. Then she said, "Are you arresting me?"

"I'll have to get with my chief on this," Candace said. "You got anyone you want to call? Like maybe any lawyer friends you might have?"

I caught Candace's eye and said, "Can I talk to you for a minute?"

Candace nodded, and we walked a few feet away into the living room.

I whispered, "This woman needs to see a doctor. Her hip and her claim she's been drugged make me think you'd better check her out before you put her in jail."

Candace stared at me, considering this. Sounding deflated, she said, "You're right." She pulled her two-way radio from her pocket and spoke into it. "Morris?"

"Yeah?" came his staticky reply.

"Paramedics still hanging around?"

"Oh yeah," he said.

"Send them up to the house," Candace said. She looked at me. "Man, I sure wanted to get this woman out of here before Lydia made her way back up here. Not too much chance of that now."

"I don't want Lydia hanging around any longer than necessary. But I honestly believe Ritaestelle is telling the truth—for what that's worth. And she is having a difficult time walking. I suspect she's in considerable pain."

Candace sighed. "I'm sure you're right—about the pain."

We walked back to join Ritaestelle, whose tears had dried. She was looking rather stoic now. "May I see my cat before you lock me up?"

"I didn't say we're arresting you, Miss Longworth. I need a heck of lot more information before we go down that road," Candace said.

"May I *please* see my cat?" she repeated.

"Sure," Candace said. "Jillian?"

I left to find Isis, thinking that in believing Ritaestelle, I was following my heart rather than my head. That blood on her robe sure was telling, and I didn't know if this whole "I was drugged" thing was true. Plus, I now recalled that Ritaestelle had been holding that rock in her hand when I first saw her on the dock. I needed to tell Candace about that when I got the chance.

I opened the door to my quilting room, not prepared for what I saw. Fabrics that I kept in color-coordinated stacks on a bookshelf littered the floor. And the drawer where I kept my quilt bindings must have been left ajar because Isis had various bindings wrapped all over her. Chablis was in a corner, grooming herself. I wished I had had time to clean the blood off her before she took care of the problem herself. Too late now.

Syrah was sitting and staring at Isis, while Merlot, wearing one bright yellow binding around his neck, lay on his back at her feet. Bet she liked that. Another adoring fan.

"All four of you have been up to no good all night," I said. I walked over and disentangled Isis. She didn't resist, didn't even hiss or try to bite.

A terrible thing happened tonight, and yet in this, the room I called my safe haven, four animals had been doing what cats do—exploring, playing and letting their curiosity take over. Their world would not be darkened by tragedy. They were loved and cared for, and how I wished it could be that way for every living thing. If that ever came to be, it would be too late for Evie Preston. Far too late.

I sighed, picked up Isis and carried her to the living room. All three of my cats followed.

Two paramedics were with Ritaestelle—Jake and Marcy. Marcy was kneeling by Ritaestelle and gently probing the older woman's hip. Jake stood on her other side checking her blood pressure. Cats have been known to help lower blood pressure just by sitting in a person's lap. I was willing to bet Ritaestelle needed that kind of help right now.

Once Jake took the cuff off her arm, I walked over and held Isis out to her.

She smiled feebly and took her cat. Isis pulled her head back immediately so she could look at Ritaestelle's face. And then she leaned into her mistress's chest, closed her eyes and began to purr.

# Thirteen

The reunion between Isis and Ritaestelle was short-lived. The cat belonged to me again once the paramedics decided that Ritaestelle needed her hip X-rayed. Candace went with her in the ambulance to the county hospital.

Which left me with Lydia Monk. That was because she is a county "investigator" and not a medical examiner—she's not even close to being a doctor. I had to tell her everything that went on before I found Evie in the water. But I got to ask a few questions of my own after I told her all I knew.

"Do you think Evie Preston drowned?" I asked.

I'd changed my clothes and we were sitting in my living room with glasses of sweet tea. Even though I do not care for Lydia, that doesn't mean I can't be polite. Besides, I needed a little sugar boost after the evening's stressful events.

All four cats had disappeared as soon as Lydia came in through my back door and hadn't shown their furry faces in the last thirty minutes. I sure could have used a cat in my lap to keep *my* blood pressure in check. But I was doing an adequate job keeping my emotions under control even though the image of Evie's wide dead eyes kept reappearing. And I had to admit that this conversation between Lydia and me was going well insofar as there'd been no remarks from her about our imaginary romantic triangle.

Lydia said, "I can't be certain about whether she drowned until I find the doc on call to do an autopsy. But that blow she took to the head? My guess is that was what did her in. I saw no evidence of drowning. Her face was pale, but her lips weren't discolored and I saw no frothing at the mouth. Believe me, I've seen more than my share of drowning deaths, what with all the lakes around here. She didn't look like a drowning victim."

"All that blood came from her head?" I asked.

"Oh yeah. Head wounds bleed like crazy. There were blood on the dock, a bloody broom, bloody slippers." Lydia paused. "You didn't notice? Because the way folks talk, you're supposed to be so damn observant."

I literally bit my lip to keep from firing back that I was pulling a woman out of the water and not checking around for blood evidence. Keeping my voice even, I said, "I never went up onto the dock."

"Ah, that explains it, I suppose. Anyway, I suspect you won't want that broom back—ever," Lydia said.

"W-was that the murder weapon?" And could Ritaestelle have wielded enough force to kill Evie with a broom? The thought made me shudder. Maybe I was wrong about Ritaestelle. Maybe something awful went on before I got down to the dock.

"I have no idea if that broom did the woman in," Lydia said. "Until a doctor examines the skull, we won't know. From what I overheard, that Longworth woman is a little off, though. Maybe capable of attacking Evie Preston. You're probably lucky she didn't take a swing at you for having her cat."

"She's grateful her cat is safe. And she doesn't seem like a violent person to me," I said.

Lydia said, "And just what does a violent person seem like?"

Good question. But I didn't have a chance to respond because my front doorbell rang. That brought cats running from various hiding places to see what was up. Even Isis. They all gathered in the foyer, anticipating more nighttime adventures. It was well past midnight now, and I wondered if Candace had returned from the hospital to gather more evidence or ask more questions.

I went to the door and saw Tom through the peephole. "Oh no," I whispered. The sound of my voice had all thirty-two muscles in each of Syrah's ears twitching. I opened the door, knowing I couldn't pretend that no one was home.

"Hi there, Tom," I said loudly when I opened the door.

Then I whispered, "*She's* here. Think of some great reason why you've showed up."

Tom nodded and said, "Is something wrong with your security alarm?"

Lydia was at the entrance to the foyer when I turned around.

"Hi, Lydia. What are you doing here?" Tom said.

She smiled—and I couldn't read her. Was that a sarcastic smile or a stalker smile? Maybe both. "You know what I'm doing here, Tom. I show up at every murder scene. Better question: What are *you* doing here?"

"My job. According to my control panel for my clients, Jillian's alarm was engaged, disengaged within a few minutes and never reset. I thought that was suspicious. Just wanted to make sure everything was okay."

Ah. He'd checked my system—probably after he heard what had happened on his police scanner.

"Everything's not okay," Lydia said. "Murder. Again."

"Really? What happened?" Tom knelt and my three cats hurried to him for some head scratching. An aloof Isis stayed back.

"Who do you think you're kidding, Tom? My guess is your wannabe girlfriend, Jillian, called you over here. She thinks she has a chance with you, but we both know she's dreaming. Isn't that right?" Lydia's penciled-in eyebrows rose.

"Who died?" Tom always avoided these crazy Lydia questions far better than I could ever manage.

"Seems Jillian got all curious again, went to Woodcrest on some animal rescue mission at Shawn's command. Now we've got a bona fide tragedy. Some chick from Woodcrest came here and got cracked over the head. Jillian is always sticking her nose where it doesn't belong—and I hope you're taking note of that."

My jaw dropped. She was blaming me? Saying that my going to Woodcrest led to Evie's death? That made no sense, and yet guilt niggled at me anyway.

"You must have reports to write, mustn't you, Lydia?" Tom said.

She glanced at her watch, the one with the wide gold lamé band. "I do. But I haven't finished my tea. Jillian and I were having a nice little talk about her involvement in this latest crime."

"You have more questions?" I asked.

"You want me to leave so you can be alone with him, don't you?" Lydia turned to Tom. "She won't come between us. Ever."

Oh boy. Cue the *Twilight Zone* music.

It was a cat who managed to do what I couldn't accomplish. Isis came sauntering over from her corner of the foyer and began rubbing against Lydia's leg. Cats can always pick out the people who like them the least and make them uncomfortable.

Lydia looked down at Isis and then back at me. "Get that cat away from me."

"She seems to like you," I said, making no move to halt Isis's marking activity.

A smile played at Tom's lips.

"I said, make this animal go away." Lydia sidestepped, but Isis followed.

"I'm kind of afraid to do that. This is the cat that belongs to Ritaestelle Longworth, and I have to say, she's not as well behaved as my cats," I said. "If I touch her, she might bite me."

"You're scared? Well, I'm not." Lydia made the mistake of reaching down and attempting to shoo Isis away.

Isis, in good goddess form, screeched and made an attempt to bite Lydia's hand.

Lydia jumped to her left, her eyes wide. "What a nasty little creature."

Isis's black coat puffed out, and she arched her back. But she didn't run off.

My turn to stifle a smile. "I have no control over this one. Sorry."

Tom reached down and swooped Isis up, then held her up to Lydia's face. "Come on. You two can be friends."

Isis offered one of her trademark fang-baring hisses.

Lydia craned her head away. "I think I'm done here. For now." She pointed a bloodred fake nail at me. "But you keep your cat paws off Tom, you hear?"

Tom handed Isis to me. "Can I walk you out, Lydia? You never know. There could be a killer lurking."

"Why, that would be so nice." She smiled, looking almost giddy. With Lydia carrying her stiletto heels, they went out the front door.

I breathed a sigh of relief and hugged on Isis. "Thank you, sweetheart. You have redeemed yourself." I set her down and she raced off after Syrah. He was batting yet another button down the hallway.

Tom returned a minute later. "Keep your friends close and your enemies closer, I always say. I checked, and it looks like the crowd out back is wrapping up. Was it a drowning or definitely a murder?"

"Murder." I sighed heavily. "Come on in and I'll tell you what I know." We went into the living room, and when I finished I said, "I don't think Ritaestelle did this, Tom."

His face was expressionless. He was probably thinking like a cop—not ready to rule out anyone as a killer just because I had an opinion about suspect numero uno.

Morris came through the back door then and said they were done for the night but would be back early in the morning.

After he left, Tom stood. "You look like you could use some sleep." He pulled me up and gave me a much-needed hug, promising to return in the morning. Before he left, he reminded me to reengage my security alarm. Like I would have forgotten after all that had gone on. But the fact that he'd voiced his concern felt good.

When I went to my bedroom, whom did I find waiting to cuddle up with me? Isis. She *had* saved me from a sticky circumstance, so I could hardly send her to the basement.

"Come on, wild one. You're welcome to join me," I said once I settled in under the sheets. As if I had a choice in the matter.

I hoped for a peaceful night. The feline crew had to be tired, too. Cats aren't truly nocturnal—they prefer dusk and dawn antics, making them crepuscular.

Isis, I soon learned, preferred sleeping by my head and taking up half the pillow, but before I even had to remove one long black hair from my face, I nodded off. And I would need that sleep in the next few days if they proved to be anything like the last two.

# Fourteen

"Where's the rest of the police force?" I said when I led Candace, Morris and Mike Baca into the kitchen at seven the next morning.

Mike wore his forest green uniform—hardly ever saw him in that. "Probably asleep if they're smart," he said. "All twenty Mercy officers met at the station last night. We were all briefed by Morris, and I thought we had completed the initial paperwork, but then Lydia showed up. She kept everyone way too long with her questions."

His tone was restrained, very professional, but he and Lydia had been in a relationship once. Everyone in Mercy knew how embarrassed Mike was about that fling. How those two had ever hooked up in the first place was beyond me—but then I knew he'd made several bad choices in the relationship department.

I gestured at the coffeepot and mugs on the counter. "Help yourself. I'm sure you guys will need plenty of that."

Murmuring thanks, they all made their way to the coffee. Candace looked the most alert of the three this morning, but, then, she was young and eager and an evidence hound.

Though Merlot, Chablis and Syrah had joined me when I'd gotten up, they didn't greet my guests this morning. They'd eaten and taken off to find their favorite sunning spots. Trouble was, it looked cloudy this morning. As for Isis? She stayed in bed. It was probably far too early for goddesses.

"Can you tell me about Ritaestelle? What happened at the hospital?" I asked Candace.

"She spent the night. Still there as far as I know." Candace sipped her coffee.

"Because of her hip?" I said.

"She had one giant bruise. Saw it myself when she changed clothes after I took that robe into evidence. But I don't know if her hip is cracked, sprained or what," Candace said.

Morris stirred sugar into his mug. "The hip is definitely a problem, but I heard she needed her head examined, too. Kept talking conspiracy theories."

"Deputy Ebeling," Mike said sharply.

"It's true," Morris said.

"She required a neurological workup and a tox screen," Mike said. "She kept saying she'd been drugged, and we have to follow up on that. No one but you is implying she has psychiatric problems."

"But you have to admit, Miss Longworth is odd, Chief," Candace said. " 'Course, if she was really drugged like she claimed, that could have caused all sorts of mental stuff."

"*Claimed* she was drugged is the key," Morris said. "I say you folks are blinded by the gleam off all her gold bricks. She's guilty as sin."

"That's *not* how we begin an investigation in Mercy— with the presumption of guilt." Mike's tone was still stern.

And Morris wondered why Candace was leading this investigation and not him. Sheesh.

Mike continued, saying, "And when Chief Shelton shows up, you better keep your opinions to yourself, Morris. Miss Longworth has practically bankrolled Woodcrest singlehandedly."

"That's what I'm sayin'. Money blinds people to the truth," he said.

Mike said, "Morris? Zip it, okay?"

"Yes, sir." But Morris Ebeling didn't sound contrite, and I had the feeling his silence wouldn't last.

Feeling a tad tense, I busied myself by grinding more beans. I had to practically shout over the noise when I said, "Um . . . Chief Shelton's coming here?"

"She is," Mike said.

The grinder stopped. I dumped the old filter in the

trash and started a fresh pot. "I've met her—twice. The first time she was pretty unhappy with me. I was driving a little too fast. Something about her demeanor scared me—something more than what I expected from a traffic stop. But then yesterday, when Tom and I went to Woodcrest, she was different. Nice. Concerned for her friend."

"Candace was telling me about your trip on the way over here. Just so you know, I've known Nancy for years. She's all bark and no bite," Mike said. "Since both Miss Longworth and Miss Preston are from her town, I decided she should be involved in the investigation."

"Speaking of that," I said, "there is something I learned from Chief Shelton. Maybe it's important." I glanced back and forth between Candace and Mike.

Candace said, "I thought you told me everything yesterday before we watched that movie."

I blinked. What had I told her? Obviously stress had taken a toll, because I couldn't remember. "Did I mention that Evie Preston told the police chief about the shoplifting?"

Candace nodded. "You did."

I sighed. "Good. I was worried, because I was pretty adamant last night that Ritaestelle didn't kill Evie—but then I thought, what if she thought Evie considered her a thief? That could have made her pretty angry. Though I'm still not convinced Ritaestelle is capable of violence. There's this sweetness about her."

"Sweetness, huh? Confusion was about all I saw. Anyway, I put the shoplifting in my report, so quit worrying. What I'm talking about is anything Miss Longworth might have said when she arrived at your door, anything you recalled after I left to go with her to the hospital." Candace eyed me expectantly.

"What sticks in my mind the most is how upset she was that someone was drugging her. She wanted my help, but the only thing I could do was to return her spoiled cat."

"You mean this one?" Mike was looking down, and sure enough, Isis had arrived. She was rubbing against his leg and depositing long black hairs on his uniform trousers.

"That's her," I said. "Wait a minute." I thumped my forehead with the heel of my hand. "What the heck is wrong with me? There is something I never told you. When I went outside and found poor Evie, Ritaestelle was holding something besides my cat. And when I was pulling Evie out of the water, I believe she dropped whatever it was and it fell into the water. I heard a splash."

"Holding something? Like what?" Candace said.

"It was dark, but I think it was a rock. It wasn't the broom—that's for sure."

"Which hand?" Candace was definitely excited.

Of course she'd want to know which hand. I hesitated, picturing Ritaestelle standing on the dock. Chablis had been clutched close in her right arm. "Her left hand was hanging down at her side. Yes. Left hand. Do you think she hit Evie with a rock?"

"Maybe," Candace said.

"If it helps, Ritaestelle is right-handed," I said. "I definitely remember she took the glass of water I gave her with her right hand."

"She could have switched the rock to her left hand to pick up Chablis," Candace said. "Do you know how deep that water is on that side of the dock?"

"Three feet at most, but it drops off quickly once you get to the end of the dock. What are you thinking?"

"Yeah. What *are* you thinking? 'Cause I didn't bring my swimming trunks," Morris said sourly.

"You can actually swim? That takes a certain amount of energy," Candace said.

"Cut the crap, you two. Don't make me feel like a middle school teacher trying to keep the bickering students in line," Mike said. "We'll have to look beneath the surface before anyone goes wading in and disturbing whatever might lie underwater. That means goggles, a special camera and someone with the skill to handle this. I got a person in mind, so I'll make some calls."

"We better get busy looking for any other evidence we missed last night in the dark," Candace said. "Might rain, and that's the last thing I need—a washed-out crime scene and a stirred-up lake." Candace set her mug down and started for the back door.

Grumpy Morris hung his head and followed her, muttering, "Yeah, yeah, yeah. Wet evidence. Wouldn't want *that*." Guess he liked the role of snarky middle schooler.

Mike stopped punching numbers on his phone and

looked at me. "When Nancy arrives, I'll be on the deck." He checked his watch. "She should have been here already."

But the knock that came on my front door a minute later wasn't Nancy Shelton arriving. It was Kara and Tom. After they both greeted the three cats—mine, not Isis, who had disappeared again—we all went into the living room. The cats went to finish off any food they'd left earlier.

Tom carried two boxes of donuts from Wanda's Bakery, and the smell of icing and yeast made my mouth water. When was the last time I'd eaten a donut?

"Why didn't you call me last night, Jillian?" Kara said.

"I'm sorry. I wanted to, but it was late. You might have already been asleep, and—"

"You could have used the support," Kara said. "I mean, you found a dead woman in your lake. This place is your sanctuary, and now it's been tainted by a vicious death."

"Nothing will ever taint this place for me, Kara. And I planned to call you first thing this morning—at a decent hour, of course, and—"

"I still could have come over. I do want to be here for you," she said.

"I suppose it's all over the newspaper," I said.

I caught Tom's glance—he was shaking his head slightly—and I instantly knew that this was a sore subject.

"You would think a story this big would be above the fold, wouldn't you? But no. It's *not*." Kara's jaw tightened.

"That's not good, is it?" I said.

"A story like this? No. It's plain embarrassing, if you ask me," she said.

"You'll own the paper soon enough, and then you'll make sure something like this makes the front page right away." Secretly I was glad the story wasn't running already. People in Mercy loved to talk, and they'd probably be calling me or stopping me in the grocery store once the news spread.

Kara said, "The *Mercy Messenger* needs this kind of story to boost sales. But that idiot Buddy who works the night desk didn't even get off his butt and come here, even though he heard the 911 call on the scanner. He sat in the office eating those five tuna sandwiches he always brings with him. The entire office always smells like tuna. Guess he figured the current owner, editor, do-everything-by-himself, Mr. Mortenson, would handle this today. Do you know how dumb that is?"

"I do now," I said quietly.

Kara's expression softened. "Damn. I am so sorry." She came over and hugged me. When she released me, she said, "I sound like I used to. I sound like the person I was running away from in Houston. Tell me how I can help."

"You're here. You've already helped." I looked at Tom. "Do not let Morris see those donuts, or Candace will not be happy. They'll distract him. I suggest you set them on the counter in an inconspicuous place until the evidence gathering is complete."

"Rain might end that endeavor," Tom said. "By the way, Kara tells me Scott Mortenson is happy to let her do the story and all the follow-ups."

"Oh. That's great," I said, trying to sound like this was a wonderful development. But I had mixed emotions. From Kara's smile, I knew she was thrilled. Despite settling in a small town, she had journalism in her blood. Her first Mercy bylines would be big ones. But would I be her first interview? That might be awkward. I hoped I got a chance to talk to Candace about being in the middle—between Kara and the investigation.

Kara said, "I saw the cop cars out front, and I was hoping—"

The doorbell rang. This time it was Nancy Shelton, but she wasn't alone. A tall man with a shaved head, maybe midthirties, was with her. She wore her navy blue suit—but this one was different. She wore slacks, and the trim along the edges of her jacket was metallic blue. These suits she wore, with the gold buttons to match her badge, had to be custom-made. I knew plenty about fabrics and sewing. A skilled seamstress had been at work—and had done a marvelous job.

The man with her wore a summer-weight suit with a silk brown-and-pink-striped tie. I instantly envied his thick, dark eyelashes. He probably had a wonderful smile, but right now he looked as serious as a politician giving a concession speech.

When I ushered them into the living room, Nancy Shelton introduced him as Liam Brennan, the county assistant district attorney. "Mr. Brennan will be coordinating the joint efforts of both our towns' law enforcement to solve this murder as soon as possible."

She sounded like she was giving a press conference— especially since she was staring straight at Kara the whole time. Did she know Kara was journalist?

I made my introductions then. "This is Kara Hart and Tom Stewart."

Brennan's brown eyes were on Kara, too. "Aren't you buying the newspaper?"

*Yup, they know,* I thought.

But I caught a flicker of surprise in Kara's eyes. "Yes," she said. "And though I'm Jillian's stepdaughter, I need to be clear that I'm also here because of my connection to the *Mercy Messenger.*"

"I didn't see any story in this morning's paper," Brennan said in an almost taunting way.

I glanced at Kara, feeling the need to protect her. "You *will* see a story. Isn't that right, Kara?"

She was staring Brennan down, not appearing the least bit intimidated. I should have known she didn't need any protection from me.

Kara said, "Since I'm already taking over many aspects of the newspaper's day-to-day operations, you'll be seeing my byline. A lot."

Brennan smiled, and that smile was as charming as I'd imagined it would be. "Look forward to it." He turned to Tom. "And you own a private security business. But weren't you a police officer at one time, and then you—"

"Good for you. You've done your homework," Tom said tersely.

The escalating tension in the room had my stomach churning. Those donuts smelled sickly sweet and unappealing now. I said, "Let me get Mike. He was trying to round up some underwater equipment."

But Mike must have heard their arrival because he came in through the back door.

Suddenly I felt the need to sit before my legs gave out. For the first time, the enormity of what had happened overwhelmed me. I found the closest easy chair. All of this bantering and the apparent need for one-upmanship seemed ludicrous. A young woman was dead. And yet politics, news scoops and evidence collection were all anyone seemed to care about.

Kara addressed Mike as soon as he came into the living room. "Do you mind if I see the crime scene for myself?" She pulled a camera from the hobo-style bag slung over her shoulder.

"From a distance."

Brennan held out a hand to Mike. "Good to see you again, Mike."

The two shook hands, and Mike said, "Nancy told me you'd be involved—help us share information. Thanks for that."

Brennan glanced back and forth between Tom and me. "You two please stay inside." He turned to Mike. "Lead the way."

When they were gone, Tom came over and took my hands. "You're cold, not to mention pale as a polar bear. This isn't what you signed up for when you told Shawn you'd help with Isis. Where are the cats, by the way?"

"I don't know. Let's find them," I said. "I could use a cat in my lap right now."

And find them we did. In my quilting room. And guess who was stuck in my sewing cabinet drawer while my three sat in a half circle staring at her latest dilemma.

# Fifteen

I carefully extracted Isis from the cabinet drawer while Tom crouched beside me and petted my cats.

I said, "Isis apparently thinks she's thinner than she actually is. Maybe her whiskers are too short. Whiskers should warn a cat about whether they'll fit into a space."

"I get the feeling that Isis does what Isis wants, regardless of the consequences," he said. "Sounds like a little criminal, if you ask me."

I held her up and looked into her green eyes. "Is he calling you names? Doesn't he know you're a goddess?" I smiled and set Isis down. She strolled away as if nothing had happened.

I said, "Why do cats act like they had no part of an embarrassing situation? Is it that little human section of their brain at work?"

"I haven't gotten stuck in a wicker basket or a drawer lately, but I'd pretend it was no big deal if *my* peers were watching," Tom said.

I laughed. "Guess I would, too."

Chablis was attempting to climb up on his knees, probably because she'd been traumatized by last night's events and was looking for any comfort she could find.

He picked her up and stood, scratching her around her neck where she liked it the most. She was purring so loud they probably heard her down at the lake.

The lake. The investigation. This stranger Brennan. I couldn't wait for this morning to end. "How long do you think they'll be hunting around in my yard?" I asked.

"You know Candace," Tom said. "She'd do a grid search like when they're looking for buried remains if it were up to her," Tom said. "But with the assistant DA and Mike around, they'll keep her on task. I'd say an hour or two."

Isis reappeared and led the way as we walked back into the living room. She seemed to want to take over as top cat, and I wondered how long Syrah would put up with that. More reason for this cat to go home. But with Ritaestelle in the hospital, would that happen anytime soon?

"Have you had breakfast?" I asked.

"A donut. And you should have one. I got to the bakery the minute they opened. Those were still hot when they were boxed."

"A bagel sounds better—if the ones I bought the other day aren't as hard as hockey pucks by now."

Turned out they were *harder* than hockey pucks, and I had a banana instead. Even the fruit didn't set well. A small part of me wondered what they were doing outside, but a bigger part didn't even want to look out the window. When Deputy Tony Martinez, who I knew usually worked the late shift, showed up dressed in shorts and carrying a camera case, I figured he must be the underwater specialist.

Kara came inside about fifteen minutes after his arrival. Tom had watched the goings-on through the kitchen window, but I stayed in the living room—surrounded by felines.

Kara grabbed a mug and poured herself some coffee before she and Tom joined me. She sat in her dad's recliner and set her bag with the camera on the floor next to her.

"Will my backyard be gracing the front page of the newspaper?" I said.

"Just the dock," she said. "If that's okay with you."

I took a deep breath and stroked Merlot, not answering right away. He was stretched out between Tom and me. Chablis immediately climbed into Tom's lap, and Syrah stayed where he'd been, on the sofa back close to my head. Isis had disappeared yet again. Maybe if she stayed stuck in whatever object she'd crawled into this time, she'd learn a lesson.

"Please let me do this story the way it should be done, Jillian? That means interviewing you, too," Kara said.

There it was. The very thing that concerned me. "I'm not sure I should do that," I said. "Somehow it seems unfair to

Ritaestelle. She's in enough trouble without me adding to it by talking about her."

"I've interviewed Mike Baca—an interview he was happy to provide, by the way—so I know most of the facts. But the duty of the press is to inform the public, to provide answers. I want to do the job right. You're a witness with a unique perspective."

Unique? Was that what this sick feeling was called? "If you spoke to Mike, don't you have what you need? Besides, you haven't lived here long enough to understand that even if you put out the facts, folks will still think up their own scenarios about what happened here."

Kara leaned toward me, her tone soft but insistent. "That doesn't matter to me. Besides, both Mike and Liam said an interview with you might stir up even more talk in town—talk they can follow up on."

He was already Liam to her? Hmm. He certainly had a great smile. You can tell a lot by a person's smile, and I kind of liked what I'd seen. Guess Kara did, too. When I didn't say anything, Tom put his arm around my shoulder and squeezed me gently. "The press and the police have a funny relationship. It can be an unpleasant one, but they need each other. Tips are often generated from press coverage. Think about it as doing a service to Ritaestelle. If you honestly believe she's innocent, your interview might just help her."

I glanced back and forth between them. "Why do I feel like I'm betraying her trust?" Unfortunately, what bothered me more than betraying Ritaestelle was upsetting Kara if I refused to cooperate. That could put a strain on the new and still tenuous relationship we'd formed since she'd arrived in Mercy. That fear is what finally tipped the scales. I sighed and said, "Ask away."

She asked about how I knew Ritaestelle—even though she already knew this—and went on to quiz me about the woman's arrival and then the discovery of the body.

"Is it true you did CPR on the victim after you pulled her out of the water?" Kara said.

Those horrible moments from last night flashed through my mind. I felt the unexpected sting of tears but blinked them back. "Yes. But could you leave out the part about the CPR? I couldn't help her. She was dead."

Kara hesitated. "You tried to save her. That's a fact, and I need to print it."

"I failed Evie Preston, Kara. I don't want to have that written down for everyone to read." I blinked harder, really fighting the tears now.

Kara's tone softened when she said, "Putting the story aside for a second, I want to say that I believe you were a hero out there. You did everything right. And I know that's how other people in town will look at this."

I took a breath, told myself to calm down before I said, "Can't you please just write about what the police know?"

Kara sat back. "The last thing I want to do is upset you, but I need to verify with you what I learned from the police."

I trusted Kara, didn't I? She would get the story right. "Go ahead," I said.

She recited what she'd heard from Mike, and I nodded to confirm everything she said until she asked, "And Rita-estelle Longworth appeared mentally unstable, correct?"

With that, I stopped nodding. "Not to me. And I'm the one she came to see. I understand she's had her share of recent troubles, but—"

"But," Kara said, "this once well-respected woman in her community has become a laughingstock. Your visit to Woodcrest confirmed that, correct?"

I felt anger bubbling up. "Only one person in my back-yard could have said such a thing about Ritaestelle. Nancy Shelton, right?"

"The chief said she's very concerned about Miss Long-worth's mental state." Kara paused, taking the time to re-move the elastic that held her long dark hair in a ponytail and gather up wayward strands before she refastened her hair at the nape of her neck.

Maybe she was giving me time to think about this state-ment, because it sure wasn't a question.

But Tom spoke before I could. "What does that mean, Kara?" Tom asked. "I was there when Jillian talked with Chief Shelton yesterday. She's friends with Ritaestelle, and nothing she said made me believe she considered the woman a *laughingstock*."

"Okay, those are my words, and I would never print

that," Kara said, sounding sheepish. "But I do like you step-ping in to support Jillian. That's sweet."

I said, "Is this the path the police have chosen to follow? To make Ritaestelle seem like a nutcase?"

"Not necessarily." Kara paused to sip her coffee. "But since it was brought up and since Miss Longworth came to your door not exactly appropriately dressed for a visit, it's an angle worth pursuing. Despite what you think, I've learned plenty about small-town life in the last few months. When the rich and powerful fall, people are quick to be-little them—even stomp on them. Besides, I understand there have been other incidents that call into question Miss Longworth's mental health. Can you tell me more about what you learned?"

I was beginning to lose patience with Kara the Journal-ist, but I kept my tone even when I said, "No, I can't. You should talk to Chief Shelton about what's been happening in Woodcrest. The most important thing to me is that that this lady came to me for help and that her employee has been murdered."

"In your backyard," Kara said. "How did Evie Preston end up here?"

I shook my head. "I can only guess—and that's not something you'd print."

"You're right," Kara said, "but I still want your take. Did she follow Ritaestelle? And if so, why?"

"M-maybe Evie saw her boss leave the house and was concerned about her, so she followed," I said.

"That's sort of giving credence to the idea that she's emotionally unstable, don't you think?" Kara pressed.

"Why? Because Evie was worried enough about her to follow her? I don't know. But how else did she get here?" The room seemed to be closing in on me. Why was Kara being so . . . *intense*?

"Or," Kara said, "could it have been the other way around? Miss Longworth followed Evie here. After all, you spoke with Evie when you went to the estate, and she knew who you were. But you never spoke with Miss Longworth that day."

I shook my head, but the small fear that had been hiding in the back of my mind was pushed front and center now. What if that were true? What if Ritaestelle followed Evie here, they somehow ended up in my backyard and Evie was killed? But then, why would Ritaestelle come to my door? That didn't make sense.

I said, "I don't believe Ritaestelle murdered Evie. She simply didn't have time."

Kara said, "Can you be sure how long you were in that closet with the cat?"

"I can't. Five minutes? Ten minutes? I'm not sure," I said.

"Miss Longworth claimed to have taken the broom outside to use as a cane, but what if she took it to use as a weapon? Have you considered that possibility?"

"Kara," I said sharply, "she couldn't have planned on her cat causing the delay in my getting back to the living room. Besides, the woman could hardly walk. I honestly have no idea how she made it down to the dock. And aren't you speculating now, and not merely confirming what the police told you?"

Her features softened. "I am. Sorry. Let me ask you this. Did you get any hint when you were visiting with the woman that she was nervous, upset, that something terrible had happened before you let her in?"

"No. She was as calm as I'd expect any person who'd just fled their home in fear would be. Her robe was clean when I let her in and—wait a minute. The cars." Morris had mentioned both a Cadillac and a Ford when he came out to the backyard and talked to us last night.

Tom said, "What are you thinking?"

"When you walked Lydia outside, where were all the cars parked? Because if Evie followed Ritaestelle here, her Ford would have been parked *behind* Ritaestelle's Cadillac," I said.

"The Caddy was in your driveway, but that's it. I parked on the street along with everyone else. Morris was dusting a Ford Focus's doors for prints—and it was on the side of the road. I'm assuming that car belonged to Evie Preston."

"Wait a minute," I said. "I saw that Ford Morris talked about. When I went to get Candace's evidence kit, it was parked on the road then, too. None of the police would have moved it, would they?"

Kara said, "I doubt it, but I'll ask."

"Kara, please listen. I promise you that if Ritaestelle was

killing Evie out on my dock before she ever knocked on my front door, my cats—well, Merlot and Syrah, anyway—would have been at that window seat. They always check out strange goings-on—even if it's a moth fluttering around. Besides, why would that ... that *possible* altercation between Evie and Ritaestelle have happened here?" But I was thinking about Merlot. About him pacing, checking out what I had assumed were insects flitting outside. But what if he'd heard something? Heard Evie Preston out there. Was that why he'd seemed so nervous?

"We might not yet understand why Evie or Ritaestelle came here, and we don't know much about their relationship, either," Tom said. "They could have had a nasty history. But you're right about the cats. They may not be as good as a watchdog, but I've seen them pay attention to even small noises coming from outside. Of course, convincing the police that your cats' behavior is important is a different story."

Kara smiled. "I don't think you can sell that one—even to Candace. Anyway, thanks for giving me some excellent questions to ask the police. If the Ford was moved, that might prove to be important."

Tom said. "I wonder if they found Evie Preston's cell phone. I'm sure she had one."

"Could be underwater," I said.

"If so, that will be a problem," Tom said. "A little bit of water or a phone being briefly submerged can often be fixed and the data retrieved. But overnight? Nope. And phone calls these days are invaluable to the police in establishing a timeline. If Evie made any recent calls, perhaps one that came *after* Ritaestelle arrived here, then—"

"Funny you should be talking about her," came a voice from behind us.

I turned and saw Mike Baca standing in the kitchen. "I've just spoken to the doctor, and Miss Longworth wants to see you, Jillian. Would you mind coming with us to the hospital? She says she'll talk to us if you're there."

I closed my eyes. I was in this up to my eyeballs. And all because of a narcissistic black cat.

# Sixteen

The county hospital was a half-hour drive, even though it's only fifteen miles away. That was because only a two-lane road goes from my place to the hospital. Tom and Kara agreed to stay at the house—Kara, I'm certain, because she wanted to learn as much as she could from the assistant DA and Deputy Martinez. Morris, meanwhile, had asked Tom to go over my security-camera footage, since I have several cameras that watch over my house near the windows. Tom installed them after Syrah was catnapped last fall. Even though it was doubtful they'd find anything of use, no stone could be left unturned.

Stone. That noise out on the dock, I thought, as Police Chief Shelton, Mike and I got out of Mike's Mercy PD SUV in the hospital parking lot. Had Ritaestelle dropped that rock into the lake last night on purpose? And if she was about to confess to murder, why did she want me present?

But I wouldn't be asking her that question. I was told not to ask her anything, to just sit quietly. Ritaestelle apparently wanted support, and that was what I would offer. No one had to force me to do that. She needed a friend right now.

As we took the elevator up to her third-floor hospital room, I wondered if she so distrusted all those people who lived with her that she'd invited a virtual stranger for support. If so, that was as heartrending as when a person moves away and leaves his or her cat behind—something that happened all the time, according to Shawn.

We walked side by side down the corridor to Ritaestelle's

room, the disinfectant smells surrounding us making my already queasy stomach protest even more. I glanced over and saw that Mike carried an eight-by-ten leather-covered notebook, but Shelton was the one who appeared most official. Her navy suit, her stiff demeanor, everything about her seemed to say, "I'm really the one in charge."

Mike rapped on Ritaestelle's door and didn't wait for an invitation to enter. Five people, three women and two men, were clustered around the bed. I recognized only Augusta—the woman who had been with Ritaestelle when she'd fallen the other day.

"I thought she wasn't supposed to have visitors," I heard Shelton whisper to Mike. But then she smiled and said, "Look here at all of you. How's our patient?"

Ritaestelle's gaze locked on me, and she held out both hands. I slid between these strangers and took her hands in mine. She squeezed, and her bony fingers were ice-cold.

"Jillian, you dear woman," she said. "To come here after all I've laid on your doorstep. I want to say that I will never forget your kindness and hospitality. How is my precious Isis? Not causing too much upheaval, I hope?"

"Isis is fine," I said, wondering why she was talking about hospitality when I'd arrived with two bigwig police officers right behind me prepared to grill her. But maybe her little speech was intended for the other people in the room.

"Let me introduce my friends and family," Ritaestelle began. "You have seen my cousin Augusta at my home."

Augusta nodded, her hands clasped beneath her large chest.

Ritaestelle said, "Muriel here is her sister, and—"

"I'm your cousin, too, Ritaestelle," the woman with cherry red hair said.

"You are indeed, Muriel." Ritaestelle gestured at a thin woman and a man about my age standing beside her. "Justine was my late brother's wife, and this is Farley, his son." She looked pointedly at Muriel. "My nephew."

"Excuse me, Ritaestelle," Shelton said. "We have a serious situation. We need your visitors to leave." By her tone, she might as well have added, "This isn't Sunday brunch at your estate."

"And why must we leave?" the older gentleman who

hadn't been introduced said. He placed a hand on Rita-estelle's shoulder.

He had thick white hair, faded blue eyes and a smile that baffled me. It seemed pleasant enough. But there was disingenuousness there. I had the feeling something else was going on between him and Chief Shelton. His body language—chin lifted and cold stare—had me thinking he was in control rather than the police.

Shelton said, "Desmond, I don't need to tell you anything. So leave. Now." Ah yes. This was the Nancy Shelton I'd encountered when she'd pulled me over.

Desmond sighed heavily. "If you insist." He bent and kissed Ritaestelle on the cheek. Augusta and the three others all bid farewell, too, and the visitors filed out of the room. Farley offered me a contemptuous glance when he passed.

*What was that about?* I wondered.

Shelton turned to Mike. "Everyone visiting, except for Desmond Holloway, lives in the Longworth house. He's an old friend." She switched her gaze to Ritaestelle. "But wait. Don't tell me Desmond's moved in recently."

Ritaestelle stared up at her sweetly. "I thought we had crossed that bridge a long time ago, Nancy. He most certainly has not moved in."

Mike cleared his throat and opened his notebook. "We brought Miss Hart as you requested. Now, if you'll please think very hard about last night's events, because we have a few more questions."

"That is all I have been thinking about, sir, and I have questions myself—what is your name, by the way? I see that you are wearing a name badge, but I do not have my reading glasses. I did leave my house in a such a rush, and then of course I ended up here and—"

"Mike Baca. Mercy PD," he said tersely.

"Oh. The police chief. I read about you in the newspaper when that woman—"

"Ritaestelle. Please," Shelton said. "We need to get down to business."

Mike's face was flushed, and I felt like I'd been caught in a small room with several buzzing, angry wasps. I swallowed hard.

"First," Ritaestelle said, "would you mind pulling over that chair in the corner for Jillian? She is looking very pale.

Hospitals do that to certain more sensitive souls." She obviously wasn't the least bit bothered by Shelton's tone or Mike's discomfort.

Before Mike could move, I dragged the chair over myself. We did need to get these questions over with.

Mike said, "First of all, we'd like a look at your car, Miss Longworth. We can get a warrant, but you could give us permission. Then we wouldn't need to bother a judge. Same for your house."

"Well, for heaven's sake, why? What are you looking for?" Ritaestelle said.

"We need to corroborate your story that you drove directly from your house to Jillian's," Mike said. "Your GPS should tell us that. You found her place by using the GPS system, I understand."

"I have managed to comprehend certain newfangled gadgets. Though I am not a fan of cellular telephones or computers, GPS is quite useful. I believe my keys are in my bag—in the closet." She pointed across the room at the peach-colored laminate cupboards. "You can look in my car all you want."

"And your house keys are there as well?" Mike said.

"I do not believe I can give you permission to search my home," Ritaestelle said. "I have seen on the television how untidy you police officers leave a house once you are done searching. My housekeeper, Hildie, would be most put out having to straighten up after a search that I imagine would prove to be quite invasive." She smiled as she glanced back and forth between the two stoic police officers.

"They'll get a search warrant, anyway, Ritaestelle," I said. "You might as well give them permission." I wasn't supposed to say anything, but she needed to cooperate and clear her name.

"I understand, Jillian," she replied. "But I remember my dear brother speaking about search warrants and other various legal matters. The police do need a good reason to search a person's home, correct?"

"Um, I think they have one," I said.

"Oh. You mean Evie's death?" She looked at Shelton. "You still believe I killed her? I suppose it is troublesome and very strange indeed that she showed up at Jillian's home. That poor girl. Why was she out by that lake?"

Shelton said, "If we search your house, are you afraid we might find, well . . . other things?"

"You mean stolen items like the kind some cruel person planted on my person in Mr. Perry's pharmacy? Or the ones Evie found in my lingerie chest?" Ritaestelle's smile had faded. "You do understand those two events have Evie in common."

Oh boy. Had she just given them a motive? Was Ritaestelle so angry with Evie about this shoplifting thing that she'd murdered her?

"We're getting off track," Mike said. "If you want us to get a warrant, we will. And like Jillian said, it won't be a problem. And now that we've dealt with that, I—"

"Oh, for heaven's sake. Please search my house. But make sure that includes all the rooms where my relatives reside. They come here pretending to care, but all they are truly concerned about is my money." Ritaestelle's lower eyelids reddened and her lips trembled. "And after all I've done for them."

I understood now why she'd asked me to come. She certainly *didn't* trust her family. But for some reason, she trusted me.

Mike shifted his weight, his gaze on the floor. After a few seconds of awkward silence, he pulled out a sheet of paper from his notebook and placed it on the bedside table. "This is permission to search your car and your house." He handed her a pen.

She scrawled her signature at the bottom and pushed the paper toward Mike. "I hope you will note that I am a cooperative witness. Not a felon, but a witness."

"We appreciate your cooperation, Miss Longworth," he said. "Now, tell me everyone who lives in your house."

"I can give you all that information later, Chief Baca," Shelton said.

"I know you can. But I want to hear about them from Miss Longworth, if you don't mind." He kept his eyes focused on Ritaestelle.

"The folks who were just here, or everyone?" Ritaestelle said.

"Everyone," Mike said.

"Well, there are my two cousins, Augusta and Muriel. You saw them. Augusta is the one with the large bosom.

Muriel has that rather ridiculous red hair. They are my dear departed aunt's girls. Listen to me. Girls. They are as old as I am. Then there is my sister-in-law, Justine. She does not look her age, does she? Pretty hair, plump lips. As they say, she's *had some work done*. She was married to my brother and is apparently just too fragile to make it on her own. So I took her in. And her son, Farley, was here as well. Steaming mad, too. He stays that way. He has tried all manner of professions. But he is attempting to become an accountant this time. He is broke, of course, and—"

"Chief Baca wants to know about the rest of the household, too," Shelton said.

Mike was writing quickly and didn't look up when he said, "Yes. Who else lives with you?"

"George, my wonderful butler—seems an old-fashioned word, does it not? But he likes the title. He is tremendously proficient at what he does. I never have to ask for a thing. He anticipates my every need." Ritaestelle shifted so more weight was on her right side—and she moved with some difficulty, as the strain on her face indicated. I noticed the ice pack on her left hip for the first time.

She went on, saying, "And Hildie is the housekeeper and cook. She is from Germany and can make a strudel like nobody's business."

Mike looked at her. "Anyone else live with you?"

"I do have more room if you ever find yourself in need of a roof over your head, Chief Baca." She paused and shook her head slightly. "Listen to me making a joke when this is one of the most somber times in my entire life. Please forgive me."

"That's everyone? No other servants?" Mike said.

"No others," she said. "The groundskeepers come every other day. They do not reside on the estate, though when my father was alive, they did. We have turned the building where they used to live into a guesthouse."

"We'll need those names, too. But I'll get Chief Shelton to give them to me," Mike said.

I saw discomfort tighten Ritaestelle's face again.

"Are you in pain?" I said.

"It is nothing, dear. I have a bruised hip, and if not for all these X-rays and tests, I would be home by now," she said.

Mike said, "I have more questions, but first I'll find a couple more chairs."

As he left, I noticed him reach for his cell phone. His departure wasn't all about chairs.

Shelton stepped closer to the bed. "Let me see that bruise, Ritaestelle."

She lifted the covers before Ritaestelle could protest. The ice pack fell off as Shelton revealed a huge black-and-purple bruise partially hidden by the hospital gown.

I stifled a gasp. I'd heard her fall but hadn't realized how much damage she'd done to herself.

"My goodness. That must have been some fall," Shelton said.

Why hadn't I thought to call an ambulance that day rather than race out of town like a scared rabbit?

Ritaestelle pulled the covers back over her, and I saw blotches of color high on her cheeks. "You should have asked my permission to look at me in all my glory. I mean, I hardly have a stitch of clothing on." But she only sounded sad, not angry, at this breach of privacy.

Shelton said, "Like you would have given me permission. They're sure it's not broken?"

"No. Seems I have very strong bones. There is some concern about blood clots, so they will be doing some fancy tests to check on that before they release me," Ritaestelle said.

"I'd like to photograph the injury, if you don't mind," Shelton said.

"Candace, that cute little police officer I met last night, took enough pictures to fill an album. Quite embarrassing, too. I have not known her for fifty years like I have known you, Nancy."

"All right. I'll ask her for copies," Shelton said.

Mike came back in the room with two chairs, and he was followed by a tiny black woman wearing pink scrubs.

"Vital signs, Miss Longworth," the woman said. She was pushing a small contraption with a blood pressure cuff and an electronic thermometer. "And it's been four hours since they gave you that pain shot. Do you want me to ask the nurse for more? I'm seeing pain written all over your face."

"Elsa, you are so very observant," Ritaestelle said.

We all moved aside so the woman could do her job.

When she was finished, she said, "Now, what about that pain medicine?"

"My muscles are simply sore from thinking I am twenty years younger than I actually am. I believe I will be fine with a new ice pack." She handed the disposable packaged blue gel to Elsa and then looked at me. "Your yard is quite expansive, Jillian. I do not know what on earth I was thinking last night walking out in the dark."

Elsa said, "I'll get you a new one, but ice won't do the trick. You need that shot. Give the nurse about fifteen minutes." Elsa nodded at us and left.

Mike and Shelton pulled their chairs next to Ritaestelle's bed.

Mike said, "I've made some calls, and I want you to be aware that officers will be sent to search your house for any evidence that might be connected to Miss Preston's death. I assume the victim didn't live with you."

"Oh no. She had an apartment in town and—"

"After you called me to make the notification last night, Chief Baca, I took it upon myself to search Evie's apartment," Shelton said.

I saw Mike's eyebrows come together. "You searched her apartment?" he said.

"I, like you, know how to run an investigation. First I went to see Evie's mother, though. Wise of your officer to ask me to make that notification. Since we had probable cause for a search and Evie's mother didn't have a problem, she gave me the key. She's very distraught, as you can imagine."

Ritaestelle turned her head away so we couldn't see her expression. But her voice was thick with emotion when she said, "I am hoping to speak with Mrs. Preston soon. A mother should not outlive her daughter."

Mike leveled narrowed eyes at Shelton. "Wouldn't have been too hard to get a warrant."

The spirit of cooperation between them that had seemed too good to be true apparently was.

"Wouldn't have been hard to get a warrant for Ritaestelle's car and her house, either." Shelton picked a cat hair off her navy slacks. A long Chablis-colored hair.

"Touché," Mike said. He turned to Ritaestelle. "Do you want to change your mind and have us get warrants?"

"I have nothing to hide—and that sounds exactly like a line from a movie. I know my brother is turning over in his grave about my decisions, but I did nothing to harm Evie. And if I could have managed to get down into that water like Jillian did, well—" She took a deep breath. "But I did not. I could not. Now, I imagine you have more questions. Please go on."

Mike cocked his head. He seemed to be trying to read Ritaestelle, see if her emotion was for real. After a few seconds he said, "The chronology of events is what's most important right now." Mike readied his pen to write down more information. "Tell me when you decided to leave your house and go to Jillian's place. And be as specific as you can."

Ritaestelle explained about pouring out the tea she suspected was drugged around dinnertime, waiting for her watchdog cousin Augusta to fall asleep and sneaking out of the house down a back staircase. Seemed that her nephew never went to bed before four a.m., so she was worried he'd spot her if she went down the main stairs.

"You're talking about Farley Longworth?" Mike asked.

"Yes," Ritaestelle said. "I cannot tell you how distressed I am that he will be carrying on the family name. Too bad he will not have the family home or the family money to go with it—unless there's a miraculous change in him before I die. Longworths should be ambitious and outgoing. He is neither. I have put instructions in my will that if he has not earned at least five hundred thousand dollars of his own by the time he turns sixty, then most of the money I have set aside for him will go to charity."

Mike said, "Interesting. Does he know about this?"

"Not yet," Ritaestelle said.

"Did you drive straight to Jillian's house?" Shelton asked.

Ritaestelle offered a knowing smile. "You above all people know you cannot get straight to anywhere in these parts. But I traveled the most efficient route. The GPS directed me in an Australian accent. That is my most favorite voice. So entertaining."

"And you don't have a cell phone?" Mike asked.

"Not our Ritaestelle," Shelton said. "Which is why I'm

quite surprised to hear about her using GPS. A system like that is actually a computer, you know."

"Why, that surprises me. Perhaps I will have to learn to use one of those before I die," Ritaestelle said. "As for the GPS, I do not often get out, as you know, Nancy, but when I do attend a function in an unfamiliar location, I find the computer, as you called it, simple to use. I found Jillian's house easily." She paused, her gaze unfocused. "Evie must have followed me . . . and look what happened to that unfortunate girl. I never thought anyone was watching me."

"Watching you? Following you?" Shelton said. "How would she know you'd be sneaking out in the first place? She doesn't stay at your house past five or six in the afternoon, does she?"

Ritaestelle cocked her head, looking puzzled. "Why, those are very good questions, Nancy. I had not thought about that."

"She came to work as usual yesterday and left on time?" Mike said.

"As far as I know. But Farley has taken a liking to her, so perhaps they were together last evening in the library or more likely in the room set up with that giant, awful television. Not my idea to have a sixty-inch television. Anyway, they might have heard me leave the house—which was certainly not my intent."

Mike scribbled in his notebook while the look on Shelton's face told me she wasn't buying this explanation.

"How old is Farley?" Though I wasn't supposed to be asking questions, I was curious.

"Forty," Shelton and Ritaestelle said in unison.

Then Ritaestelle added, "Too old for Evie, if you want my opinion. But a man who acts like an adolescent is likely to have an attraction to an accomplished and attractive woman like Evie, wouldn't you agree?"

I nodded. "I'd say most men would have found her attractive."

Mike stared at me, saying, "I'll be asking plenty of questions of all the people who knew Miss Preston."

*Message received, Mike,* I thought.

Another woman, this one in beige scrubs, entered the room. Her name tag said, JENKINS, RN. "The doctor has changed your medicine to pills." She glanced at all of us. "Um, I need to talk to my patient in private."

"You may say whatever you need to, Nurse Jenkins," Ritaestelle said. "I have no secrets."

The nurse said, "Are you sure?"

"Absolutely," Ritaestelle replied.

"All right. After more blood work and an MRI of that hip, you're being released, Miss Longworth. We know your hip isn't fractured, but we can get an extent of the inflammation with the MRI." She pushed a small cart that had several drawers to the bedside after we all moved aside to allow her to get close to her patient. She checked Ritaestelle's hospital bracelet, administered the medicine and left.

Meanwhile, Ritaestelle never took her eyes off me. "I do not feel inclined to go home. After what's happened I believe I am far less safe than I was yesterday."

That stare turned pleading and bore into me.

I knew what she wanted. Yup, I was *still* in this up to my eyeballs.

# Seventeen

Mike Baca dropped me off at the Main Street Diner when we returned to Mercy. I walked into the restaurant and was met with the smell of fries and grilled meat. This place always made me hungry—and I was grateful that my stomach had finally settled down. That didn't mean I wasn't worried about my offer to have Ritaestelle stay with me for a few days. But deep down I knew it was best for her. She needed help, and after learning about her family, I feared they weren't the right crew for the job.

Mike hadn't objected when I'd haltingly told Ritaestelle she could stay with me if she was afraid to go home. But Shelton sure hadn't liked the idea. That was when I realized that having Ritaestelle in Mercy, rather than back in Woodcrest, was fine with Mike. Not so from Shelton's point of view, though. Police are so territorial. But she'd forced a smile and said she wanted her friend to be comfortable.

I leaned on the counter near the cash register. Besides their trademark Texas chili dogs, they made wonderful burgers with chipotle mayo and sweet onions served on toast. I was craving one of those, so I took out my phone and called Tom for a headcount at the house. After I got the number—everyone wanted burgers—I placed my order and then walked down the street to Belle's Beans. During the walk I took time to check my cat cam. Tom was sitting in the living room with Morris. They were surrounded by sleeping cats. Except for Isis, that is. I wondered where she was. Still stuck somewhere? Probably.

The owner of Belle's Beans, whom I called the *real*

Belle, was sitting reading the paper at one of the tall tables. Meanwhile, a young woman with a BELLE name tag stood behind the counter taking coffee orders.

When the real Belle saw me, she practically jumped off her bar stool and came over to greet me. She is spry for a woman in her late sixties—maybe as spry as Ritaestelle was before her fall. Belle's lipstick, an almost Concord grape color, did not serve her well. Seemed to me that white-haired ladies should go for pinks and corals. Plus, as usual, she'd spread the lipstick well below her lower lip.

Belle gave me a bear hug, saying, "Oh, my goodness gracious, I heard what happened. I am so sorry."

When she released me, I said, "It's a terrible thing. Evie Preston was so young."

"Have some coffee and tell me all about it." Belle started for her table.

"I ordered takeout from the diner, so I can't stay. I came to pick up coffee beans, and I am dying for an iced vanilla latte."

Belle pouted, only emphasizing her awful makeup job. But then she called out to the Belle behind the counter. "Large iced vanilla latte to go and a bag of Kenyan beans for Miss Jillian."

I knew that the real name of the young woman behind the counter was Wendy, but it was Belle's practice to have every employee wear a name tag with BELLE on it. She felt it added to the friendly atmosphere. I couldn't argue. This cute little coffee shop with its wonderful drinks and delicious pastries and cakes was probably the friendliest spot in Mercy.

"Listen, Belle, I promise to tell you everything when I can," I said, keeping my voice low. "It's a long story."

"I'll tell you this: Ritaestelle couldn't possibly have killed anyone. She has been a pillar in that town of hers. Yes, a pillar. Helped anyone in need. But did she really come to your house in her dressing gown?"

I averted my eyes, thinking, *Everyone knows. Heck, Belle probably knows more than I do.* I met her eager stare. "It was a bathrobe. But are you saying you know Ritaestelle?"

"Why, yes. We are of the same generation, after all. But her cousin Muriel is the real connection. She married my cousin, so we're sort of related," Belle said.

"I believe Muriel was at the hospital this morning. Plump woman with red hair?"

"That would be her," Belle said. "Not long after my cousin and Muriel were married, he took off with a nineteen-year-old nanny who lived at the Longworth Estate. The girl was supposed to be taking care of Farley Longworth, but apparently she was busy doing other things."

"That was a while ago, then?" I said. "Because Farley is approaching middle age."

"Yes. You do the math." Belle grinned. "I don't measure anything by years anymore. Helps a girl stay young."

I grinned. "Is that why you chose grape lipstick today? For the youthful look?"

Belle touched her lips. "Yes, but I nearly scared poor Java to death when I put it on this morning. I don't think I'll try it again."

Java was her cobby kitty, a lovely brown Persian.

"Cats know best," I said. "I pay attention to what they tell me in their own way. But back to Farley. You knew him, too?"

"Not really. When my cousin was part of the Longworth family, my late husband and I were invited to a few gatherings, but aside from Ritaestelle, I didn't care for that bunch. Maybe that's why my cousin ran away from all that money. He couldn't stand them either. He stayed away, too. Had his happily ever after life in Wisconsin until he passed away two years ago."

Wendy boomed, "Large iced vanilla latte."

Belle muttered, "I'm gonna have to talk to that particular Belle. Guess her mama never schooled her about using her inside voice. She's not calling across a football field, for heaven's sake."

"Gotta go," I said, giving Belle a hug. I paid for my coffee and latte and walked back to the diner. Now that the morning clouds had cleared, the sun shined bright and hot. No rain today, which I'm sure made Candace happy. Indeed, it was such pretty weather that the tourists who frequented Mercy in the summer were out in droves visiting the specialty shops and antiques stores on Main Street.

I was surprised to see Tom standing under the diner's green awning when I arrived back there. I had been just about to call him to pick me up.

He said, "Food should be ready, right?"

It was, and ten minutes later we were at my house. As we took the back steps, I saw Candace traipsing up from the lake carrying a wad of used yellow crime scene tape.

She called, "We're done."

"Come on in for a burger," I said. "I have a few things to tell you."

Tom headed straight to the table in my breakfast nook and set the bag of food down.

I waited at the back door for Candace.

"Did she confess?" she said as she climbed the porch steps. "'Cause outdoor crime scenes are trouble with a capital *T*. Didn't find any fingerprints on the dock, and Martinez didn't have any luck looking underwater either. We need a confession."

"Sorry to disappoint you, but she didn't confess. And I really don't think she did it, Candace," I said.

A muscle in Candace's jaw tightened. "The lady was standing out on your dock while a dead woman floated in the water not three feet away. That's evidence of something, I'd say. Mike's pussyfooting around on this one, and I don't get it."

"You think he has an agenda?" I asked.

Candace and I came inside and she shoved the wad of crime scene tape in the trash can in the utility room. She glanced at Kara, who was walking toward us.

"Can we shelve this discussion for now?" Candace whispered.

I nodded, realizing she wasn't about to talk about police business in front of someone following developments for the newspaper.

Morris joined us, too. Kara was holding Chablis but set her down when she reached the table. The other three cats trailed behind her. Syrah was sniffing the air like a bloodhound. He does have a taste for people food on occasion.

Tom found paper plates and napkins while I put the coffee beans in the airtight container where I keep them. Once we all had a burger and a stack of fries on our plates, I decided I'd better tell everyone the news.

I took a fortifying sip of my latte before I said, "Rita-estelle is coming here to stay after she's released from the hospital this afternoon."

Kara's eyes grew wide, and Candace blinked about a dozen times.

Candace finally broke the silence. "Are you kidding me?"

"The woman's afraid to go home. She's convinced someone was drugging her tea and making her look like a thief," I said. "And besides, she's still hurting. All those stairs at her house would be a big problem."

Candace set her untouched burger on her plate, her cheeks vivid with anger. "This is not good, Jillian."

"Mike doesn't agree. Besides, you should have seen her hip. I have no clue how she got down to the lake last night in the shape she was in," I said.

"I did see her hip—last night," Candace said. "She's a little hobbled. So what? I agree with the chief that she needs watching, but you're not the one to do it."

"You both saw her leg? You have proof she was truly injured?" Kara said.

Candace stared at Kara. "The whole world doesn't need to know. You get what I'm saying, right? We need to keep a few details out of the news."

These two had trouble getting along when they first met in the spring, and with Candace running hot right now, I hoped her temper wouldn't cause them to take several steps backward in what had become a decent friendship.

"Are you telling me what I can write and what I can't?" Kara said.

Before I could say something—anything—to smooth the waters, Tom spoke. "That's not true, right, Candace?" he said. "You totally embrace freedom of the press."

Candace took a deep breath and turned back to me. "Of course I do. But still, why did you agree to take that woman in? You realize you could have a murderer sleeping down the hall."

"I have to trust my heart—just like you have to trust the evidence," I said evenly.

Candace took a deep breath, and the color on her cheeks faded. "I get that. I'm sorry, but I worry about you."

"I know, and I appreciate that," I said. "Here's something else that will interest you. Mike has the keys to Rita-estelle's car and permission to search it."

Candace stood up so fast, she nearly knocked over her

chair. "When is he coming? Maybe I should put crime scene tape around the Cadillac so no one will touch it before he gets here."

Morris stopped eating long enough to say, "Jeez, Candace, sit your butt down and eat. We're the only ones here, and we're not messing with that car."

Candace hesitated before sitting back down. "Sure. I know that. Do you think the chief will let me do the search?"

"You're his little princess and lead on the case, so why not?" Morris picked up about ten fries and shoved them in his mouth.

I started when Syrah suddenly jumped in my lap. He stretched his neck toward my burger, his nose twitching. I pulled off a small piece of meat and set it on the floor by my chair. He jumped down, but not fast enough. Isis came from out of nowhere and gobbled up the morsel.

Syrah swatted her on the nose for this infringement. But she didn't run off like Merlot or Chablis would have done. She just sat and stared into his eyes.

Oh boy. Candace and Kara first, then Candace and Morris, and now this. I needed some peace and quiet before I went to the hospital to pick up Ritaestelle.

As we waited for Mike to show up with the keys to the car, Candace passed her time wandering down by the lake, probably hoping to find any additional bit of evidence after once again complaining about outdoor crime scenes. Calls for new security systems started coming in to Tom just as we'd finished eating—probably because of the murder. He and Kara left for a consultation soon after. She still worked for him part-time installing systems and handling contracts. I finally had a few minutes to myself and settled on the couch along with the cats.

Isis soon discovered that Merlot was too big to bully. He gently nudged her away when she tried to take his spot next to me. Syrah was above me on the couch cushions, and Chablis sat in my lap. Isis weaved in and out of the coffee table legs before deciding that her place for now had to be the other end of the couch—a good three feet away from Merlot. With size comes intimidation. That was for sure.

I leaned back, feeling tired enough to fall asleep, but my cell phone rang. I took it from my pocket, and before I could say hello, a male voice said, "Why is my aunt staying with you? She needs to come home to her family."

"Um, is this Farley?" I said.

"You bet it is. Farley Longworth the Fourth. What is going on between you and Aunt Rita? Are you after her money?"

What in the heck was this guy talking about? That should have been my first question, but instead I said, "How did you get my phone number?"

"I have connections. Lots of connections. Now, answer my question," he said.

"I don't have to tell you anything, Farley," I said as kindly as I could. "Your aunt is capable of making her own decisions, and that's all you need to know."

He said, "I don't think she should be staying with someone like you."

"What do you mean?" I said, not appreciating his arrogant attitude.

"You come to South Carolina, build a big house, and wham, suddenly your husband's dead and the property's all yours, free and clear. I checked, you see. No mortgage. That makes it quite the easy life for you. You have to know there's talk that you actually killed your husband. They just couldn't prove it."

I was too stunned to speak. Too hurt to even think of a reply to this horrible accusation.

Farley was more than willing to fill the silence. "Did Evie figure out why you came knocking on our door the other day? That you planned to extort money out of my aunt for the return of her cat?"

*"What?"* was all I could manage.

"Did Evie confront you about this cat business, so you killed her?" Snide didn't begin to describe his tone.

I closed my eyes and took a calming breath. Discussing any of this with him would be fruitless. I disconnected—and realized that tears were streaming down my cheeks. The thought that anyone—even one person—suspected I could have harmed John made me feel like a hole had been seared through my heart. Grief washed over me, almost as intense as on the day he died.

I felt Syrah's paw on my shoulder, then his face close to mine.

*What an awful man,* I thought, reaching back to scratch Syrah's head. And who could I talk to about this? Who could possibly understand how wounded I felt? I wasn't even sure if Kara would identify with these emotions.

As my heartbeat slowed and the tears dried, I thought more about the other things Farley Longworth had said and what he had *not* said. Did he know that Ritaestelle expected him to get his act together? Was that why he felt I was some sort of threat to any future money he hoped to inherit?

Seemed like I'd landed smack in the middle of a family feud. And now I was about to pick up the person at the center of all this. Maybe Candace was right. Asking Ritaestelle to stay with me might have been a huge mistake.

# Eighteen

Since my minivan was blocked in by Ritaestelle's Cadillac, I called Tom to see if he could drive me to the hospital to pick up Ritaestelle—that is, after he'd finished his security system consult.

But after I asked the question, he said, "What's wrong? You sound upset."

"A woman died in my backyard, Tom," I said.

"I know, but something else is going on. Come on. Spill it."

I sighed, and though I appreciated how perceptive he was, I wasn't ready to tell him what that awful person had to say about John's death. Instead, I gave an abbreviated version. "I received a call from Farley Longworth. He isn't too happy about Ritaestelle staying at my house while she recovers."

"Because ... ?"

"He believes the day I went to see Ritaestelle I wanted to trade Isis for a wad of cash."

"That's plain stupid," Tom said. "I'll check up on this guy, maybe see if he's the one who needs money."

"It's not that big a deal, and—"

"Jillian, you don't sound like yourself, so this *is* a big deal. I'm a PI. I check up on people every day. In fact, I think I'll start digging up anything I can find on all those people you said were visiting Ritaestelle. Now, as for picking her up, I have another job after this one. But Kara could help. She's just finished the paperwork for my client and she's right here. Let me put her on."

I talked to Kara and she agreed to drive me to the hospital. Tom would drop her at my place in a few minutes and we'd take her car—currently parked out front.

I patted several kitties good-bye and waited outside. The sun felt good on my skin. Candace, gloved and ready with her little hand vacuum, was standing by the Caddy. Apparently Mike Baca was on his way with the keys.

I walked toward her but stopped when she held up a hand.

"Don't get too close," she said.

I smiled. "I promise not to touch the car. Will the GPS system tell you exactly where Ritaestelle was before she came here?"

"Yes, if she didn't delete her last trip. GPS systems are quickly becoming a cop's best friend." A thin sheen of sweat covered Candace's forehead. Those cop uniforms must be brutal in the summer, even though Candace told me she had both summer and winter uniforms.

I turned, hearing a car pull into my driveway. Not Kara. It was Mike in his police SUV.

Candace's eyes glittered with anticipation, and after he greeted me, he and Candace got to work. Tom dropped Kara off a minute later, and I called to Mike and Candace that we were going to the hospital and that the house was locked up. Neither replied. They were too busy tearing that car apart looking for evidence.

When we arrived at the hospital, we found that Ritaestelle was checked out and waiting in her room. But she wasn't alone. Muriel and Augusta were with her. Seems she'd told her cousins that they could follow us to my house. I wanted to say they could have saved us a trip by bringing the patient to me.

But when Kara had to drive twenty miles an hour as they puttered along behind us in their big, ancient Lincoln—we wouldn't want to lose them, after all—I began to believe those two might need more help than Ritaestelle did.

I was sure Kara was chomping at the bit to ask our passenger questions, but before she could get out even one sentence, I asked her if we could have a peaceful ride home. I'd not had much peace of late, and neither had Ritaestelle. Thank goodness Kara reluctantly agreed. That phone call from Farley was still bothering me, but I willed those thoughts to the back of my mind and enjoyed the landscape of South Carolina in summer: wildflowers, trees greener than green and lush fields lined the road. I concentrated on that.

When we returned to my house, the police presence and the Cadillac were gone. For the first time in nearly twenty-four hours my property wasn't the center of an investigation.

The hospital had provided Ritaestelle with a walker, which she adamantly refused to allow Kara to remove from the car.

She said, "If I can make it down to a lake in the dark, I do not need hospital equipment."

We'd parked near my front door, where there were no stairs to maneuver. Ritaestelle limped ahead of us. She was wearing a sea foam green terry-cloth warm-up suit. Muriel and Augusta trailed behind, with Augusta carrying a tapestry satchel that I assumed held more of Ritaestelle's clothes.

All four cats sat waiting in the foyer. Isis shocked both Kara and me by taking a running leap into Ritaestelle's outstretched arms. She immediately nuzzled close to her owner's face.

Kara's eyes were wide with surprise when she glanced my way. Once Muriel and Augusta joined us, I closed the door behind them and shut out the summer heat.

Muriel perused the foyer and peered beyond into the living room. "Why, this is so much nicer than I thought. You'll do quite nicely here, Ritaestelle."

"Muriel seems to have left her manners at home," Ritaestelle said. "I suppose she believed you were taking me to some hovel out in the country."

"Why, I never—" started Muriel.

Augusta pinched Muriel's elbow. "Oh yes, you did. Always with the double entendres. Do you think we don't know you and your ways?"

Oh boy. *This ought to be fun,* I thought.

Aloud I said, "Ritaestelle needs to get off her feet. Let's all settle in the living room."

My three cats had already left the foyer, anticipating a human gathering. There were five women, after all, and they knew that meant there would be talking.

Turned out Muriel was diabetic, so she opted for water while the rest of us had sweet tea. I offered a late-afternoon snack—cheese and crackers was about the best I could do—but everyone turned it down. Ritaestelle said she was still recovering from the "revolting" hospital food. Muriel had to have her special diet and said she and Augusta would be leaving soon, anyway.

"We did want to see Ritaestelle get here safely," Muriel said. She'd taken John's recliner.

"That was your idea," Augusta said.

She was sitting in the overstuffed chair with a sleepy-looking Chablis on her lap. Syrah and Merlot had chosen to lurk under the coffee table.

"And *safely*?" Augusta went on. "What is that supposed to mean, Muriel? Did you think they were going to drive their automobile into a ditch or something?"

"Why, it's simply a figure of speech, Augusta." Muriel clasped her hands in her lap, looking insulted.

"I believe this is Ritaestelle's business," Augusta said. "Though I suppose there is a concern that she will be that much closer to the police officers investigating poor Evie's death. Being here in Mercy provides such easy access, while if we were at home, we could protect her while she's healing." She tilted her head and focused her deep brown eyes on Ritaestelle. "Does that bother you, Ritaestelle? The hovering police presence?"

*Smart lady,* I thought. And the way Augusta talked, she could have been Ritaestelle's twin—not just in her manner of speech, but even the tone of her voice.

Ritaestelle was stroking a purring Isis. "Since I firmly believe someone in my circle of friends and family drugged me, where do you think I feel more protected, Augusta?"

"Are you accusing me—or us—of doing you harm?" Augusta's turn to sound offended.

"Yes, are you, Ritaestelle? Because that's an awful thing to say," Muriel chimed in.

I was sitting on the couch between Kara and Ritaestelle, and when I started to speak, Kara tapped my foot with hers. I'd hoped to interrupt this argument with some sort of distraction, but Kara obviously wanted their spat to play out. Maybe that was best, but it sure made the muscles at the back of my neck tighten. I set down my glass of tea, leaned back and kept my mouth shut.

"What I believe about the two of you, whether you have involved yourselves in nefarious behavior or not, is of no consequence until I am apprised of the facts," Ritaestelle said. "And the facts will come out, ladies. You can trust me on that, because this woman here"—she patted the space between us—"will find the answers."

Muriel and Augusta looked at me like I was a two-headed snake. But perhaps it was the other way around. Maybe they were the two-head snake. I stared at them and blinked, much as one of my cats might have done.

Kara leaned around me and spoke to Ritaestelle. "You seem to have great faith in Jillian. Why is that?"

"Excellent question, Kara," Ritaestelle said. "May I ask you a question that might provide an answer? Did your stepmother prove to be heroic in extricating you from a difficult situation in the past?"

Kara nodded. "She did."

"Is she a kind, generous woman who believes in the truth?" Ritaestelle went on.

Kara said, "Yes, but—"

"I believe you have your answer," she said with a smile. This was said in an extra-polite way, and yet I had no doubt that Ritaestelle knew exactly what she wanted and no one would obstruct her path. Her idea to stay with me was all part of the plan. I sure hoped she would let me in on her reasoning when we were alone.

Muriel and Augusta left after thirty minutes of squabbling about everything from the weather to the need for Hildie, their housekeeper, to polish the wood floors back at the "estate." Both of them had to use "the ladies'" as they called it, so that took at least fifteen more minutes before I could usher them out.

I felt tired when I closed the door after them. And a little sad. They'd mentioned Evie once, and only when Ritaestelle asked if they knew when the services would be. They didn't. Probably hadn't even thought about it.

But if I was tired, Ritaestelle had definitely perked up. She said, "I cannot tell you how sorely I have needed a respite from those two. If only I could have come here under better circumstances. When this is over, I intend to take a vacation with Desmond—as far away from Woodcrest as I can get."

"Desmond?" Kara said. She'd moved over to her father's recliner, where Muriel had been seated.

"Desmond Holloway," Ritaestelle said. "He is a dear friend, has been for many years. I am so glad he has returned to his roots."

"His roots?" I asked.

"Yes. He came to Woodcrest when he was a young man. He was a Realtor and came to know everyone in town," Ritaestelle said.

"But he never went to school with you—like Nancy Shelton and Ed Duffy did, for instance?" I said.

"Are you curious or suspicious, Jillian? Because I can assure you that Desmond is harmless. When he left town to 'see the world,' he was missed. He can be a very entertaining gentleman."

She cared about him—more than she cared about her own relatives. Somehow that seemed sad. "Would you like more tea?" I asked, glancing back and forth between Kara and Ritaestelle. I could tell Kara wasn't asking about Desmond just to be polite. She wanted a story. Maybe— hopefully—I'd interrupted her, at least for a while. After all, Ritaestelle had just gotten out of the darn hospital.

"My dear Jillian, if I drank anything more, I might float away as if I were riding a wave on your beautiful lake," Ritaestelle said. "But if the offer for a snack still stands, I would appreciate one."

"Cheese and crackers?" I rose.

She nodded. "Anything, dear."

"Tell me about Desmond," Kara said. "I saw a sparkle in your eye when you spoke about him."

I went into the kitchen, with three cats on my heels. Isis remained in Ritaestelle's lap. I should have known it was futile to stand between Kara and a story.

"You are discerning, Miss Kara. Just like your stepmother. But Desmond is simply a friend these days. Years ago, it might have been a different story. We might have married, had children, but he was a bit of a philanderer." Ritaestelle's voice quavered a little. "He returned only two months ago."

I wondered if Desmond was the reason she'd never married. Had he been the love of her life? Had she turned Ed away for Desmond?

As I sliced cheddar on a cheese board, I heard Kara say, "But you want to go on vacation with this *philanderer*?"

"Why not?" she said. "He's without adequate funds—same as he was back in the day—so he needs a friend like me to take him around the world. And I am foolish enough to enjoy his company, even knowing his character is not completely stellar."

Kara laughed. "You seem to know exactly what you want."

"I suppose that's true to a point. But why are all my relatives still living with me? Because *that* is not truly what I want. Obligation gets in the way of want too much, I fear."

I added a row of crackers to the cheese board and carried it out to the living room. I set the dish on the coffee table in front of Ritaestelle. I gave both her and Kara napkins thinking that this conversation was getting interesting, and maybe Kara's questions weren't all simply because she wanted a story. Maybe she did want to get to know Ritaestelle better.

But the doorbell interrupted any further questions. I saw Lydia Monk through the peephole and stifled a groan. Not her again. At least Tom wasn't here this time.

I opened the door and said, "Hi, Lydia. The police have all left, so—"

She pushed by me and came inside. "I didn't see his car. Where is he?" Her burnt orange T-shirt had beading and pearls around the V-neck. She wore white capris and strappy wedge-style sandals. Lots of cleavage showing today, so she must have dressed expecting to find Tom here.

"Who are you talking about?" Playing innocent with her was about the only way to deal with her delusions.

"Never mind. I heard that woman is staying with you. What's with that?" she said.

"I offered to help Ritaestelle out until she feels better," I said.

"I came to talk to her." Lydia strode past me into the living room. But Kara drew her attention first, and she pointed at her. "You. Out of here. I need to talk to the, um . . . *witness* without you hanging around."

Kara didn't move. "This isn't a police station, and you're not a cop, so why do I—"

"I'm hired by the county to investigate suspicious deaths, and you know that as well as anyone," Lydia said. "Leave." She turned to me. "And if you could busy yourself elsewhere, please?"

*Please?* Wow.

Before I could respond, Ritaestelle said, "There is nothing I can tell you that these kind women do not already know. If you want to interrogate me, you will do it with them present."

Lydia rested a fist on her hip. "Really? You're telling me how to do my job?"

I said, "I have quilt orders to work on. I can go in the other room."

"You will not," Kara said. "This is your house, and this, this—"

"Please go ahead with your questions," Ritaestelle said to Lydia. "I do not want to use up too much precious time in what I assume is your very busy day."

Lydia smiled. "At least someone understands. I suppose we can do this your way." Lydia opened the patent leather purse slung over her left shoulder. She removed a small notebook. She sat across from Ritaestelle and laid her bag in her lap to rest her notebook on top. "I hear you've been in trouble in your little hometown down the road before any of this happened. Tell me about that."

Ritaestelle seemed surprised that this was the first question.

Before she could say anything, Kara said, "What does that have to do with the murder? Do you have something that connects those two things?"

"Am I talking to you?" Lydia said.

I was standing behind Lydia, not knowing exactly what to do with myself. Sit? Go away? Run away? Or pick a cat up off the couch, where they'd all gathered? The last option seemed excellent, but I felt the need to protect Ritaestelle from Lydia's blunt approach first. I said, "Lydia, this woman just got out of the hospital, and—"

"I know. That's why I couldn't question her before." Lydia smiled at Ritaestelle and said, "Tell me about your troubles in Woodcrest."

"But—" I started.

Ritaestelle held up one hand. "Thank you, Jillian. I most certainly do appreciate your concern." She returned Lydia's stare. "You may talk to Chief Nancy Shelton about certain accusations directed at me. She has all the details."

Kara, whose expression showed keen interest in this subject, said, "This prior history goes to motive, Lydia?"

"That's Assistant Coroner Monk to you," Lydia said. "And it's none of your business. Now, Miss Longworth, tell me why your personal assistant, Evie Preston, came *here* of all places? Or did you two come together?"

"I had no idea she was following me," Ritaestelle said.

"So she followed you and not the other way around?" Lydia was scribbling in her notebook as she said this.

"Why would Evie come here if she wasn't following Ritaestelle?" I asked.

"Because," Lydia said, "you, Jillian, had unfinished business with the victim. I know you went to see Miss Preston and spoke with her."

"But I went to see Miss Longworth, not Evie." What in the heck was Lydia getting at?

Lydia twisted in my direction. "That's what your story is today, but for some weird reason, you're harboring a suspect. Did you and Evie Preston get into it the other day?"

Kara said, "You think Jillian had something to do with the murder?"

Lydia glared at Kara. "I'm asking the questions here."

Ritaestelle said, "I understand your desire to do your job, Assistant Coroner Monk. My, that is a mouthful. Anyway, I believe I have asked and answered every question more than once prior to now. Surely you can consult with your fellow law enforcement professionals. I am very tired and I do not believe I could offer you any coherent answers at this time."

Lydia leaned forward. "Are you aware that I have to get documents ready and issue a death certificate?"

"Oh my." Ritaestelle lifted a hand to her lips. "I had not considered that. Of course you do. I want to help, but you seem so . . . angry with these kind women for some reason. May I assure you that they have done nothing wrong."

I walked around Lydia's chair and over to the couch. I sat next to Merlot, who lifted his head and croaked a meow before resuming his nap. Guess he was getting used to the crazy lady coming to call.

But I could see that Lydia had gotten to Ritaestelle. She now looked exhausted—probably because no one ever gets to sleep in the hospital and no one can take very much of Lydia without getting tired.

Lydia said, "I am aware you have an upstanding reputation, Miss Longworth, but I need answers. You say Miss Preston followed you here. Why would she do that?"

"I have no earthly idea," Ritaestelle said. "That seems to be the biggest question—that and who followed *her* following me? It is all very confounding. My fear is that Evie had something to do with the events of the past few months, that perhaps she was in cahoots with someone at my home to make me look foolish."

"Like who?" Lydia asked.

Kara looked at Ritaestelle with interest. Lydia seemed to be on point for once, and both Kara and I wanted to hear the answer.

"I do not know that either, but someone in my house was drugging me. Evie could have been part of that. Or she could have seen me leave and followed to protect me. Do you not agree that is what needs to be sorted out?"

"Oh, I do. Did you hit that young woman with something? Did her tailing you make you that mad?" Lydia said. Though she'd at least been polite to Ritaestelle up until now, that seemed to be over.

"I—I tried to help her as best I could. Why, if not for those voices I heard, and the cats escaping, poor Evie might have lain on that dock all night," Ritaestelle said.

"What voices?" Kara said.

Lydia offered Kara a withering glance before saying, "What voices? The ones in your head?"

"No. Outside. I was *not* hallucinating, despite what people may think," Ritaestelle said. "I do believe I heard an argument. That part is hazy, I am sorry to say."

"Convenient." Lydia looked at her watch. "My time is up here. I have an appointment with Miss Preston's mother. There will be an autopsy, which she is resisting. But we have no choice."

"Will you tell Evie's mother that I send my sincere condolences?" Ritaestelle said.

"Do I look like a mail carrier? That's *not* my job." Lydia rose and waved me off when I started to accompany her to the foyer.

The slam of the door that came with her departure sent Merlot running for cover.

# Nineteen

After Lydia's not unexpectedly dramatic departure, Kara, Ritaestelle and I remained still and silent for several seconds.

Finally Ritaestelle said, "Might I use your telephone?"

I pulled my cell from my pocket and held it out.

Ritaestelle shook her head. "I am quite uncomfortable with cellular telephones. Do you have a real one?"

"Real one." That was an interesting way to put it.

"I'll get the landline." Kara rose and went into the kitchen.

"I almost feel like I should apologize for Lydia. I see that she's upset you," I said. "But I have to admit, I'm not fond of her myself."

"She is quite blunt, but that is not what I would call a bad thing, in this case. I should have already called Evie's mother. In that tapestry bag that my cousin carried inside you'll find a small address book. Would you mind fetching that for me?"

A minute later, Ritaestelle was speaking with Evie's mother and saying how sorry she was that Evie had died so tragically.

Meanwhile, I put away the leftover cheese and crackers and Kara washed the cheese board and knife. Isis appeared at my feet after I closed the pantry door and began to mew repetitively—tiny little meows intended to inform me of something.

"Are you hungry?" I said.

Apparently not, because she trotted off toward the living room, fluffy tail high. Did she want to play? But then I tuned in to Ritaestelle's voice.

She was pleading with Evie's mother, saying, "Please give that coroner woman your consent, Loretta. Otherwise they will involve the county authorities and drag this thing on and on. You need to lay poor Evie to rest, and that cannot happen quickly without your help."

I walked quietly to the edge of the dining room table that separates kitchen and living room. Isis was rubbing against Ritaestelle's shins and still meowing. I stepped closer and saw tears streaming down Ritaestelle's face. Even so, her voice was supportive and kind as she again encouraged Mrs. Preston to cooperate with Lydia.

I could see why Ritaestelle had been so respected in her community. She was strong but kind; she'd probably been an adviser to many. The accusations dogging her lately must have hurt her deeply, just as her nephew's words had stung me.

Even her little goddess Isis wanted to help—or get me to help. I went to the couch and sat next to Ritaestelle, taking her free hand in mine. I squeezed it and she looked at me, gratitude evident in her eyes.

Ritaestelle's grip relaxed and she smiled. "I believe you are doing the right thing, Loretta. I can be reached at Miss Jillian Hart's residence, so if you will call me—oh my, I do not even know the number." She looked my way.

But before I could give her the number, Ritaestelle said, "Oh, you have it from the caller ID? Good. Such a fine invention when our memories are beginning to dim. Please call me when the visitation times are settled. You take care, Loretta."

Ritaestelle took the phone away from her face and looked at it in confusion. I released her hand, took the receiver and ended the call.

"Thank you, my dear Jillian. And thank you for your kindness."

Isis stared up at her mistress. Ritaestelle reached down and picked her up. "You were quite the noisy one while I was trying to speak." She looked at me. "I would very much enjoy a nap about this time. Is that possible?"

"Certainly," I said.

I helped her to her feet and led her down the hall to

the guest room, grabbing her overnight bag on the way. Isis stayed with her on the bed as I closed the bedroom door.

Back in the kitchen, Kara was rummaging through my freezer. "Do you have anything for supper? Or should I pick something up?"

"There's a chicken in the fridge. But I have no idea what I should do with it. My brain has quit on me," I said.

"You do look tired," Kara said. "And a little sad. Is something bothering you?"

Was I that transparent? Because my brain hadn't really quit. It was simply filled once again with Farley's ridiculous accusations. "I'll be fine once this murderer is caught. Plus I am a little worried because I'm so behind on Christmas orders."

"It's only the end of July," Kara said.

"Custom cat quilt orders have been pouring in— especially after your article about the cats we rescued from that professor was syndicated," I said. "And there are the hundreds of e-mails from people who think I can solve their pet troubles."

Kara smiled. "Which you can't. Let me worry about dinner, and you take some time to yourself."

"I don't want to bother you with—"

"Please. Let someone take care of you for a change." Kara extended her arm toward the foyer. "Go. Quilt. Nap. Soak in the tub. Do whatever you need to feel better."

I chose quilting. Nothing is more relaxing. My three cats joined me. Chablis settled in my lap as I sat down in the comfy armchair in my quilting room. I picked up the small quilt I'd been working on—the appliquéd one for Kara. Then I remembered that the buttons for this project had been scattered everywhere—some of them in this very room. I'd collect them later. Instead, I switched to quilting on a custom order as Merlot and Syrah continued the button game. Yup, they were still finding buttons I didn't even remember being in that box. One day they would tire of this, but for now, they were having fun.

The rhythm of the work settled me, and I began to think about the poor victim. Had my visit with Evie Preston somehow put her in danger? And if so, why? Then it dawned on me that I had forgotten the *why* that began my involvement. What was Ritaestelle's cat doing so far from home? Did Isis ending up near that highway figure into Evie's death in some way? That might not be of interest to Candace or Mike, but I wanted to know.

The smell of chicken and herbs filled the hall when I emerged from my little retreat at about seven that evening. The cats ran straight to the kitchen, and I wanted to run myself, the smells were so wonderful. But the doorbell sounded and stopped me as I entered the foyer. I checked the peephole and saw Tom.

After I let him inside, he said, "I smell something that had my mouth watering the minute I got out of the car."

"That's Kara's doing. Let's see what she's up to."

Tom put his arm around my shoulder as we walked toward the kitchen, but Kara was sitting in the living room working on her laptop.

"Hey, Tom. Hope you can stay for dinner," she said. "Apparently Jillian likes to buy chickens as big as turkeys."

"You do not have to ask me twice. Working on a story for tomorrow?" he asked.

"Yes. This morning's edition sold better than any *Mercy Messenger* in two years, even if the murder was already a day old." She closed her laptop and set it on the floor beside the recliner. "Unfortunately, tomorrow's story will have little new information. And before you say anything, I did not mention Ritaestelle is staying in Mercy."

"Thanks," I said. "I don't want people calling me and asking me questions. Some folks might accuse me of harboring a criminal."

Tom said, "I met with three potential clients today, and two of them knew. I'll bet most of the town already knows she's staying here."

Kara's lips pursed as she nodded in agreement. "I figured as much. I have never seen news travel as fast as in this little town."

"Where is your houseguest?" Tom asked.

"Napping," I said.

Tom glanced back toward the hallway. He whispered, "Got the dirt on the nephew."

Just the mention of Farley Longworth made my stomach clench.

He went on, saying, "In fact, an unnamed source—that's

for your benefit, Kara—told me plenty about the money problems that all those relatives living with Ritaestelle seem to have."

Kara leaned back against the recliner cushions. Chablis appeared from behind the sofa and jumped into her lap. "Go on. This should be interesting." She began stroking my cat.

I figured I'd learned plenty about Farley Longworth already and wanted to know nothing more. "Do we have to talk about this right now?"

"With Ritaestelle asleep, this is the perfect time," Kara said.

Tom took my hand and led me to the couch, but when he sat down, I remained standing.

"Maybe there's something I can do to help with supper?" I looked at Kara.

Tom tugged at my hand. "This guy upset you when he called here, and—"

"He called you?" Kara said.

"Yes, but it's no big deal," I said. "Maybe he was upset about Evie's death and decided to take it out on me. Now, what can I do in the kitchen?"

"Nothing. Everything but the chicken is ready, and that will take another thirty minutes," Kara said. "What did this guy say to you?"

I reluctantly sat next to Tom and said, "He accused me of trying to extort money for the return of Ritaestelle's cat. Ridiculous, huh?"

"Ridiculous, yes. What a jerk," Kara said. "What else did you find out, Tom?"

"I got plenty of info about the rest of that Longworth clan, the hired help and that Desmond character. He's a real loser." Tom said. "So is Farley, and everyone in Woodcrest knows it. Flunked out of college twice. Has two DUIs that I uncovered—but who knows how much stuff his father 'took care of' before dying in a hunting accident. Farley's mother, Justine, continued to live at the estate, and he eventually joined her after a stint in rehab. See, Farley's father left his share of the Longworth money to his sister, Ritaestelle—not to his wife and kid. They are a 'feckless pair,' as my source said. Feckless. Hadn't heard that one since I finished high school required reading."

I wasn't surprised by any of this, but it didn't make me feel better. What Farley had said about people talking behind my back, his inferring that I'd killed my husband, still bothered the heck out of me. This must be how Ritaestelle felt, too. Those implications that she was losing her faculties, that she'd become a shoplifter despite being wealthy, must have been so hurtful. But what if she wasn't wealthy at all? What if that's why she was stealing things from the drugstore? I looked at Tom. "Did you find out anything about Ritaestelle's finances?"

"You bet I did," he said. "You can't investigate the relatives of old money without learning how much old money there is. Ritaestelle is rich enough to own a controlling interest in South Carolina if she wanted. I'd say that's millions and millions of reasons to want *her* dead rather than Evie."

"Yes, that's something I've been contemplating," came Ritaestelle's voice from the foyer. She limped toward us. "I should have been the one to die out on that dock."

My cheeks felt hot with embarrassment. We'd been talking behind her back—doing exactly what bothered me so much about what Farley had said was going on concerning me.

I went over to help her into the living room. Isis trailed behind as I led Ritaestelle to the couch, saying, "Tom is a private investigator, and since I had a call from Farley, Tom decided to see why he seemed so . . . so upset when he phoned."

Ritaestelle sighed heavily as she sat on the couch. "First, in my opinion, 'unpleasant' better describes his behavior than 'upset.' What did Farley want? Because he always wants something."

"He seemed bothered that you were staying here rather than at home." I was trying to sugarcoat this, I knew. The poor woman had enough on her mind.

"And," Kara added, "Farley's got some crazy notion that Jillian wanted money for your cat's return."

"What?" Ritaestelle gripped her left fingers with her right hand so tightly her knuckles whitened. "I must speak with that man. For now, all I can do is apologize for his behavior. I am quite familiar with apologizing for Farley."

"I never did get to tell you about why I came to your

house," I said. "Shawn Cuddahee sent me to check you out. He wanted to know if it was safe to return Isis to your home."

At the mention of her name, Isis jumped on the coffee table. Ritaestelle held out her arms, and the cat leaped onto her lap. "That was the tipping point, was it not? Your arrival at the estate to check on me?"

"What do you mean?" Kara said, sounding curious.

"I had been accused of stealing, been drugged, but you, Jillian, caring only about this precious black cat, brought it all to light. You came thinking you would find an addled old woman. Instead, you saw me lying on the floor. You knew something was very wrong."

I nodded. "True. But that doesn't explain how Isis escaped in the first place."

"Indeed, that is a mystery in and of itself," she replied. "My sweet girl here has great disdain for the outdoors. I once bought her one of those catios—you know, a screened building that can allow your cat to be outside but still not wander off?"

"Catios?" Tom said. "You have got to be kidding."

I smiled at him. "I've seen them advertised at cat shows. You would not believe the things people will buy for their cats—like special little quilts."

He looked flustered. "I didn't mean what *you* do is anything but great. Dashiell loves his quilt."

"You have a cat, Mr. Stewart?" Ritaestelle said.

"He does," Kara said. "And I have two kittens. But tell us about the day Isis disappeared. This might make a good story."

"I would be happy to," she said. "The police do not seem the least bit interested in that event, so perhaps a little publicity would not hurt. I consider that a seminal moment. My tormenter, whoever it is, took things to the intolerable level with that dirty trick. First, though, I smell something wonderful, so perhaps we could chat over dinner?"

# Twenty

The herbed chicken, rice, peas and salad that Kara made for supper brought compliments from everyone. As we ate the delicious meal, I realized just how much home-cooked food can ease the mind. Between the quilting earlier and this meal, I felt more relaxed than I'd been in days. The wine Tom opened helped, too. Ritaestelle was quite appreciative of her glass of white wine since she'd had nothing alcoholic to drink ever since she had suspected she was being drugged.

As I loaded the last of the peas and rice onto my fork, I said, "Now that we've all had a chance to adore this food, tell us about Isis's disappearance."

Ritaestelle dabbed at her lips with one of my homemade plaid napkins. Bet she had nothing but the monogrammed kind at her house, but she didn't seem to mind my more modest table setting in the least.

"I believe that someone took her and tossed her by the road. That's the only explanation," Ritaestelle said.

"Why do you say that?" Kara said.

"She was sleeping on my bed the first day I could no longer fight whatever was in that tea. I am assuming it was the tea. Anyway, she always stays close by. When I awoke, she was gone. And no one could explain it," she said.

"Did you call animal control? Put up flyers?" I asked.

"Unfortunately, I was in no shape to even punch numbers on the telephone," Ritaestelle said. "Evie told me she would find Isis, but she was beginning to act very suspicious of me. I think she believed I had gone completely mad by then. She did have to pull items I supposedly stole out of my bag at the pharmacy."

"She seemed a little cool when I arrived on your doorstep the other day." I paused, recalling a visit that seemed aeons ago. "But Evie did say that Isis needed to come home. Why wouldn't she have returned Shawn's phone calls if that were the case?"

"He called me?" Ritaestelle said.

"More than once. I never questioned him about who he spoke to, though. Might be worth asking now," I said.

"If it was one of my relatives, I am sure they simply ignored him." Ritaestelle pulled a piece of chicken off a breastbone and offered it to Isis. "That is how they have always done things, which is extremely impolite—and I have told them as much on many occasions. That is why, when I am able, I always answer the phone or greet guests at the door myself."

"We heard that's your routine," Tom said, "but the explanation is new."

"Yes, amazing what goes around town. Getting back to my cat's mysterious disappearance and rescue, I must thank this gentleman Shawn in person. Can that be arranged?" Ritaestelle said.

"Sure," I said.

"Oh my. That sounds so pretentious. I can do the arranging. Since numbers on the telephone are no longer blurry, I will call the man myself. Now, I heard part of what you all were discussing when I came into the living room earlier. Tell me about the rumors. I would appreciate hearing them from your point of view." She glanced back and forth between Tom and me.

"Actually," Tom said. "We'd like your version."

"Hmm. I suppose you would." She stared up at the ceiling, ostensibly to collect her thoughts.

All the cats had taken spots beneath the table in anticipation of a chicken treat like Isis had gotten. Merlot was lying on top of my feet, and I took a peek and saw the other two beside him. Chicken scraps are something all my cats enjoy.

Ritaestelle drew in a breath and went on. "This all began about two months ago. Earrings from a local merchant suddenly appeared in my handbag. They still had the price tag on that little cardboard piece that held them. I was with Desmond at a restaurant and took out my wallet to pay—I always pay when I am with him. I believe I let out quite an audible gasp when I saw them."

"Had you recently been to that store?" Kara asked.

"Yes. The man who owns the shop designs and makes his own jewelry. He takes other items on consignment. I am a frequent buyer because he certainly can use the business." Ritaestelle lowered her voice. "Bless his heart, the poor man does give his best effort."

"How do you think the earrings got into your handbag?" Kara said. Her tone was formal. She was in journalist mode again.

"I have no earthly idea," she said, "but the next day I promptly returned them. I must say it was humiliating, especially since the owner seemed less than gracious. I suppose some of the talk already started after that very first incident."

"What about your friend Desmond? If he knew about the earrings, could he have told others?" I said.

Ritaestelle narrowed her eyes in thought. "Perhaps. Desmond is quite the conversationalist. He will engage anyone about anything. But I have always assumed the most intense gossip began after a similar incident a week later. Evie was with me at the pharmacy, as you know. Her turn to be humiliated. She asked me if I had forgotten those items were in my bag."

"What items?" Kara asked.

"Small things—nail polish, a few emery boards, perhaps a lipstick. But I was quick to notice that others in the store saw Evie point this out to me. The very next day Nancy paid me a visit and told me that several people had informed her that I might have a *problem*. She wanted details."

Tom shook his head, apparently not buying this. "The police chief came to you about this piddly stuff?"

"She came as a concerned friend, not as an officer of the law," Ritaestelle said. "Despite what went around town, I was never 'let off the hook' by her. Yes, that is what people said. A rich woman steals things and gets away with it. But I returned the earrings and never took anything from the pharmacy. Nancy wanted to make sure I was all right, even suggested I visit my physician."

"Did you?" Kara said.

But before Ritaestelle could answer, there was the familiar sound of a knock at the back door.

Merlot stood, obviously anticipating that I would get up. "That's Candace."

"I smell supper," she said once I let her in. After she came into the kitchen she, added, "And I see a party I wasn't invited to."

"I am so sorry. I should have thought to call you. Can I fix you a plate?" I said.

"I'm just giving you a hard time. But I am hungry." She craned her neck, looking over the counter to see what was on the table.

"Hey there, Candace," Kara said.

I noticed that Candace had a large manila envelope in one hand, and as she offered a "Hey there" back, she walked over to the built-in kitchen desk and set the envelope down.

Meanwhile, I got another plate from the cabinet above the dishwasher and silverware from the drawer.

Candace grabbed the plate and took off for the dining room table, saying, "My stomach thinks my throat has been cut."

Ritaestelle laughed for the first time since we'd met. "Sounds like something a police officer would say."

"How are you feeling, Miss Longworth?" Candace asked as she piled leftovers on her plate.

Guess it was a good thing I'd bought a chicken as large as a turkey after all.

"I am feeling quite well, thanks to the generous hospitality of Miss Jillian Hart," Ritaestelle said. "I might have to adopt her."

"She's bighearted—that's for sure." Candace sat, and I handed her the knife and fork. She looked at Tom. "Did you move in when I wasn't looking?"

Tom's turn to laugh, but all this good humor from Candace had me thinking that she must have found something in the Cadillac—perhaps some piece of evidence that was now in that envelope she obviously didn't want anyone to see.

While Candace dug in, Tom stood, checking his watch. "I have to go. All these new orders for security cameras and alarms have to be to my supplier by tomorrow." He looked at me. "Walk me to the door?"

Once we were in the foyer, Tom took me in his arms. He whispered, "Tell Candace about Farley. After that phone call to you and what I learned about his less than stellar character, I don't trust that guy."

He kissed me good-bye, and as I rejoined the others, I felt guilty for kissing another man while my heart was once again heavy with grief. I could only keep telling myself that John would have wanted me to move on.

I put these thoughts aside when I realized that Kara and Candace were feuding again. These two were friends, even lived in the same apartment complex, yet here they were, sounding angry with each other—and not for the first time.

Kara was saying, "You can't kick me out of my step-mother's home." She leaned back, arms folded across her chest. "I'm staying."

"Then I'll have to haul Miss Longworth down to the police station for questioning." Candace took a large bite off her chicken leg and started chewing, never taking her eyes off Kara.

Kara raised an eyebrow. "That's how you're going to play this?"

As Candace finished chewing, Ritaestelle spoke up. "Kara, honey, I will be happy to share whatever it is Deputy Carson questions me about afterward, if you would like. I have no secrets. Can you abide by her request for now?"

Candace waved her chicken leg at Ritaestelle. "There you go. Problem solved."

I didn't say anything to Kara, but I implored her with my eyes and she finally relented. Her irritation seemed gone when she said, "I'm not allowed in a police interrogation room, and I suppose this is the equivalent for now." She stood, smiling at Ritaestelle. "But I intend to take you up on that offer. I'll be finishing up my work for tomorrow's edition by midnight. Please call me."

Time to walk Kara to the front door. I gave her a big hug, saying, "Thank you for making such a lovely dinner, and for being so nice about being kicked out. I'm sorry, though."

She withdrew and gripped my upper arms. "The last thing I want is to stress you out. But make sure Ritaestelle calls me."

I nodded and she left.

This time when I returned, Candace was clearing the table and Ritaestelle was standing at the sink, filling it with steaming, sudsy water.

"You need to be off your feet. This nurse's orders." I handed her a dish towel to dry her hands, gripped her elbow and led her into the living room.

"I can handle a few dirty dishes, Miss Jillian," she said. "I sometimes help Hildie out at home after we have had guests. She is a stern woman unless she is in her kitchen. Then her personality simply brightens the world. I was hoping some of that might work for me tonight. And besides, you should not have to tidy up after me."

"Please let me help you sit down. I'd feel terrible if you injured yourself again," I said.

"She's right," Candace said, placing the last of the dirty dishes on the counter. She fetched the envelope from the desk.

"Candace came to talk to you," I said. "I'll handle kitchen duties while you two talk."

Candace joined Ritaestelle.

Meanwhile, with the platter holding a chicken carcass nearby, I had four cats to please. I pulled off a mound of scraps and divided them on to four saucers. I set each dish down on the floor by the back door, giving each cat plenty of space. Isis wasn't big on sharing, and I hoped to avoid a spat.

I used the full sink to soak the dishes. Everyone had filled their bellies, so there were no leftovers to put away. After I took out the trash, I joined Candace and Ritaestelle. While I'd been cleaning up, I'd tried hard not to listen to their conversation. But not listening was easier said than done. I'd heard, "Well, I never," more than once from Ritaestelle.

The envelope and the pictures it had held were sitting on my coffee table. Ritaestelle's face was ashen. I was instantly worried. She looked terrible. What if she had a heart condition I didn't know about?

Ritaestelle looked up at me. "I can see that you are fretting about me, Miss Jillian. Calm yourself, dear. I will be fine once I understand all this better." She turned to Candace. "If it is agreeable with you, I would like my friend to see these pictures."

Candace gestured at them. "Sure. Have a look. We found these things in Miss Longworth's car."

I picked up the pictures. The first several were photos of the outside of the Cadillac. They were taken in a progression to show the seats and then the console that separated the front seats. The next picture showed the open console and revealed a Ziploc bag containing unopened cheap cosmetics, candy bars, a three-pack of Sharpie markers, and several pieces of turquoise jewelry with little price tag strings. It was impossible to see everything. But the next shot had the contents laid out on a cloth. It looked like someone had been to the Dollar Store and made a killing. Oh. Bad word choice.

I glanced at Candace. "Wow."

She in turn looked at Ritaestelle, who said, "I know nothing about any of these items."

"Next pictures," Candace said.

This photo was of the open glove box. A small red velvet box was visible. The next shot showed the box open and holding a diamond engagement ring. The stone was small and the setting looked less than modern.

"That belongs to my cousin Muriel," Ritaestelle said. "How in the world did that—how did any of this—end up in my car?"

"Good question," Candace said. "Seems we found only one print—beneath the glove box. I'll be comparing it to yours, but I should have found dozens of prints, and I didn't."

"I am sure Muriel went into a hysterical episode once you showed this to her. I certainly do not blame her. She adored the man who gave her that ring."

"She was a little upset when I asked her if she gave it to you," Candace said.

"Muriel was married to Belle's cousin once," I said to Candace.

"Belle Lowry?" Candace said.

"Yes," Ritaestelle said. "Of course, I assume living here in Mercy you both know Belle. How is the dear woman?"

"She's fine. Everyone loves her coffee shop. But back to the matter at hand," Candace said. "You're certain you have no idea how these items ended up in your car?"

"This is more of the same, Deputy Carson. It has been

going on for weeks. Have I not been forthright about everything?"

"You have, but it still doesn't explain this," Candace said.

"Someone must dislike me very much to do this sort of thing." Ritaestelle shook her head, and though her color had returned, her eyes were filled with misery. "Someone in my family, I am assuming. Who else had access to my car?"

"I don't know," Candace said. "The absence of finger-prints is suspicious. Someone wiped it down."

"You've decided there's no evidence that Ritaestelle took those things?" I said.

"That's right. Pardon me, Miss Longworth, but that doesn't mean you didn't. I just don't have any proof. To-morrow I'll try to find out where these items came from." Candace leveled a gaze at Ritaestelle. "Am I gonna find you on some security camera footage from a store stealing things, Miss Longworth?"

Ritaestelle's lips tightened into a thin line. She hesitated before looking at me. "Your friend, Mr. Stewart? I under-stood someone to say he was private detective of sorts. Is that correct?"

"He is, but—"

"Could I impose on you to bring me your telephone, Miss Jillian?" Ritaestelle said. "I would like to hire Mr. Stewart. I want him to find evidence that will prove that I am telling the truth."

"You understand I have to follow the evidence, don't you, Miss Longworth?" Candace said.

"I completely understand. But I hope you understand that it is time I took action to protect myself from the lies some terrible person is trying to spread across the entire county."

# Twenty-one

The next morning, I awoke with Isis sitting on my chest staring at me. Must be time for breakfast. I checked the alarm clock and saw that it was eight—late for me—and realized I hadn't stirred all night. I'd sure needed a good night's sleep.

But why was Isis in my room and not with Ritaestelle? I got up, put on my cotton robe and slipped my feet into the handiest shoes—a pair of flip-flops.

My own cats were not in my room. Another mystery—as if I didn't have enough of those.

Last night, after deciding she'd needed a private investigator to help clear her name, Ritaestelle had refused to speak about anything else to Candace. Candace had left, saying she was only trying to be as open as she could concerning the investigation. I had the feeling she was beginning to think Ritaestelle was innocent after all.

Still, I felt caught between Candace and Ritaestelle, between Kara and Candace, even between Isis and my own cats at times. Plus, I'd started out by agreeing to be the middle person between Shawn and Ritaestelle. Maybe hiring Tom was the best thing for Ritaestelle. Still, since she was obviously a suspect, I wondered why she wasn't calling her lawyer rather than Tom.

I passed the guest room as I walked down the hall and saw that Ritaestelle's door was open and her bed neatly made. *She's an early bird,* I thought as I went out to the kitchen with Isis leading the way.

No Ritaestelle to be seen in the living room or in the

kitchen. But my three cats were all sitting like little statues, their faces intent on the back door. My heart skipped. Was something wrong? Did Ritaestelle attempt another trip to the dock?

I shooed all the felines away from the back door and went outside. I saw Ritaestelle sitting in the wicker rocking chair staring out at the glassy lake. The morning sun spread its golden warmth across the water and gleamed on the backs of five ducks gliding their way to shore. There were times I wished I were an artist so I could capture this morning beauty, something I was treated to so often.

"Pretty, huh?" I said.

"Absolutely lovely. And so soothing," Ritaestelle said, not taking her eyes off the lake.

Though the chair did have a floral cushion, I wondered how comfortable it was for someone with a bruised hip. "Can I get you a pillow? Wicker isn't always friendly when you're sore."

She looked at me and smiled. "No, thank you, dear. I am feeling simply fine, good enough to take those ballroom lessons I always intended on doing. I do not suppose they offer those in prison."

"You aren't going to prison." I dragged a lawn chair over next to her and sat. "Tom will make sure of that. But couldn't you use a lawyer, too?"

"I am putting my faith in you and in Mr. Stewart, as well as the Lord. My brother may have been a lawyer, but he did not much care for his colleagues who specialized in criminal law. Said they were a different breed. The only lawyer I trust is our family attorney. He specializes in estates and trusts. I do not believe he would be much help in this situation."

"I suppose not. But he, or even Tom might know someone—"

Ritaestelle held up a heavily veined hand. "If I need to go down that road, I will seek counsel. For now, as I said, you and Mr. Stewart will continue to be my guides through this terrible journey. That is, if you are willing to put up with me a bit longer."

"Of course we are," I said.

She looked at me for the first time since I'd come out on the deck. "Since I would like a visit with Belle, I took the liberty of calling Mr. Stewart and asking if he could meet us at her place of business. Would you very much mind driving me there?"

"Why Belle?" I asked.

"Because she was part of my family once," Ritaestelle said, "and I was very preoccupied with my charities and the socializing involved at the time. Perhaps I was not as welcoming as I should have been to her cousin or to her. I want to apologize. She might also have a perspective on relatives who I saw in a different light back then, but who have for the most part been quite cold and uncaring in recent years."

We arrived at Belle's Beans about an hour later, and though I didn't think Ritaestelle was ready for ballroom dancing, she did seem less hobbled by her injury.

Tom waved at us from one of the larger tables he'd nabbed in the far corner.

"What would you like?" I asked. "Coffee, latte, cappuccino?"

"I am quite fond of cappuccino. Does Belle take credit cards? Because I do not have a red cent with me," Ritaestelle said.

"You can pay me back. Join Tom, and I'll be right with you." I literally put my hands on her shoulders and turned her in Tom's direction before she could protest. See, I'd spotted a problem. Waiting in line was none other than Morris Ebeling, who I swore spent all his free time here. This ought to be fun.

I was hoping he would get his coffee, leave and not notice me—or Ritaestelle. But though Morris is cantankerous even on a good day, he is still a cop. He's observant, and I could tell by his expression when he greeted me that he'd definitely seen us arrive.

"This where Tom is meeting with his new client?" Morris turned and said as soon as I stepped in line. "Last I knew, he had an office."

Guess Candace had already filled him in. "I wanted coffee, so we agreed to meet here," I said, sounding cheerful. I was hiding my guilt at withholding the other reason we were here—to see Belle. But my loyalty toward Ritaestelle, my belief in her, was making me do things that surprised me. Why? Was it because she reminded me of my dear,

dear grandmother who had been Texas Southern, not Deep South Southern, but shared so many of Ritaestelle's traits? I truly had no idea.

Morris pointed at me. "I know you, girl. From the look in your eyes, I'd say that ain't the truth, the whole truth and nothing but the truth. But I forgive you—mostly 'cause I know we'll find out the reason soon enough." He turned back and ordered his coffee and Danish from the fake Belle behind the counter.

I arrived at the table a few minutes later with a tray carrying our coffees, several pastries and two yogurt, fruit and granola cups. Though Tom had his large coffee in a to-go cup, I'd made sure ours was in china cups. Had Ritaestelle ever had anything to go in her life? I thought not.

The whispering and stares had already begun, but Tom and Ritaestelle seemed to be ignoring this, so I did the same. Really, what else could I do?

"Where's Belle?" I said as I took a spoon to one of the yogurt cups.

"Said she'd be here in about fifteen minutes." Tom reached for a raspberry and cream cheese Danish.

Ritaestelle, as I expected, chose the other yogurt.

"Miss Longworth and I were talking about exactly what she expects of me—actually of us, Jillian," Tom said.

I stopped my spoon before it reached my mouth. "What does that mean?"

"These cousins aren't likely to open up to me. From what Miss Longworth tells me, Muriel, in particular, isn't exactly fond of men after what Belle's cousin did to her. I was hoping you could help with them." Tom bit into his Danish.

"What am I supposed to do?" I was about to put myself in the middle of Ritaestelle and her cousins. I felt like I was becoming the town go-between.

Tom finished chewing and then said, "Engage them. Get them to talk. You're excellent at winning friends. In the meantime, I'll deal with Farley and his mother, as well as Desmond Holloway."

"Desmond?" Ritaestelle said. "What could he possibly have to do with this? The man is harmless."

"Miss Longworth, with all due respect, you'll have to let go of the reins if you expect me to do my job," Tom said. "Desmond's part of your life and needs investigating. I might also be able to wrangle information out of Nancy Shelton. I've been a cop. I know what buttons to push with her."

"You may know, but I sure don't, Tom." I set the spoon down. I'd lost my appetite. "I'm no private investigator. Can't Kara help you?"

"Kara? Think about that for a second," Tom said.

"Oh. The *Messenger*. I get it," I said. "But—"

"Listen, Jilly. Doing private eye work is about being charming, nice, and a little manipulative," he said. "That's the part you don't like, and I know that. There's also times when you have to be confrontational, but since that is way outside your comfort zone—like on another planet and in another lifetime—we'll leave that to me."

Ritaestelle was paying close attention to her yogurt and coffee. She probably felt as if she couldn't ask me to do anything else for her. But as strange as that may seem, that was what sold me. Being needed was important to me. And she needed my help.

"I'll do what I can," I said. "But you'll have to be very specific about what I'm supposed to do."

Ritaestelle reached over and put a hand over mine. "Thank you, dear. You have no idea what this means to me." Her eyes filled. "If only I had a family that included the likes of you two."

I smiled at her. "It's okay, Ritaestelle. We'll get to the bottom of this."

"The bottom of your cups, I hope," came a familiar voice behind me. Belle had arrived. She smiled and nodded at all of us, and I was happy that she'd chosen pink lipstick. But the applying of said lipstick? That hadn't changed except that today she'd spread a straight line across her upper lip.

"Why, Belle Lowry, you look amazing," Ritaestelle said. "I must apologize to you for so many things, but why not start with how sorry I am that I did not keep in touch."

Belle sidled over to Ritaestelle's chair, put an arm around her and squeezed her close. "You do not have to apologize to me. I am so thrilled to see you enjoying a cup of my coffee."

"I must say, this is the best cappuccino I have ever had—and this is from a woman who has enjoyed the same in Italy." Ritaestelle held up her chocolate spoon. "But this cute little utensil? I don't want to spoil it by stirring my coffee."

Belle grabbed a chair from the table next to ours and sat. "I understand from Tom there's trouble and that we need to clear things up. How can I help?"

Tom explained that we needed more information about the family from someone who might have a fresh perspective. "You pick up on the unspoken, Belle. You can read people. Tell us what you know from the days when your cousin was part of the family."

Belle cast a glance at Ritaestelle. "This is a tad awkward."

"Do not feel that way," Ritaestelle said. "I have come to understand that something went quite wrong with my family a long time ago. I chose to pretend. I chose to look the other way. I can no longer do that."

Belle cleared her throat. "You want to know what I saw? Or what my cousin told me?"

"Both," Tom said.

"Guess we should start with my cousin Ronnie." Belle looked at Tom. "He's the one who married Muriel. Loved her, too. He never cared about the family money, but apparently Ritaestelle's sister-in-law Justine accused him of just that. Said who else would marry Muriel if it wasn't for her money?"

Oh boy. *Why not get right to the heart of the matter, Belle?* I thought. But if this bothered Ritaestelle, she didn't let it show.

"Anyone else have issues with your cousin?" Tom asked.

Belle didn't look at Ritaestelle when she said, "Ronnie was the one with the issues. He felt like Ritaestelle wouldn't give him the time of day. Same thing with her brother, rest his soul." She looked Ritaestelle straight in the eye. "He never felt part of the family. You were just too busy."

Ritaestelle closed her eyes and nodded slowly. "I have come to contemplate that very issue. I reached out to the needy in the community when the neediest of all were right next to me every day."

Belle's already rosy cheeks turned a deeper shade. "Please don't take what I've said the wrong way. You have done some fine things. Ronnie could have chosen another path. Sought guidance from our pastor. Seen a marriage counselor. Cheating on his wife? There's no excuse for that. I told him as much, too."

"What else did you observe about the family?" Tom asked.

Belle pondered the question for a few seconds. "I must say Augusta was always ready to tell it like it was. I appreciated that about her. But I also sensed some jealousy on her part. She was bothered that Muriel landed a husband and she hadn't."

"Did the cousins seem jealous of Ritaestelle?" I asked.

"You want my take, they were scared and jealous," Belle said.

"Scared?" Ritaestelle sounded genuinely surprised.

"Scared you'd cut them off. You and your brother held the purse strings, plus those two did like to be in your company. Lord knows they weren't the prettiest or most popular girls in school, were they?" Belle laughed, her gaze far off. "When you're not pretty or popular, you tend to want to hang around those that are. And you and your brother were certainly the most popular pair in Woodcrest."

"Probably because of the family name, not because of our personalities," Ritaestelle said.

"Why, I never thought I'd hear you sell yourself short. You must feel very troubled," Belle said.

"These past few months have worn me down, Belle," Ritaestelle said. "My reputation as an honest woman has been tarnished. All I can say is, some person knew exactly how to get to me."

"And had the access to do it," Tom said. "That limits the possibilities. I know that you don't want to go home, but can you call one of your cousins and ask that the people who live in the house be available for interviews?"

"I'll telephone George. He will make sure you have access to anything you need," Ritaestelle said.

"I forgot about the butler and the housekeeper. We'll need to talk to them." Tom looked at Belle. "Let's get down to some real dirt, now. What have you heard?"

Belle's lips twisted into a pucker as she bit the side her mouth. She glanced at Ritaestelle.

"Come on. This woman is tough. She can take it." Tom lifted his cup and drained what was left of his coffee.

"People think you did it, Ritaestelle," Belle said softly.

"They say you killed Evie Preston because she wouldn't cover up for your shoplifting anymore."

"Do you believe that?" Ritaestelle said.

"No. And here's why. If you put up with that bunch of freeloaders living with you, and you never murdered one of them, why in the heck would you kill a girl you'd only known for what? A year, tops? Doesn't make sense." Belle nodded. "And that's the truth."

Ritaestelle smiled. "I always did like you, Belle Lowry. Thank you for your honesty."

"We've got to get answers," I said. The thought of helping Tom no longer seemed quite so daunting. I could always count on Belle to say things that just plain made sense.

# Twenty-two

We finished our breakfast and coffee and walked outside, with Tom supporting Ritaestelle. This day promised to be a scorcher. The sign above the bank across the street told us that even though it was a little after ten in the morning, the temperature was already eighty-five degrees.

Just as Tom was helping Ritaestelle into the front passenger seat of his Prius, Candace and Chief Shelton hurried toward us.

"Glad we caught y'all." Candace eyed me and mouthed the words, "We're okay." She certainly looked less stressed than she had when she left my house last night.

"Caught? That could be taken more than one way," Tom said.

"Don't be funny, Tom. We'd like to talk to Miss Longworth for a few minutes," Candace said.

"Is something wrong?" Ritaestelle said.

"Not any more wrong than it already is," Shelton said. "But I don't think you want to discuss matters outside in this heat."

*I wouldn't want to either if I were wearing a blue suit like you are,* I thought. Bet she wore those slacks to avoid the whole pantyhose thing.

"I believe I have told you everything I know," Ritaestelle said.

"She's done talking." Tom looked down at Ritaestelle in the passenger seat of his car. "Buckle up, Miss Longworth. Wouldn't want to give these officers any excuse to haul you down the street to the police station." He shut the car door.

Candace, hands on hips, looked steaming mad. "What is this about, Tom?"

But Tom matched her with some anger of his own. "This is about the two of you bullying this woman. Do you honestly believe she had the strength to hit a vital young woman so hard that she knocked her out? Where's the common sense in your investigation, huh, Candace?"

Candace's mouth opened, but no words came out.

Shelton blurted, "Okay, so you've got a point. Plus we know she was drugged. Her urine test proved it."

"How did you get access to her medical test results?" Tom said.

I felt a wave of relief wash over me. Maybe now they'd start listening to Ritaestelle.

"We had a warrant." Candace's tone was flat. "Remember that little thing called probable cause from your police days, Tom? Miss Longworth found a body. Regardless of what you think or what Miss Longworth thinks, I'm doing this the right way. I'm collecting and following the evidence."

"I know you are, Candace." I looked up at Tom. "And you know that, too, right?"

Tom smiled. "Yeah, I do know. Not easy, is it, Candace?"

She squinted at him for a second, and then cracked a smile herself. "Tom Stewart, you are gonna pay for this one day."

"You're doing a damn fine job, Deputy Carson. If you weren't, I wouldn't have this little PI assignment." Tom turned to me. "Come on. We've got another stop to make."

I opened the back passenger door, and Tom started for the driver's side.

Shelton said, "Wait. When will Ritaestelle be coming home? Her family has been asking after her."

As Tom opened the car door, he said, "You'd like that, wouldn't you, Chief? But she's staying away from Woodcrest for now."

As we drove away, Ritaestelle said, "I am unclear about that particular interaction, but I do appreciate you speaking up for me, Mr. Stewart."

"That's what you're paying me for. Your friend Chief Shelton, I'm guessing, would love to have you back in

Woodcrest so she could take over this investigation. Cops are territorial like that."

"Ah. Are you saying I should not trust Nancy?" Ritaestelle said.

"For now, trust us," Tom said. "But in the end, my money's on Candace to figure this out—with our help."

I saw Ritaestelle nod her head in agreement. "Can I ask where we are driving to now in your precious little car?"

"You are about to be reunited with another old friend," Tom said.

Five minutes later we pulled into the driveway of Karen Stewart's cottage.

"Why are we visiting your mother, Tom?" I asked.

"You'll see." He slid from behind the wheel, came around and helped Ritaestelle get out.

But as we walked up the steps of her latticed porch, it dawned on me. Karen was in a relationship with Ed Duffy. And Ed had told us he'd once cared very much about Ritaestelle.

Sure enough, both Karen and Ed met us at the front screen door. Karen wore a vintage-looking cotton print dress, belted at the waist and buttoned up to her neck. Ed's shirt was clean and pressed—as Karen always made sure of when he was at home.

"We've been expecting you," Karen said as she opened the door for us to enter.

The ceiling fan in Karen's small, darkened living room was churning at high speed. She never ran the air conditioner, and I assumed all the heavy drapes were closed to keep the heat out as much as possible.

Tom helped Ritaestelle to a mustard-colored velour rocker in the corner while saying, "Mom, this is Ritaestelle Longworth. Ed, you already know her, of course."

Ritaestelle's eyes grew wide and her fingers covered her mouth for a few seconds. "Sweet Lord. Edwin Duffy? Is that really you?"

"Yes, ma'am. Nice to see you again." Ed stared at the floor, not at the woman he told us he had once loved.

"I am never *ma'am* to you, Edwin. I will always be Ritaestelle." She blinked rapidly, and I could see this was a poignant moment for her.

"I've made fresh lemonade, so I'll be right back," Karen said.

"Let me help you." I followed her into the kitchen, wondering what in the heck Tom thought he was doing. Why did he want his poor mother to endure this reunion? I'd have to get some answers about this move.

Unlike the cluttered shop where Ed spent most of his time, Karen's small house was tidy and spotless. Just like the clothes she always wore, her kitchen was vintage—a stainless toaster still as shiny as the day she had bought it, a gleaming glass whistling teapot on the old gas range. The refrigerator was turquoise, rounded on the edges and small. She opened the door and took out a Fiestaware pitcher. Another pitcher holding ice water and sliced cucumbers sat near the sink.

She placed the lemonade on a wooden tray she'd already set up with six glasses. Why six? Maybe she liked even numbers. That was something I would expect of Karen. Tom's mother was an odd lady, with her dark, slick hair, deep blue eyes and commanding presence. Seemed like Ed preferred women who took charge.

Karen said, "I never would have thought I would be entertaining one of Ed's old girlfriends. Old in more ways than one. Forced him to tell me all about her, though. The man could have married into money. Instead he ended up with me."

"I'd say he got lucky," I said with a smile. Karen might be peculiar, but she was good for Ed and he adored her. That gave me a hint about this visit. Karen, a recovering alcoholic, didn't need secrets between herself and Ed. She'd found happiness, and my guess was that Tom wanted to keep it that way.

"Would you mind carrying the ice water, Jillian?" Karen said.

We both walked back into the living room, and soon everyone held his or her beverage of choice.

Karen sat next to Ed, who'd trimmed his beard in the last few days. I had to say, at times his clothes and limited grooming reminded me of a cult leader, but not today. He sat as stiff as a soldier on the plaid couch with its wooden arms. But perhaps because of his confession to Karen about his old love Ritaestelle, he didn't seem as anxious today as when we'd talked to him about her the other day.

"Ritaestelle and Ed were just catching up," Tom said. "But the reason we came today is that we hoped that you, Ed, could offer insight into why someone might want to set up Ritaestelle—make her look bad." Tom went on to explain the details about the shoplifting accusations, the drugging, and a beloved cat that mysteriously found herself wandering by a busy highway.

While Tom talked, I kept glancing at Ritaestelle, but she kept her eyes focused on the cold glass she clung to with both hands.

"I ain't sure why you're goin' back fifty years, Tommy," Ed said in his slow, measured tone. "Sure, everyone, 'specially the girls in school, suffered from envy when it came to Ritaestelle. Class president, valedictorian, and a pretty thing to boot. Seemed natural they'd be wantin' some of that. But what's that got to do with anything?"

I noticed Ed was careful not to say he had also "wanted some of that." Karen stared at him intently when he spoke of Ritaestelle. But not in a jealous way. Seemed to me she'd had a long talk with Ed about this woman.

"Maybe history has nothing to do with the murder, though I doubt that," Tom said. "Here's the deal. Before I start talking to Ritaestelle's family, I want to be armed with as much information as possible. Mom's insistence that I become a Boy Scout taught me one thing—be prepared. This is personal to someone. Close and personal. A serial killer didn't chase Evie into Jillian's backyard."

"I sure as hell hope not," Ed said.

"What about her cousins Muriel and Augusta? Did you know them?" Tom said.

"Sure. Everyone knew everyone in Woodcrest. Augusta was a year ahead of us and Muriel a year behind. Needy girls, but their daddy died young and I could see they were troubled and missin' him."

"That's very true, Edwin," Ritaestelle said. "Especially because my aunt—their mother, Estelle—was ill. Part of my name came from her. Unfortunately she became quite neglectful due to her sickness and died of cancer when we were all in our twenties. But her funeral brought Edwin and me together. We were close for a time. What did happen to us, Edwin?"

Oh boy. *What happened to their relationship?* Did Ritaestelle realize what she was saying? I felt the need to protect Karen and get this conversation back on track.

"This crime *was* personal, not random," I said. I'd known this and guessed Candace and Mike knew this as well. But Tom's approach wasn't about finding evidence he could hand to that prosecutor we'd met, or to a judge. Maybe that was why he quit the force—so he could do things his way.

"Yes. Highly personal murder, I'd say," Tom said. "Evie Preston followed Ritaestelle and was confronted by a killer. Sorry to say this, Ritaestelle, but you seem to have lived your life with blinders on. Now they've been ripped off, and you're in big trouble. Still, I can't rule out that Evie had some secrets herself. I'll be checking on her, too."

"Blinders," Ritaestelle said, as if to herself. She looked at Tom. "That is a very insightful observation, Mr. Stewart."

"Gaslighting," I murmured.

"Ah, yes. That's exactly what this sounds like." Karen, sitting between me and Ed on the couch, patted my thigh. "I didn't know you enjoyed the 1940s as much as I do."

"Whatever are you talking about?" Ritaestelle said.

Tom glanced back and forth between Karen and me, looking lost.

"Gaslighting," I said. "The term comes from an old movie. Karen, you probably know more about it than I do."

"If I remember right," she said, "in the film *Gaslight*, a woman is almost driven mad by her husband's manipulations. One of the things he does is dim the gas lights in their home and then make her believe she's imagining that they've been turned down."

Tom nodded. "I get it. That's like what the Manson family did when they broke into houses—that was before they got into more violent stuff. They would rearrange the furniture and steal nothing."

"I'm not a cinema expert, nor do I know much about Charles Manson," Ritaestelle said, "but, Karen, your explanation is such a relief. There is actually a word for what someone is trying to do to me."

"We find the reason, we'll get answers. Money seems the most likely motive. Someone drives you crazy, gets you de-

clared incompetent and ends up in control of a fortune."
Tom looked at Ed. "By the way, did you know Ritaestelle's
brother, too?"

"Nope. He was older than us by—what? Five years?"
He looked Ritaestelle's way.

"That would be correct," she answered. "You have a
good memory, Edwin."

Ed took a long swig of his lemonade, looking more embarrassed than I'd ever seen him.

The awkward silence was broken by a knock on the
door.

Tom rose from the recliner he'd been sitting in. "I'll get
that."

He let Desmond Holloway in, and the two shook hands.
What the heck was he doing here?

But I remembered that sixth glass and understood then
that he'd been invited.

After introductions he went straight to Ritaestelle,
bent and kissed her lightly on the lips. "I came to help you,
princess."

The cramped living room and the late-morning air
that whooshed in with Holloway made me feel so warm I
gulped down half my glass of cucumber ice water.

Ed offered Desmond his spot on the sofa closest to
Ritaestelle. Then he walked to the hall closet and brought
out a folding chair. But Tom took the chair from him, set it
up and told Ed to have the recliner. That was the spot I was
most used to seeing Ed in, and for some reason the tension
that had arrived with Holloway seemed to ease. But why
did the man bother me?

He chatted on for several minutes about missing having coffee with Ritaestelle every morning, not talking to
her on the phone, not sharing dinner a few times a week. I
noticed that Ritaestelle seemed like a schoolgirl, hanging
on his every word.

"You two have coffee every morning?" Tom asked.

He and I must think alike, because if they shared a drink
every day, maybe the tea hadn't been drugged. Perhaps it
was the coffee. But what motive would he have to harm
Ritaestelle?

Tom got straight to that. He looked at Ritaestelle, un-
smiling. "You leaving anything in your will for this guy?"

"Thomas Lee Stewart," Karen said. "You're bordering on rude."

"Mom, you may have grown up in the South and have all the same manners the Longworth bunch has, but I need to get to the bottom of this mess. If you think that's rude, you can head for the kitchen or bedroom."

"I don't appreciate your tone," Karen said. "And you shouldn't tell your mother what to do in her own house. But I understand, and I forgive you." She folded her hands in her lap and spoke to Ritaestelle. "I believe you should answer my son's question."

Ritaestelle cleared her throat. "Desmond and I are quite frank with each other. He is well aware that I will not be bequeathing anything to him."

Tom looked at Holloway. "What about spending time together? When Ritaestelle was stumbling around her house in a stupor and her cat went missing, where were you?"

Wow. Tom sure didn't like Holloway, and I wondered if he knew something he hadn't shared with me.

Holloway's ears were bright red even though he had a pasted-on smile. "We spoke on the phone. When she wasn't feeling well, Ritaestelle didn't want to see me."

"That's true, Mr. Stewart," Ritaestelle said. "Besides, Desmond would never harm me."

"Really?" Tom looked at Holloway. "Who else were you messing with when you were hanging out with Ritaestelle before you skipped town way back when? Word is, Augusta was on your list of conquests."

This time Desmond's entire face lit up with embarrassment. "I—I suppose Augusta told you that?"

"No, she didn't," Tom said.

"Who told you? And what else did they say?" Holloway was fidgeting with a diamond ring on his left pinkie, turning it around and around.

But before Tom could answer, Ritaestelle said, "Augusta, too? I knew about Nancy, and Charlotte, that girl who went on to sing in the opera, and even my friend Raye. I knew there were others, too. But *Augusta*? She is related to me, for heaven's sake."

Yup, Tom knew exactly where he'd been headed with this and wore a satisfied smile as Holloway fought to find the words to get out of the trouble he suddenly found himself in. The fact that he'd even been involved with Chief Shelton made me think this Desmond character went after anything in a skirt.

"She meant nothing to me, Ritaestelle," Holloway finally said.

"You mean she did not have enough money. You discarded one paramour after another and kept returning to me because I was wealthy. I forgave you, though I knew your true colors, but this? I am sorry, but this is too much." Her jaw tightened, and she looked at Tom. "Is there anything else about Desmond I should know?"

"I can give you a complete report later. He does get around—like all over the world with wealthy women," Tom said.

Holloway rose. "I will allow you time to digest this information, but do be careful believing everything you hear. I care very much about you, Ritaestelle."

Once he was gone, Ritaestelle glanced back and forth between Ed and Karen. "I must apologize for taking up your time with my problems—some of which I obviously knew nothing about."

"You're a good woman, Rita," Ed said. "Don't let nobody, even yourself, convince you of anything different."

We talked a while longer, but I realized why Tom had brought these particular players together today. He wanted happiness for his mother, he wanted Ritaestelle to hear an unpleasant truth, but most of all, he wanted Ed to be at peace. Ritaestelle had hurt him once, but that was over. He'd found love again, a love with Karen that I knew would last. Yup, I had a new insight into Tom, one I liked very much.

# Twenty-three

We left fifteen minutes later and returned to my house for lunch. Ritaestelle said little during the drive, and she didn't talk during our meal of salad and sandwiches. Once Tom left to begin his case file and set up interviews with Farley, his mother and others, Ritaestelle asked if I'd join her outside.

She seemed to be walking better, but I did take her elbow once we were out on the deck and helped her settle into the wicker rocker. The warm breeze began playing with her silver hair. I remembered that red Velcro roller in her bangs when she came to my door what seemed like a century ago. Her hair had gone flat and wispy in the last couple of days, but that seemed to be the last thing on her mind. She rocked and stared out at the water, seemingly lost in thought.

I sat next to her in the lawn chair. I usually sat at the glass patio table behind us in one of the wrought-iron armchairs. I'd read or stitch and listen to the water lapping and the birds singing. But for now I wanted to be close to my new friend.

After about five minutes of silence, I mustered enough courage to ask Ritaestelle about Desmond Holloway. Since I had the feeling the meeting with him was what had brought her outside to think, she might need to talk about him—get that bad taste out of her mouth.

"From what I understood today, you were willing to forgive Desmond's other indiscretions, but not when it came to Augusta. Tell me about that," I said.

Ritaestelle's rocking tempo picked up when I posed this question.

"I thought he was being completely honest," she said. "I believed him when he told me he had revealed everything about all his lady friends. That was the condition I'd set for me to allow him back into my life—that he tell the truth. Now I know that not only did he lie by omission, but Augusta did, too. I feel like a fool."

"You knew about your friend Nancy, though?" I said.

"That was aeons ago. She cannot stand the man now. She, too, realized that he was not to be trusted. But unlike me, she gave up on him, while I welcomed him back with open arms. I suppose that her being a police officer helped her see him for what he was. She warned me when he returned to Woodcrest that he was a deceiver, but did I listen?"

I could picture Nancy Shelton giving him a *big* piece of her mind when she found out he was a cheater. She might have even broken a few of his fingers. "Are you finished with Desmond now?"

"Most definitely. My relationship with Augusta is what concerns me. I certainly need to discuss *her* betrayal— though I would never toss her out the door. She is family and a most devoted soul, despite what might have gone on with her and Desmond." Ritaestelle's rocking slowed.

"Um, I may be out of line, but why are all these people living with you?" I asked.

Ritaestelle looked over at me. "You are not out of line. I have asked myself the same question, especially in the last few days. I am what you might call a *soft touch* when it comes to them. Whatever would they do without me?"

"They might have to fend for themselves," I said. "The question is, would that be a bad thing?"

I didn't get an answer because Candace came around the side of the house and said, "Hey there."

I stood, and after she climbed the deck steps, she nodded at Ritaestelle and said, "Afternoon, Miss Longworth."

"You look quite tired, Deputy Carson," she said. "Perhaps it's the heat? Seems quite warm to be wearing that dark green uniform."

"You get used to it," Candace said. "I have a few questions. I've just come from the initial interviews with your family and staff. Going back for the search of your house. It may sound like more of the same stuff, but I've found that after a few days, certain things someone witnessed become clearer."

"Please ask whatever you want. And may I take this moment to say that I am sincerely sorry I have caused so many problems," Ritaestelle said.

Candace dragged a chair over from the patio table and set it between Ritaetelle and myself, with her back to the lake so she could see us both at once. "Before I start with the questions, you should know the autopsy is complete and Evie has been released to her family."

"Bless her heart," Ritaestelle said. "Bless her poor mother's heart, too."

"What was the cause of death?" I said.

"We don't have the *official* word, but the blow to head's what killed her. Probably something round and irregular, the doctor said. Like a rock. Miss Longworth, I'm hoping you've recovered your memory enough to recall more details about what you had in your hand when Jillian found you out on her dock."

Ritaestelle closed her eyes. "I have indeed given this some thought, Deputy Carson. Events do seem clearer now. I remember that before poor Evie tumbled into the water, I tried to catch her. That's when my knee hit an object." She lifted up her cotton pant leg and revealed a purple bruise.

I winced.

"It's nothing, dear," Ritaestelle said. "Not until precious Chablis joined me on the dock and I nearly tripped over whatever it was did I pick the rock up. I swooped the kitty up at the same time, very afraid she would end up in the lake as well. I was so frightened, I suppose my mind went blank."

"Did the rock feel wet or sticky?" Candace said.

"Since my hands were already sticky from what I later learned was Evie's blood, I cannot be sure." Ritaestelle squeezed her eyes shut. "What a horrible way for that girl to die."

"Sure was. There's something else I wanted to go over with you again. You told me you were drawn to Jillian's back door by voices. The other night that was about all you could recall. Have you remembered anything else about what you heard? Knowing if they were male or female might help us a lot," Candace said.

"That coroner person asked me about the voices, and I had no definitive answer. If you could give me a few seconds to concentrate on exactly why I went to the back door that night, I might recall." Ritaestelle rubbed her chin with an index finger and focused on the lake.

This line of questioning sounded like Candace might be beginning to buy Ritaestelle's story. I wondered if something had happened at the Longworth Estate to sway her toward a family member as a better suspect. Now was not the time to ask Candace any questions, however.

Candace patiently waited, and finally Ritaestelle said, "I heard one voice that I am certain was a woman. That could have been Evie, but as for the other person, I cannot say. My hearing is not what it used to be."

"Was the woman shouting? Did she sound angry?" Candace said.

Ritaestelle stopped rocking and her spine stiffened. "Why, she *did* shout. What I heard was a long, loud *no*."

"That's good. The word *no*. Anything else?" Candace said.

"I do believe what followed was not words. More like a primal cry." She stared at Candace. "That is when I rose from the sofa. Yes. I knew something was very wrong. Why didn't I remember this before?"

"Probably because of what you encountered on that dock," Candace said. "Shocked the heck out of you. But you couldn't tell if that cry was male or female?"

Ritaestelle shook her head no.

"How long do you think it took you to get to the back door once you heard the voices?" Candace asked.

"Oh my. I could not move very fast, but one of the cats—Syrah, I think—had been sitting at the window, and he leaped like a leopard in the direction of the back door as soon as he saw me get up."

"See?" I said. "Didn't I tell you that my cats would have been paying attention to what was happening out there? Did I tell you that Merlot was focused on that window before I went to rescue Isis from the closet?"

"You didn't," Candace said. "But that's okay." She

turned back to Ritaestelle. "Can you guess how long it took you to get to the back door? A minute? Five minutes?"

"A minute is a long time, Deputy Carson, but that would be my best estimate. Today I do believe I could make the trip in thirty seconds."

"When you opened the door, what did you hear?" Candace asked.

"I heard the sound of Miss Jillian's cats whooshing down those steps." She pointed in the direction of the deck stairs.

"Nothing else? No more voices, no sounds that would indicate another person was lurking around?"

"I am afraid I was so focused on the cats and so upset that I had allowed them out into the night that I was only concentrating on getting them back inside the house." She glanced my way. "I am very grateful nothing terrible happened to your friends. Two of them came right back on their own when I called out—" Ritaestelle raised fingers to her lips. "Oh my. I begged your kitties to come back. I forgot all about that. And two of them did return."

"They were waiting at the back door, Candace. She's telling the truth," I said.

"Her version fits with what I learned when I canvassed your neighborhood. I needed to verify, that's all," Candace said.

"My neighborhood?" I said. "But we all live so far apart."

"Voices carry over the lake at night. You know Mr. Voigt?" she said.

"Yes. He has this big old fishing boat," I said. "But we just wave at each other and that's about all."

"The night of the murder, he was out on his deck having a smoke," Candace said. "He heard the same thing that Ritaestelle did. The word *no* and an odd cry—he called it a wail. But he also confirms he heard what he said was a high-pitched voice coming from the direction of your house, Jillian. Someone calling for the cats."

"Why didn't he phone 911?" I said.

"Said he knows you've got cats that you care a lot about. Said the whole thing only lasted a few seconds and he decided it had to do with them."

He knew about my cats, and yet I wondered if he even knew my last name.

"The questions you are asking have me wondering if you still believe I killed Evie," Ritaestelle said.

"I wondered the night of the murder, and maybe I tried to intimidate you into confessing," Candace said. "But in my training, I remember the words of an experienced officer. He told me that the only innocent person at a crime scene is the victim. That's what I was thinking about when I arrived on the scene."

"Sounds like your instructor was a wise man," Ritaestelle said.

"He was. I always follow the evidence," she said. "I've uncovered some support for your statement. I checked the GPS system in your car, and you came directly here. Plus I have corroboration that the attack on the dock apparently occurred before you even opened the door. Your voice is high-pitched and Mr. Voigt heard someone with that tone calling for the cats. Circumstantial evidence and the amount of time needed to commit the crime seem to rule you out."

"Is Ritaestelle even strong enough to . . ." I swallowed before I went on. "To do what was done to Evie Preston?"

"I doubt it, but adrenaline is a powerful thing. Let me ask you this, Miss Longworth. Who do you think wanted Evie Preston dead?"

"I—I . . . I have no earthly idea. Evie was a confident young woman. She handled my affairs competently, dealt with the philanthropic requests that came in an assured and businesslike manner."

"Did your family like her?" Candace asked.

"I would suspect not. I told Evie how much money my family should be allotted per month, and she either gave them a check or used the computer to transfer money to their accounts. Do you think that could have caused enough rancor that one of them killed her?"

Candace sighed heavily and fixed a blond strand of hair behind her ear. "People kill for all kinds of stupid reasons—and you ask me, money is one of those. Right now I need to get on with the business of figuring out what Miss Preston knew, what secret she may have held, that led to her death.

I would appreciate your continued cooperation—even if my investigation leads to someone you care about."

"Most likely the person who drugged me?" Ritaestelle said.

"Yes, ma'am. Your servant, Mr. Robertson, seems to know quite a bit about the folks living in your house. But he seemed reticent to talk about them. Maybe you can encourage him to cooperate." Candace glanced at her watch. "My break is up, and I need to get back to your house."

Ritaestelle smiled. "Do tell George I miss him, but that I am being well cared for and that he can speak freely to you."

"I'll do that. He sure seems protective of you," Candace said.

"No such attitude came from my relatives, I assume." Ritaestelle's lips tightened, and she resumed her rocking.

"I can't tell you what they had to say right now, but I told you about the neighbor because Kara will be printing what he said tomorrow," Candace said. "Casting public doubt on you as a suspect might make the killer nervous. Maybe they'll make a mistake, do something stupid." She stood and started for the steps but turned before she reached them. "I forgot one question. Who had access to your car?"

"I always hang my keys on a hook by the back door that leads to the garages," she said. "I have done so for years. Everyone in the household had access. Why are you asking?"

"Because if you didn't put those items in your car, someone else did. Seems as if it could have been just about anyone." Candace's stony cop face was gone for an instant. I could tell she was deflated.

"Have you ever heard of gaslighting, Deputy Carson?" Ritaestelle said.

"Gaslighting?" Candace sounded puzzled. "Are you talking about arson? And what would that have to do with this murder?"

"Can you explain the gaslighting to her, Miss Jillian?" Ritaestelle said.

"Sure." I told Candace what we'd discussed earlier with Karen and Ed.

"Oh. You mean you're being set up," Candace said to Ritaestelle. "Didn't know there was a name like that for it. But that's why I came today. We're on the same page."

"We'll have to rent the movie *Gaslight* if it's on DVD," I said.

Candace pointed at me and smiled. "Sounds like a film I need to see."

She hurried down the steps and was gone.

Ritaestelle and I spent the rest of the afternoon and evening indoors playing with the cats and talking. I threw together a hamburger Stroganoff that Ritaestelle thought was delicious. I wondered how many fifteen-minute meals she'd ever eaten and if she was simply being polite with her praise. After supper, while I did some hand quilting on orders that urgently needed my attention, Ritaestelle asked a million questions about my past, how I'd learned to quilt and why I'd moved to South Carolina. The conversation eventually turned to my late husband, and I was again reminded of Farley Longworth's accusation. Still not wanting to talk about what he'd said, I instead told her about John and some of the wonderful things we'd done together.

"Mr. Stewart has a genuine affection for you. Have you had enough time to heal from your loss and return that affection?" Ritaestelle said.

"Some days yes and some days no," I said.

"That is an honest answer. Life is indeed complicated." She glanced at the clock on the DVR box next to the television.

"Nine o'clock," she said. "I must say, I am extremely tired."

"Can I help you to your room?" I asked.

"I truly am beginning to heal. The more I walk on my own, the better." She left the living room with Isis leading the way.

I was about to get up, set the security system and curl up with a book when my phone rang. I saw Tom's name on the caller ID and felt a tad guilty talking to him right after my conversation with Ritaestelle about John and about my hesitancy at times to allow Tom completely into my life.

I answered with a breezy, "Hey there," hoping he wasn't as perceptive as he usually was. I did like Tom, after all. A lot.

"It's Candace," Tom said hurriedly. "I'll pick you up in ten minutes."

"What are you talking about?" I said. But the urgency in his voice told me something was terribly wrong.

"She was hit over the head in her apartment parking lot. They've taken her to the county hospital."

I could feel my heart pounding at my temples. "She'll be okay, though?"

"I don't know. She's unconscious."

# Twenty-four

As soon as I hung up with Tom, I speed-dialed Kara with a shaky hand. I couldn't leave Ritaestelle alone, but I had to get to that hospital. I was hoping she'd come over and stay with my houseguest.

When she answered, she said, "I was just about to call you. I'm on my way to the hospital. They found Candace lying unconscious in our apartment parking lot."

"Tom told me. Do you know how badly she's hurt?" My mouth was so dry it was difficult to get the words out. My three friends, realizing I was upset, gathered close. Merlot sat next to me, ears pricked, Syrah was at my feet staring up at me and Chablis had jumped into my lap.

"I don't know anything about Candace's condition," Kara said. "By the time I got out to the parking lot, the ambulance had already left. The deputies weren't about to tell the newspaper snoop anything about one of their own—even when I said I was off the record and asking as a friend."

"You didn't hear anything that went on outside beforehand?" I said.

"I was in the shower, and when I got out, the police scanner was squawking about an ambulance needing a police escort. I got dressed, saw all the flashing lights through my window, and you know the rest."

"Tom's picking me up. I was hoping you could stay here with Ritaestelle, but of course Candace is your friend, too. What should I do?"

"Arm the security system and tell the woman to stay put. She *is* an adult, Jillian."

"But—"

"Do you believe Ritaestelle is next on this hit man's list?" Kara said.

"Maybe. I'm too upset to think straight." Syrah meowed and pawed at my knee. Tears stung my eyes, but I fought them back.

"This whole nasty business is swirling around Ritaestelle. Makes sense she might need protection after what's just happened. But any Mercy cop who's free will be at the hospital," she said. "Maybe Chief Shelton can whip on over and guard your house."

"That could take a good thirty minutes. Tom will be here any minute to pick me up, and I don't feel right leaving her alone, but—"

"Leave," came a voice from the foyer. Ritaestelle was standing there in her robe, Isis in her arms. "Obviously you need to be somewhere right now."

Kara said, "I heard what she said. Listen to her. Meanwhile, I'm pulling into the hospital lot. Bye." She disconnected.

I looked at Ritaestelle. "Candace has been attacked. Hit over the head. She's in the hospital and—"

"You need to be at your friend's side. I promise you I will be fine. I will not open any doors or peer out any windows if I should hear anything outside," she said.

I hesitated, but I had to be with Candace. "Let me show you how to set the alarm. Engage it right after I leave, okay?"

"Thank you. Perhaps you could write down your cellular phone number for me?" She stroked Isis and smiled sadly. "Terrible things have happened, and I feel responsible. I should have never come here."

"Don't say that." I lifted Chablis off my lap, set her on the floor and stood. "Tom and I and every person on the police force will work as hard as we can to find the truth. If you hadn't come here, you might be dead now."

"I might indeed. But I would gladly exchange my life for Evie's or for your friend's at this juncture."

"This is *not* your fault." I gestured toward the kitchen. "Come on. Let me show you how to engage the system."

After I was sure she knew what she was doing, I told her that I would be checking my cat cameras often, so she would have another level of security.

Before I left with Tom, she said, "Please call me when you have news about Deputy Carson to share. I will be praying for her."

When a police officer goes down, the response from the community, fellow officers, fire and rescue teams, paramedics, local politicians and of course the media is almost overwhelming. So many people were at the hospital awaiting word on Candace's condition that all her visitors were directed to the outpatient surgery waiting room—even Nancy Shelton. Good choice for a gathering place since no one was having elective surgery this late at night.

Tom and I headed straight for Mike Baca. He was pacing behind a vinyl sofa at the far end of the room.

"Tell me she'll be okay." I said when we reached him.

Mike's face was drained of color. "She's been taken from the emergency room to ICU. There was a lot of blood and she was unconscious the entire ride in the ambulance."

"Blow to the head, we heard," Tom said.

"Back of the skull, so she might not have even seen her attacker." Mike focused on the floor and shook his head. "I should have handled this case myself."

"Don't go blaming yourself, Chief," came a voice behind us. It was Morris. His red-rimmed eyes betrayed how upset he was. "We're gonna find this coward and take him down—take him down *hard*."

Seeing how emotional these two strong men were brought out a part of me I usually reserved for my cats. They needed a few comforting words. "Candace is tough. She'll be good as new. I feel it." But I didn't truly feel it. All I felt was sick and scared and anxious.

Tom ran a hand through his hair, and though he'd been calm and reassuring in the car, he wasn't that way now. "Are there any leads? Like, how many of those bozos that live with Ritaestelle have an alibi?" He held up a hand before Mike could say anything. "Stupid question. You couldn't have gotten that information yet."

"I have a deputy canvassing Candy's apartment complex," Mike said, "but from the reports I've been getting so far, no one saw or heard anything. Her gun was still in her holster and her car was where she'd parked it. Nothing amiss."

I cringed hearing him call her Candy. She would hate that.

"This wasn't a random mugging if nothing was taken," Tom said. "My bet is someone got nervous after Candace interviewed them and decided to take action."

"She reinterviewed Ritaestelle this afternoon," I said. "Candace planned to give Kara a story hinting that Ritaestelle might no longer be the main suspect in Evie's death. She hoped to draw some other suspect out of the woodwork. Could that be why she was attacked?"

"That fits," Mike said. "Candy has been researching something called a forensic interview. She says that interviewing while paying attention to demeanor is almost as good as tangible evidence. That's why she came to reinterview Ritaestelle. What she saw, as well as what she heard, probably made her doubt Ritaestelle's guilt. Getting out the word that Ritaestelle wasn't the only suspect would be important."

"Did Candace talk to Kara to get these 'hints' out to the public after she left your house?" Tom asked me.

I glanced around the room looking for her. "I don't know, but when I called Kara, she said she'd be here at the hospital."

I caught Shelton's eye then, and she made her way over to us. Meanwhile, I was reminded by this crowded room, these many people with concerned faces, that I knew nothing about Candace's condition. That bothered the heck out of me. Was her mother with her? Was she awake? Was her injury so serious that she might die? No, I couldn't think about that.

Shelton said, "Do you know anything?"

"No one's given any of us a report," Mike said. "I can only hope they're too busy helping Candy so they don't have time for us."

"That's a good way to look at it," I said. Good enough that I felt like the tension that had grabbed hold of every muscle in my body seemed to ease a bit.

"She was your friend. This must be hard on you," Shelton said.

"She *is* my friend," I said.

Tom, Mike and Morris wandered in the direction of the vending machines, still talking about evidence and neighborhood canvasses and possible weapons. I felt even more relieved when they left. This wasn't procedural for me; it was gut-wrenching, and it was all I could do to hold back the tears.

"I'm really sorry this happened," Shelton said.

This was the person we'd spoken to in the park the day of the murder, not the hard, cold woman who had pulled me over. "I'm so worried."

"She's one of our own, so we're all troubled, but your worry is different. More intense." Shelton glanced at the array of sofas and chairs that filled the room. "Where's Ritaestelle?"

"I had to leave her alone. And that's bothering me, too. What if this person comes after her next?"

"Do you know of some specific reason they might do that?" Shelton had slipped back into cop role.

"Who knows what any of this is about? But she didn't feel safe at home. That should tell you something." Again, my anxiety made me sound curt.

Shelton checked her watch. "It's late. I wouldn't want to wake her, but I could park outside your house, make sure nothing happens to her. How's that?"

"You'd do that?" I said.

"She and I *are* friends, even if I was stupid enough to have been suspicious of her in the last few months."

I wanted to hug the woman. "Oh my gosh, I'd feel so much better if you'd do that."

"I'll leave right now," she said.

Nancy Shelton, always in her blue suit with its shiny buttons and those comfortable-looking shoes, left. Why couldn't Lydia take a clue from a professional? The thought of Lydia made me glance around, wondering if she was hanging around, too, but I didn't see her—and I sure didn't want to.

I checked the cat-cam feed on my cell phone and saw Ritaestelle sitting on the sofa. I noticed that she'd gotten dressed. Maybe she decided she wouldn't be sleeping at all tonight, and in her world, I imagined that being awake meant being dressed. She was entertaining Syrah and Merlot with a feather toy while the other cats were batting buttons around.

Though I hated to disturb Ritaestelle, I didn't want her to freak out if she heard a car outside. I didn't see the telephone near her when I'd been checking on them, but she answered on the first ring, so she must have put it beside her.

"Jillian? Is that you?" she asked.

"Yes. I wanted—"

"How is Deputy Carson?" she asked. "I have been so concerned."

"We don't have any word on her condition yet. I'm calling because Chief Shelton decided to drive over and make sure you're all right."

"That is truly unnecessary, Jillian," Ritaestelle said. "I have been scrutinized so much in the last few months, I must say being here alone feels safe."

"She might not even come to the door, said she planned on parking outside to watch the house," I said. "But since I saw you were awake when I peeked in on my cat cam, I wanted you to know she'd be hanging around."

"That is very kind of you, and I did not mean to sound as if I were complaining," Ritaestelle said. "You have been generous to a fault. Please call me back when you know anything about Deputy Carson. She is on my mind and in my prayers."

We said good-bye, and I slipped my phone into my pocket. I still wondered where Kara was. But of course she knew Candace's mother since Candace's mom was always dropping by the apartment building. Those two could be together.

I didn't see any reason why I had to wait here, clueless. No. I had to find them. So I left the waiting room and followed the signs to the ICU. Sure enough, they were sitting in the padded chairs that lined the wall across from the ICU doors. A desk between the doors and the visitors seemed almost like a blockade. A woman wearing scrubs sat at the desk focused on a computer monitor.

This is where I should have come to begin with—but like a good girl, I had to follow directions and go to that other place.

When Candace's mother saw me, she stood and hurried

to embrace me. Soon my shoulder was wet with her tears. "Why did this happen, Jillian? And why did she ever think she could do such a dangerous job?"

I hugged Belinda Carson tightly and said, "Can you imagine her doing anything else?"

Belinda pulled away and dabbed beneath her eyes with a crumpled tissue. "No. You're right. But if I lose her ..."

Again I said, "Candace is tough. She'll come through this just fine. They've told you she'll be all right, haven't they?" This had to be true. It *had* to be.

"They haven't told us anything, Jillian, and I am getting so upset waiting here, and—"

Kara said, "Why don't you stay off your feet, Belinda? This might be a long night." She put her hands on Belinda's upper arms and guided her back to her chair.

A large brown paper sack sat on the floor, and Belinda looked at it. "That's her uniform. There's blood on it. Her poor head was bleeding so much."

I gripped her hand, and Kara put her arm around Belinda's shoulders. We all sat in a row, silent except for Belinda's small hiccuping sobs.

Finally she seemed to gather herself. "Candace would be so angry with me for crying like a baby. But she's not a mother, and—"

"She wouldn't be angry," I said. "I'll bet she's in there right now telling them they need to make sure you're all right."

"I saw her in the emergency room," Belinda said softly. "She was so still, and her beautiful hair was all matted with blood, and they said they'd have to shave some of it away to stitch up the gash, and—"

"Shh." I squeezed her cold hand tighter. "Everything will—"

A balding man came out through the ICU doors and said, "Mrs. Carson?"

Belinda stood. "That's me. How is my girl? Will she be all right?"

The man walked over and introduced himself as Dr. Patrick, a neurologist. He then said, "Your daughter woke up about five minutes ago. She is hungry and thirsty and quite irritable." He smiled. "Those are all good signs."

Belinda's knees buckled, and it was a good thing Kara

and I were on either side to catch her or the ICU might have had another patient.

"Can we see her?" Belinda said.

"Sure." He looked at Kara and then at me. "But are these ladies relatives?"

"As good as family. Why do you ask?"

"I want her visitors limited to family, but if she has these two *sisters*, well, I see no problem." Dr. Patrick winked. "Do you mind if we discuss your daughter's condition with them present?"

"I do not mind in the least. They might have to explain everything to me later, the state I'm in." Belinda smiled for the first time. Candace's smile. It tugged at my heart.

Dr. Patrick said, "Before you visit her—and family can come in one at a time on the half hour—we're going to give Candace a mild sedative. She's being quite, um . . . *animated* right now, but since she has a grade-three concussion, she needs rest. Encourage her to stay calm. We'll be observing her for any signs of bleeding in the brain for the next twenty-four hours. I have to say, you daughter has one hard head. No fractured skull. She does have twenty-three stitches, though."

"Twenty-three? Oh my word," Belinda said.

"But you're saying she'll be okay? With this grade-three concussion? What does that mean, anyway?" I said.

Dr. Patrick looked at me. "Sorry. We do have to code injuries. Grade three simply means someone has lost consciousness for longer than, say, thirty minutes and thus the concussion is more severe. That doesn't mean she won't have a full recovery. But I also expect her to have mild neurological symptoms for the next few weeks. Short-term memory loss, the irritability we're already seeing, headaches, trouble finding the right word for something. All of these symptoms should clear up with time."

Belinda said, "You sound like a very competent doctor, so don't take this the wrong way, but the ICU seems so . . . intimidating. Can I just take her home and—"

"Absolutely not," Dr. Patrick said. "As I said, we'll be taking more pictures of her brain to make sure there's no slow bleeding in there. This is the safest place for her right now. We treat our peace officers with the special care they deserve."

"Don't forget she was attacked, Belinda," Kara said. "As far as I know, they haven't caught who did this. She *needs* to be here."

"I know you're right. It's just that—" Belinda's tears started again, and I put my arm around her shoulders.

"I will see you in the morning for an update, Mrs. Carson. Right now, I have to inform all the others waiting to hear about her condition," the doctor said. I had the feeling that tears and this man did not mix, because he hurried off down the hall like a cat with its tail on fire.

While I waited with Belinda, who was told by the woman at the desk that it would be about thirty minutes before she could see Candace, Kara went back to where all the others were waiting. She might hear or learn something that she could add to the article I was sure would appear in tomorrow's paper. The next half hour passed much more quickly thanks to the good news we'd heard. Belinda was soon her old chatty self and said that she told Candace not to give up her vacation because of a murder—that she wouldn't have been in that parking lot if she'd listened. At last she was ushered into the ICU while I waited for her.

Belinda's time with her daughter must have been great, because she wore a broad smile when she came back out through the double doors. "Candace is awake and cranky. That's my girl," she said.

"Does she remember what happened?" I asked.

"I didn't ask. I'll leave that to you. Right now, I need a Coca-Cola. Do you want one?" When I refused, she started off down the hall.

Meanwhile, Kara and Tom came by. Tom took a spot beside me, and Kara said she had to get her story to the paper as quickly as possible. She headed for the elevators after telling me to get word to Candace that she was glad she was awake and talking and probably giving the nurses hell.

I whispered to Tom how I was now officially Candace's sister—and that meant I could I visit her. Belinda returned with her Coke, and the three of us waited together.

When I was allowed in for my five-minute visit with Candace, I signed a visitor sheet and went inside the ICU accompanied by the woman who sat at the desk. She pointed out Candace's curtained-off area in the circular room.

I went to her bedside. Her eyes were closed, an IV

dripped into a vein, and she had a blood pressure cuff around her upper arm. The machinery behind her bed beeped and displayed numbers and graphs. They made me so nervous; I tried to ignore them. How could patients rest with all this going on? But they were being well cared for, and that was all that mattered.

I sat and took a deep breath, exhaling quietly so as not to wake Candace up. I was content to sit by her side and watch her breathe. But her eyes fluttered open and widened when she saw me.

In a thick voice she said, "I thought you were Mom again and I had to pretend to be too drugged up to talk. Poor thing needs to chill. I'm fine as can be."

"You got a new hairdo, I see." I smiled and rested a hand over hers. It was so darn cold in here, and her fingers felt like ice.

"What did they do to my hair?" She started to lift her hand, but I stopped her.

"Check the mirror tomorrow and have a gasp. For now, you need to stay still if you want to get out of here." I squeezed her frosty fingers.

"Listen, Jillian. I couldn't ask my mother this because she'd give the guy in that next bed another heart attack by freaking out, but what the hell happened to me?"

I smiled. "Someone bonked you on the head. Good thing you have concerned neighbors. One of them found you and called 911."

"They catch the jerk?" Her eyes closed, and she almost seemed to be nodding off.

I now understood about the five-minute visiting regulation.

"Not yet. But we will." To myself, I added, *If it's the last thing any of us do.*

Candace laughed the sarcastic laugh I was familiar with. "'Officer down. Officer down.' I can hear those words spewing out on radios all over the place. What they should have been saying is 'Idiot officer let someone get the jump on her.'"

"Hey, don't get worked up over something you can do nothing about. You need to chill more than your mom right now. Can I do anything for you before my time is up? You want some of these yummy ice chips I see?"

"I asked for a steak, but that's all they brought me. But there is something. My notes about the Longworths are in my RAV4—I think. Did I even get out of my car?"

"You must have, because they found you in the parking lot," I said.

"Anyway, find the notes. Get my keys from the uniform they took off me. Mom says she has it in a bag from the emergency room."

"You sure you don't want Mike to take care of this?" I asked.

"No. You get them." She grinned. "I went to that big old house and talked to the crazy family, but the details are fuzzy."

"You remember where you were earlier in the day," I said. "That's a good sign."

"I remember ole Chief Mike Baca making a fool of himself over Justine Longworth. She's gotta be a whole lot older than him. Why does he always pick the wrong woman?"

"Candace, your notebook contains police business. I shouldn't—"

"I'm with-it enough to know that the chief is gonna shut me down. So I want you to read them. My banged-up brain won't let me remember." She squeezed her eyes shut. "I hate that."

"Your brain will be fine and you'll solve this case. For now—"

"He'll put me on stupid sick leave. But you can help me stay connected. You and Tom. Yeah. We should get Tom on the case." She giggled. "Yup. All hands on deck."

She'd obviously forgotten that Tom was already on the case. If Candace was in her right mind—and she sure wasn't—she wouldn't want me reading her notes.

Candace reached through the bars on the side of the bed and gripped my arm. "Bring me the book tomorrow and read it to me. You and Tom want to help old lady Longworth. You believed her when I didn't. You should know what I know. Or what I don't know. Or— Jeez, I sound stupid, don't I?"

"Not at all. I'll get your notes. I promise."

But would I give them to Mike or bring them here?

# Twenty-five

Candace's mother had been happy to give me the keys to her daughter's RAV4. "If that's what my baby wants, then you can have them."

Tom and I drove to the apartment complex parking lot, now cleared of any police presence. But when Tom opened her vehicle with the remote and the headlights flashed, Mercy police deputy Jerry Raymond jumped from behind a row of shrubs, weapon drawn.

He shouted, "Mercy PD. Hands in the air." He held his flashlight and gun together, pointed right at our faces. The light was blinding.

We both did as we were told, and Tom said, "Jerry, it's me and Jillian. Candace wanted to make sure her stuff was safe. See the keys in my hand?" Tom jangled them.

"You scared the living crap out of me, Stewart," Jerry said.

We lowered our arms.

"Candy's talking?" Jerry said. "That is some major good news, man."

"She's awake and she'll be fine," I said. "But she was worried about her evidence kit, stuff like that."

"Just like her," Jerry said. "Always worried about some evidence goin' missin'. But I've been watching her RAV like a hawk. Ain't nobody stealin' nothin' from our Candy."

"She asked me to keep her things at my house until she's released tomorrow. Would that be all right?" I said.

"I can take her stuff. Drop it at the station when I clock out in the mornin'," he said.

"She wants Jillian's eyes on this," Tom said. "You know how she is."

"*Do* I? Guess it would be all right, 'cause, man, I do not want to be on Candy's bad side. Not never. But that evidence kit is police property. I gotta take care of that or the chief will be all up in my—sorry, Miss Jillian. I almost cussed. Anyways, take her personal stuff just to say you did what she asked. I'll take her evidence kit to the station."

And that was how we ended up with Candace's notebook. It was on the front floorboard along with her baton, a flashlight and an umbrella. For some reason I'd expected the notes to be in her evidence kit, where I'd seen them before. I took the time to clean out the RAV of empty coffee cups and fast-food wrappers. I also collected several sweaters that had probably been in Candace's backseat since last winter. She might not recognize her car when she got out of the hospital.

Tom and I returned to my place at about two in the morning. True to her word, Nancy Shelton was parked on the road outside my house. She got out of her car when we pulled into the driveway, told us that everything was fine and that she hadn't even bothered Ritaestelle. The tired-looking police chief went back to her car and drove off.

Ritaestelle, still dressed, was asleep on the sofa surrounded by cats.

Tom whispered, "Read through the notes if you're not too tired. I'll see you in the morning." He kissed me lightly on the lips and left quietly.

*Read through the notes?* I had a problem with that.

I turned to see Syrah stretch his legs before approaching me. He had such lovely long legs and stretched so gracefully. I heard once from a breeder that cats live into their teens or twenties because they stretch all the time. The activity apparently activates their lymph system. Maybe I should take up yoga so my fur friends wouldn't outlive me.

Syrah sat at my feet, and I knelt to scratch him behind the ears. Pretty soon I had all four cats looking for a little middle-of-the-night affection. Deciding I should wake Ritaestelle up and tell her about Candace, then make sure she slept in a bed, I walked over to the couch. I gently touched her shoulder.

Her eyes opened so quickly, I almost jumped backward.

She was probably so anxious after all that had gone on that she was only half asleep.

"Oh my good gracious, you have come home." She sat up, and I heard a few bones creak. "By your expression I am willing to wager that your friend will recover?"

"You'd win that bet," I said. "She's groggy and acting a little wacky, but the doctor said she'll recover completely. She'll probably be released tomorrow. But getting her to rest up will be a chore I do not envy her mother."

Isis jumped in Ritaestelle's lap as she said, "Deputy Carson is a very dedicated police officer. I cannot imagine her remaining on the sidelines for long."

"I can't either. Come on. It's late. We both need a pillow and a quilt." I picked up Isis, much to the cat's chagrin—and earned a hiss for doing that. Then I helped Ritaestelle to her feet. All this maneuvering was done with the notebook tucked under my left arm. Maybe I *was* a good candidate for yoga.

Ten minutes later, after I'd washed my face and brushed my teeth, I settled into bed, the notebook on my bedside table. I couldn't bring myself to open it, and yet I didn't turn out the light. Syrah showed great interest in me just lying there, eyes on the ceiling. Merlot and Chablis cared only about sleeping. I'd put three kitty quilts at the foot of the bed, mostly to collect the summer shedding, but Syrah and Merlot rarely slept on theirs. That left Chablis to enjoy all three at various times. But tonight, Merlot curled up on the one at my feet, a nine-patch with a wild-goose-chase border in blues and whites. I wondered if he was feeling insecure because of having both cat and human houseguests, not to mention so many people coming in and out. He is a sensitive soul and used to routine. We'd had anything but routine in the last few days.

Try as I might, I couldn't get the notebook out of my head. What if I only checked out what Candace had observed about the family and staff at the Longworth Estate?

Okay. But that was all I'd look at.

Propped up by several pillows, I opened the small spiral and immediately realized reading her notes would be easier said than done. I was aware that she always transferred these scribblings—and that was what they were, messy scribblings—to her computer as soon as she was able. She had grumbled about this chore on more than one occasion.

The first page had a giant red check mark through the writing, and I guessed that was her way of indicating she'd done the computer work. The first phrase was, "Morris keeping murder book."

Murder book? What the heck was that? If I couldn't even understand the first sentence, how would any of this make sense? The next words weren't what I wanted to read: "Female, white, deceased."

I skipped over pages until I found what she'd wanted me to read to her tomorrow—her interview notes. There was a semblance of order here. I saw the full name of the first person she'd talked to—the butler, George Robertson. He'd given her the names of everyone who resided in the house—and even knew their middle initials. *Smart to talk to him first,* I thought.

But that was the last thought I had for hours. I woke up to Chablis, paws tucked, sitting on my chest on top of Candace's notebook. She was purring. Because I was half sitting, my neck had a serious crick and the sunlight sneaking through the wood blinds seemed way too bright. What time was it, anyway?

I glanced over at the clock and saw that it was eight thirty. I never slept until eight thirty. I carefully removed Chablis from the notebook, closed it up and headed for the shower.

After I dressed and tried to do something with my uncooperative hair, I left the bedroom, only to see buttons littering the hallway. Where were they getting all these darn buttons? I gathered up about a dozen and dropped them off in my quilting room on the way to the kitchen. I smelled coffee and was a little amazed that Ritaestelle could even make coffee. After all, she did have people who did everything for her.

She and Tom were sitting in my living room. Huge muffins and three large coffees from Belle's Beans sat on the coffee table. But Ritaestelle held a cup and saucer in front of her.

"Good morning, dear. Mr. Stewart brought us breakfast," she said. "I did make a feeble attempt at making coffee myself. My George makes me the most wonderful morning coffee. I do miss him, but I can say I most sincerely do not miss the rest of my family."

Isis, who was sharing the window seat with Merlot, raised her head and meowed after Ritaestelle spoke. I wonder if she knew the word family. Bet it was tossed around a lot at the Longworth house.

Tom picked up one of the to-go cups and brought it to me. "We all need some of this today."

"I'm eyeing those muffins," I said.

"How about taking one with us?" he said.

"Where are we going?" I asked, my mind still muddled by too little sleep.

"To the hospital," Tom said. "After you help Candace remember what happened when she interviewed Miss Longworth's household, we're headed to the estate."

"But should we leave Ritaestelle alone? Last time the chief watched the house," I said.

"That's why I'm here," came a voice from the kitchen.

The pantry door was open and had blocked me from seeing Kara. She emerged from behind the door holding a box of granola. "Check out the paper." She nodded toward the counter before opening the cabinet where I keep the dishes.

I sipped my latte—Tom had fixed it perfectly with the right amount of sugar and nutmeg—as I walked over and picked up today's *Mercy Messenger*.

The large, bold headline read, OFFICER ATTACKED.

I felt scared all over again just seeing those huge, dark words. But Candace would be fine. Fine if she'd rest. But I wasn't sure anyone, even Belinda, could make that happen.

Kara said, "I'm hoping the story will bring in leads. Maybe someone who hasn't already come forward and saw what happened in the parking lot will call the police. Liam thinks it's a good idea to give this as much publicity as possible."

"Liam Brennan? The district attorney? When did you talk to him?" I said.

"I called him from the hospital last night. This has to be connected to the murder, so—"

Tom held up a hand. "Let me play Candace for a minute. There's no evidence connecting the two attacks. Both women were struck over the head, but that's about it."

Kara filled a bowl with granola. "Two people hit over the head in a similar fashion in a town this small? And you don't think the events are connected?"

"What I think and what the evidence shows are two different things," he said. "You know that, Kara."

"But I'm a journalist, not a cop. What I write, though factual, does allow for speculation. I like to plant seeds. It might help solve both attacks."

"She's right," I said. "Now that Candace is down and out, we need all the help we can get to find out what happened." What I'd just said gave me pause. "Candace is down and out," I repeated. "What if she got too close to the truth at Ritaestelle's house yesterday? What if that's the reason she was knocked unconscious?"

"Exactly," Kara said as she poured milk over her cereal.

Ritaestelle set her cup and saucer on the coffee table. "This sounds as if the terrible person who killed dear Evie is willing to stop at nothing to conceal himself."

"Or herself," I said. "Assuming one of your relatives is guilty, that is." But could Muriel or Augusta or Justine wield enough strength to knock not one, but two people out? I couldn't imagine any of them doing that. But anger is a powerful thing. Tom was right. We needed to get a handle on these relatives, see what they were capable of. First stop, though—the hospital.

Although the person at the desk guarding the ICU was a now a man with an unsympathetic and suspicious expression, Belinda Carson assured him that I was Candace's sister. Tom and I sat down beside Belinda to await my five-minute visit. Would that be enough time to go over the notebook entries?

"Did you stay all night?" I asked Belinda, even though I knew the answer. Her hair was a mess, worse than mine, and her wrinkled clothes told the tale.

"Leave?" Belinda said. "Never. Not until I walk out the door with my girl this evening. That's when she'll be released if the scan or whatever test they're doing today is normal."

I patted her arm. "You are a good mom. I'm only beginning to learn how to be a mom—to a grown woman who once thought I was stealing her father away."

"Kara thought you'd want to cut her off from her father? Oh, but she was a teenager then. Teenagers aren't hooked up right yet. They do think such things, I suppose."

"She was in college, actually," I said. "But you could be right about adolescents."

"Oh, I'm right," Belinda said. "I am sure that Candace was abducted by aliens when she turned fourteen. They kept her and returned her to me as a completely different girl. She gave me fits for the next six years."

The young man at the desk, who really didn't look like he wanted to be there, said, "Jillian Hart? You can visit now."

I started toward the doors, my bag holding the notebook slung over my shoulder.

"Hand your purse over to one of them." He nodded toward Tom and Belinda.

"But last night—" I started.

"Purses are filthy. You really want to bring something into our ICU that's been sitting on a public restroom floor?" He raised his eyebrows. "I'm right, aren't I?"

I couldn't argue with his reasoning. I walked over to Tom and handed him my purse. As quick as any pickpocket, he pulled the notebook out of my bag and stuck it in my waistband.

"Thank you for holding this, Tom," I said. I mouthed, "It's okay," to Belinda.

One obstacle hurdled, I was soon sitting beside Candace.

Her first words were, "Did you bring it? Because I have been awake all friggin' night trying to remember what I talked about with those people. Who could sleep here anyway? I'll bet if I'd lain on a New York City sidewalk I would have gotten more rest."

I offered her the notebook, but she shook her head. "This whole room is as blurry as the sun behind a morning fog. Read me what I wrote. Quick, too."

Thus the challenge began. I flipped to her most recent entries and started summarizing. "You spoke with George Robertson first. He told you Muriel and Augusta would bicker so much you'd be lucky to get them to give their names. He said Farley would pout like he used to when he was twelve and that his mother would want to be in on the interview with him."

"He said all that?" Candace said.

"That's what you wrote—I'm sort of filling in the words you omitted. This is pretty sketchy."

Candace's expression changed, and she said, "Now I remember. The chief took on Justine and Farley. I interviewed the cousins and that housekeeper—what's her name again?"

"Hildie."

"That's right. What did I say about the cousins?"

"By Augusta's name you wrote: *Alibi—asleep. Hates Farley. Dislikes Muriel. Says Justine acts like princess. Loves Ritaestelle.*" I turned a page. "*Refuses to discuss shoplifting. Thought Evie loyal and smart.*" I looked at her. "That's it for her."

"What about Muriel?" Candace said.

"*Alibi—asleep. Says Ritaestelle is strong. Could hurt someone. Evie treated badly by Ritaestelle. Pressed her. Wouldn't elaborate but agrees never saw Ritaestelle violent. Says Augusta would help Ritaestelle do anything.*" I looked up at Candace in surprise. "She thinks Ritaestelle killed Evie."

"I may be fuzzy about all this, but doesn't that sound more like sour grapes?" Candace looked up at the ceiling and slowly said, "*Sour grapes.*" She smiled. "Yes. That's what the chief said he heard from Justine. That everyone in the family envied Ritaestelle because she controlled the money."

I smiled. "You remembered something. But this all fits with what I observed when I met the family while Ritaestelle was in the hospital. The way they seem, I'd almost call them incapable of planning and executing a murder."

"Do not underestimate the criminal mind. My question is, why was I writing this stuff? This is nothing. Totally unfocused. Or they were playing me." She motioned with her hand for me to go on.

I looked down at the notebook. "Hildie the housekeeper was next. You wrote *uncooperative* by her name and then, *says too busy to waste time with police. Knows something or she's ornery.*" I couldn't help but laugh at that one. "Is *ornery* police terminology?"

"My shorthand. Keep reading," Candace said.

"There's not much left . . . just a few words, but—" I raised my fingers to my lips but couldn't stifle my "Oh boy."

"What?" Candace said insistently.

"You wrote: *Justine claims jewelry hidden behind a dresser in Ritaestelle's bedroom is hers.*"

# Twenty-six

My time with Candace was up, and I had to be escorted out of the ICU, perhaps not so much because of the time limit, but because Candace got cranky when she was told I had to leave. The person who took my arm and led me to the double doors said Candace's blood pressure had jumped during our conversation and maybe I shouldn't come back. Guess they were monitoring her the whole time I was talking to her. I certainly didn't want to cause her harm or have anything delay her release from the hospital. Nope, I didn't mind leaving.

As I left, I wondered how many other things that didn't belong to Ritaestelle had been found in her room. Would Mike tell me? Probably not. But I had a feeling Muriel would be more than happy to fill Tom and me in when we visited the mansion for our own interviews.

After I said good-bye to Belinda, Tom and I left for the Longworth Estate. We arrived thirty minutes later. Tom whistled in awe at the magnificent landscape and majestic house after we parked.

"I see Nancy Shelton is here," I said as we walked up to those huge front doors.

"How do you know?" Tom used the brass door knocker to announce our presence.

I gestured at the car parked on the curving drive. "That's her unmarked police car. I'd recognize it anywhere."

"That you would, you minivan speed demon," Tom said with a smile.

George Robertson admitted us a few seconds later. I

didn't have to talk my way inside this time, because Rita-estelle had called ahead and told George to allow us "full access" to her home.

Mr. Robertson said he'd assemble the family, that they were all at home and talking with Chief Shelton.

"We'd like to talk to you, first, Mr. Robertson, and then each family member in this order." Tom handed the man a list he'd pulled from the pocket of his khakis. "Is there someplace private?"

"Of course, and I am happy to help any way I can, but first, though, is Miss Ritaestelle doing okay? I miss her."

"Her hip seems to be healing well," I said. "She's hardly limping anymore."

"Good news. Come this way." Mr. Robertson waved a thin hand as he walked ahead of us down that block-paneled hallway. As we followed, he said, "How is—well, it's probably none of my business—but how's her mind? I've been worried."

"Her mind is sharp. Sharp as a between," I said.

"A between?" Tom said.

"Sorry. Sharp as a quilting needle," I said. "Those little needles that make tiny stitches are called 'betweens.'"

"Ah. I understand. She is sharp—that's for sure." Mr. Robertson stopped at a polished door with an ornate shiny knob and opened it so we could enter.

This room did not have a view of the big gardens like the library, where I'd met with Evie, did. In fact, there was only one window to the left that looked out on a small cir-cular patch of brilliant-colored pansies. What drew me the most, however, was a stone fireplace with bronze life-size cat sculptures on either side of the hearth.

Two burgundy leather wing chairs faced each other in front of the fireplace. An inlaid round oak table sat be-tween the two chairs. On the other side of the room was a Victorian sofa upholstered in gold and cream brocade stripes. Bookshelves lined the walls, and Renaissance-type artwork that was probably very pricey hung on the walls.

Though the room was elegant and tasteful, I felt un-comfortable. The atmosphere was almost sterile. But then I imagined Ritaestelle sitting in front of that fire-place, perhaps reading a book, and I began to relax. She was the heart of this house and no doubt brought the warmth. She needed to come back—and we had to make that possible.

Mr. Robertson pointed to the wing chairs. "Have a seat, if you like."

We did, and Tom pulled a small recorder from his pocket. "Do you mind if I tape our conversation?"

"I don't mind. You might not get the okay from all the folks who live here, though." Mr. Robertson stood to our left, hands behind his back. He apparently did not intend to drag a chair from another room and sit down for a friendly chat.

"I understand you were here yesterday when the Mercy police officers came," Tom said.

"I'm always here," he said, "unless Miss Ritaestelle sends me on an errand. Since she's staying with you, Mrs. Hart, my responsibility is to keep the household running."

"Because the folks who live here aren't too good at that, are they?" I said.

Mr. Robertson hung his head. "They don't know how. Never tried to learn, neither." He looked up, and I saw that his eyes were moist with tears. "That's been hard on Miss Ritaestelle. Carrying the load all these years. She won't mind me saying that. She told me to be honest, to not keep secrets. Miss Ritaestelle fears for her life, and that's got to end."

"She said she fears for her life?" Tom asked.

"Not in so many words, but I saw it in her eyes those last few days she was here," he said. "That's why she took off the other night. Someone in this house is doing harm by spreading lies. Pity after all she's done for them."

"Have you been keeping secrets?" I said.

"I guess I have. Mostly about the way Miss Ritaestelle changed these last few months," he said. "She wouldn't want people to know how she's been stumbling around in the night. How she lost her cat after she fell asleep. She loves that cat with all her heart, and I don't care what anyone in this house says, she'd never, *not never*, throw Isis outside."

I shifted in the less than comfortable chair. "I'd heard that's what happened. But you don't believe it?"

"No, ma'am. Could have been Miss Justine who said it. But when I asked her, Miss Justine didn't have no answers.

She spends way too much time playing solitaire in her room to know much of any goings-on in this house. That's why I think she's not being honest."

"My friend Shawn Cuddahee says he called several times trying to talk to Ritaestelle about Isis," I said. "No one returned his calls. It seemed to him as if no one cared."

"No one cared but Miss Ritaestelle—that's for sure. One thing I don't do is answer the telephone," Mr. Robertson said. "But if I'd known someone found that cat, I'd have gone right out and brought her back here. Miss Ritaestelle was so upset and crying over her Isis, and not one of these people here tried to help. Not until you showed up, Mrs. Hart."

"Not even Evie?" Tom asked.

Mr. Robertson looked at him. "Miss Preston was caught up in her work. She called it *putting out fires* for Miss Ritaestelle. Every time we turned around, something silly turned up in Miss Ritaestelle's room. One time it was a big old bag of rubber bands. With Isis wanting to eat any rubber band she ever saw, Miss Ritaestelle would never bring something like that into her room."

Tom said, "What does that have to do with Miss Preston *putting out fires*?"

"People in town was saying Miss Ritaestelle stole all these things," he answered. "The police chief and Miss Preston did their best to cover it up by returning whatever Hildie or Muriel or Augusta would turn up, but word was out that Miss Ritaestelle was losing her mind. Miss Preston's job was to make sure she maintained the Longworth reputation."

"You didn't think Ritaestelle was losing her mind?" I said.

"Like I told that young lady yesterday, the one who took my fingerprints—"

"You were printed?" Tom said.

"We all was," Mr. Robertson said.

There had been nothing in Candace's notes about fingerprints—but her kit was in the evidence bag. I was betting that was where the print cards were. That blow to the head sure muddled Candace's brain. She considered herself a fingerprint expert—took several classes on the

Mercy PD dime—so for her to forget about *that* was a major memory loss.

Tom's brows came together, and he seemed confused. "Did Chief Baca have a search warrant for this house? Because if he printed everyone, then—"

"He did," Mr. Robertson said.

"I thought Ritaestelle gave permission for the house to be searched and no warrant was needed," I said.

"Fingerprinting an entire household is a Fourth Amendment thing. South Carolina's pretty lenient about fingerprinting anyone and anything, but knowing Baca, he'd want a warrant," Tom said.

There was a knock on the door, but before George Robertson got halfway across the room to answer, Nancy Shelton entered.

"There you are, George," she said. Then her eyes widened when she saw us sitting by the fireplace. "Is something wrong with Ritaestelle?" She sounded worried.

Tom rose. "No. She hired me to investigate the crimes, both large and small, that have occurred over the last few months. Miss Longworth has insisted I do that with Jillian's help. As you know, Ritaestelle is awfully fond of Jillian."

"Great. More people from Mercy thinking they know what to do here," Shelton said. "I have a handle on this, Mr. Stewart. Woodcrest is my town, after all."

"Apparently there was probable cause for a search warrant," Tom said.

"That was Mike Baca's doing," Shelton said. "I didn't know he got a warrant until I came to talk to the family today."

Tom was standing, I assumed, because Shelton had been looking down on him. Knowing Tom and his old cop ways, he'd want to be at eye level with her.

"Here's the thing I don't understand, Chief," he said. "Why did Candace fingerprint everyone in the house? And did she print anything else?"

"Do you see anyone telling *me* anything?" Color rose on Shelton's cheeks.

From the corner of my eye, I saw George Robertson stiffen.

I sympathized with him, because I'd seen Chief Shelton's anger before. Not pretty, but I understood her frustration. This *was* her town.

She went on, saying, "All I know is the family is upset that Ritaestelle won't come home and that she suspects them of drugging her—and who knows what else."

"We came to talk to those people," Tom said. "If you want to help clear up this mess, ask these folks to cooperate with us."

But Nancy Shelton's red face indicated that she was livid now. "I will do nothing of the sort. This should have been my investigation from the beginning. I consider these people friends of mine. But now we've got foreign police and a private investigator invading the house."

"But Ritaestelle asked for our help." I'd kept my tone soft and even. Nancy Shelton looked ready to have a stroke, and maybe I could smooth things over.

"I don't believe you coming here is really Ritaestelle's wish. No, ma'am. This is all *your* doing." She stabbed a finger in my direction. "She loves that cat of hers, and you wormed your way into her affections by using Isis and—oh, never mind. Seeing as how I was on my way out, I'll leave you to do whatever you want."

She stormed past Mr. Robertson and out of the room.

I took a deep breath and let it out slowly. I sure hoped the upcoming interviews were less explosive, because I again felt like running out the front door. I'd probably get pulled over by the chief again, though.

Mr. Robertson brought me back to the moment, saying, "How would you like to handle your talks with the family?"

"Not here. Maybe the dining room?" Tom said. "Plenty of room to spread out there. And by the way, was everyone home last night?"

George seemed confused by the question. "They all go up to their rooms or watch the television, so I couldn't say."

I knew why Tom was asking. Mike Baca may have checked alibis for the night of Evie's murder, but so far, he probably hadn't had time to figure out where all these people were when Candace was hit over the head.

# Twenty-seven

Though Tom and I had already decided to do the interviewing together, we'd agreed that he would take the lead with Farley and his mother, while I would handle Augusta and Muriel. I already had a feel for the cousins after their visit to my house. As for the housekeeper? We'd have to play that by ear. Ritaestelle had told us she was only happy when she was in the kitchen, and we'd decided that was where we'd go when we were done with the family.

Once we were set up in the dining room and Mr. Robertson left to get Augusta, I said, "You want to see what chair they pick, don't you?" I smiled. "We might have to end up shouting out questions, if that's the case."

The mahogany dining table *was* huge. There were six tapestry-covered chairs on each side and armchairs at each end. Tom pulled out an armchair for me, and I discovered it was much more comfortable than the wing chair in the study. The buffet to my right looked like an antique with the top covered by a cream lace cloth that was obviously made to fit the piece. Large candles sat in crystal holders in the middle. In the corner, a tea cart held a silver service surrounded by four bone china cups. This place reminded me of a museum—gorgeous, yes, but I was almost afraid to touch anything.

I took out the brand-new notebook from my purse that Tom had bought for me. Meanwhile, he placed the tape recorder on the table right next to him. That thing was intimidating even to me. As for a notebook? I wasn't even good in college at taking notes. For me, writing interrupted the listening.

Augusta bustled in first, all smiles and full of Southern hospitality. But the cloud of perfume surrounding her almost made me sneeze.

"Why, heavens, you don't have a beverage?" she said immediately.

I started to say "Mr. Robertson already—" but the man arrived before I finished. He carried a tray with sweet tea for me and iced coffee for Tom.

Augusta said, "I'm fine, George," when Mr. Robertson looked at her. I was betting no one had to say a word around him; he was that quick to anticipate.

He quietly left, and Augusta took the chair right next to me and across from Tom. How would I endure the overpowering scent with her this close? I scooted my chair back a little and opened the notebook.

"I understand," Augusta said, "that my dear cousin wants all of our help in solving these problems and—" Her gaze landed on the recorder. "Oh my. You are serious about all this."

"Do you mind if we record our conversation?" Tom said.

*Conversation sounds so much better than interrogation*, I thought.

"Why, of course I don't mind." She folded her hands on the table in front of her. She wore a large emerald ring on her right hand and a diamond pinkie ring on her left.

Tom pressed the RECORD button and looked at me.

My cue to begin. I said, "Unlike the questions the police might have already asked about your alibi and other matters that I'm not familiar with, I'm interested in one thing in particular. Why would someone want Ritaestelle to look bad in the community?"

"Oh my. Is that what's happening?" She sounded so naive . . . and so fake.

"I believe you know that's what's happening. Bet after all the shoplifting and the talk about her not being quite right in the head, they even suspect her of murder." I took a sip of my tea—probably the best sweet tea I'd ever tasted.

"I suppose you cannot keep people from talking," Augusta said. Nothing like a little Southern-style evasiveness. But we have that in Texas, too, and she wasn't wiggling off the hook. "Do you think the accusations swirling around Ritaestelle made her kill Evie?"

"No. Oh, absolutely no. She is incapable. Simply incapable." Augusta licked at her lips and began rubbing the arthritic-looking knuckles on her left hand.

"We know you said you were sleeping the night Ritaestelle left the house," I said. "But from what I saw when I was here the other day, you seemed to be her caretaker. Was she upset the evening she left? Different in any way?"

Augusta closed her eyes briefly and then fluttered her lashes at Tom. She leaned toward him and in a low voice said, "Did she seem upset? Hmm. Perhaps you could say so, but in the quiet way I am familiar with. Ritaestelle is never one to lose her temper—unlike some folks in this house."

I wanted to pursue that statement, but Tom said, "How did you know she was upset?"

"She'd muttered over the last several days about being drugged and that she didn't know why someone would do that to her. She never accused me, mind you. She knows I would never do anything like that. Then she started pouring her tea out. I watched her do it that very night. But I never did anything to her food or drink. Do I seem like that sort of person, sir?"

Tom offered Augusta a sardonic smile. "You seem like the kind of person who knows a lot more than she's saying."

Augusta leaned back in her chair, considering this.

"You weren't drugging her, Augusta?" I asked.

"Why would I do such a thing?" she said.

Tom said, "That was a yes-or-no question."

"No. Absolutely not," she said, offering a wintery smile.

"Did you brew her tea?" I said.

"That is *not* one of my responsibilities," she said.

"Whose responsibility is it?" I asked.

"Why, Hildie, of course," Augusta said. "Then George would carry the tray upstairs and leave it on that table at the end of the hall. I would carry it in when Ritaestelle was ready. It became necessary for Ritaestelle to take her meals in her room after she became so unsteady on her feet. She was embarrassed, I believe. Wanted to keep to herself as much as possible."

"Embarrassed about what?" The perfume was giving

me a major headache, and I rubbed the spot between my eyebrows to ease the pain.

"All right, I'll admit there was talk about her competence. And I'll answer your next question before you ask. Who was talking? Just about everyone in this house and in town." Augusta stared beyond Tom, her hands still now.

"Did everyone also know that Ritaestelle's meal trays were set in the hallway that led to her room?" I said.

Augusta turned to me, head tilted. "I suppose everyone might know, though only Muriel and I have rooms on the same floor. We've all lived here together for decades. And we all knew about her tea as well. Twice a day with the tea, always taken in her room. Justine and Farley are up one story. There's an elevator you can take from the kitchen, and they usually use that, rather than climb all those stairs. I'll admit I tend to use it more and more of late."

"You spent a lot of time with Ritaestelle," I said. "Did you ever once catch her stealing anything?"

"Never. Not once. She is not a thief. And she's not a drug addict, even if they did find that bottle of pills in her room yesterday."

Uh-oh. That wasn't in Candace's notes. "What kind of pills?" I asked.

"Tranquilizers. I heard that police chief tell that little girl policewoman that they were prescribed for Ritaestelle." Augusta smiled with satisfaction. "Muriel's going a little deaf in one ear, but not me. No, I can still hear a pin drop."

I sat back, not sure what to think about this. Ritaestelle insisted she was being drugged, and yet she had a prescription for tranquilizers and never mentioned it.

Tom must have realized I was a little stunned—yup, I'd completely lost my train of thought. He wrapped up with Augusta by standing and saying, "Where were you last night?"

"Why, here, of course. Where else would I be?" she said.

"Thanks for your time. You've been a big help," Tom said.

"It's been my sincere pleasure," Augusta said before she bustled out of the room.

Between the lingering smell of the perfume and the news about the pills, I needed to clear my brain. I took the notebook I'd not written a word on and waved it at the spot where Augusta had been sitting.

Tom said, "Why don't we move to the other end of the table? Mr. Robertson will be sending in Muriel next."

"Good idea," I said. "I thought I might suffocate if Augusta stayed any longer."

Once we were settled in "fresher" spots, I said, "What about these pills? Ritaestelle never said anything about medication."

"Did you ask her directly?" Tom said.

"No. Guess I'm not very good at being direct, huh?"

"You did a fantastic job with Augusta. Look at what we learned in a few short minutes." His reassuring smile made me feel a little more confident.

But I was up again with Muriel. Would things go as well?

Mr. Robertson brought her in a minute later. He walked in behind her and was carrying a large tray.

Muriel, in her bright green silk dress and heels that I feared might land *her* in the hospital after a fall, chose to sit next to me. But she left a chair between us. She was keeping her distance. The red hair and the green dress had me thinking about Christmas.

Mr. Robertson set the tray down on the table. "Miss Hildie insists you eat. Doesn't want anyone hungry in this house."

It was past lunchtime, but I'd been too nervous about playing detective to pay attention to my stomach. One plate held triangle sandwiches, some filled with pimento cheese and others with what looked like chicken salad. There was a bowl of frosty red grapes and a platter of broccoli, carrots, celery sticks and cherry tomatoes surrounding a bowl of creamy dressing. What really caught my eye was the sliced apple strudel sitting on a small silver tray and dusted with confectioner's sugar. Suddenly I was *very* hungry.

Mr. Robertson left, and I took a napkin from the pile of folded white linen at one end of the tray and laid it across my lap. I'd start with the sandwiches, but I couldn't take my eye off that strudel.

"How are you—may I call you Muriel?" Tom said.

"That is my name, so most certainly," she said.

Mr. Robertson returned carrying another tray. This one held three pitchers—ice water, sweet tea and iced coffee.

Fresh glasses surrounded the pitchers, and there was also a bowl with sliced lemons. Mr. Robertson left without a word, my "thank you" echoing after him through the gigantic room.

*I could learn to like this sort of treatment.* But as I bit into the delicious chicken-salad sandwich—was that dill she'd added?—I realized that perhaps this was the reason no family member left this house and went out on their own. Being waited on hand and foot might be almost *too* comfortable.

"Muriel," I said once I'd finished off my little sandwich, "do you mind if we tape our conversation?" I nodded toward the recorder sitting in front of Tom.

"Oh dear. The police didn't even do that. Why would you ever want to record what I have to say?" She ran a thin hand through her vibrant red hair.

Tom tapped his temple. "I'm not good at remembering. Do you object?"

Ah. *Object.* Good word choice, I thought.

"I—I suppose not," she finally said after some hesitation. "But I do have an appointment this afternoon, so if we could get on with this?"

Tom pressed the RECORD button.

"Did you know we have a mutual acquaintance?" I said.

"You mean aside from Ritaestelle?" Muriel replied.

"Belle Lowry. She tells me her cousin was married to you for a time." I hadn't wanted to start out the interview this way, but Tom had told me I should—that it would put her on her heels right from the start.

"He was. What does ancient history have to do with anything?" Suddenly Muriel's face almost matched her hair.

*Ancient, but not* forgotten *history*, I thought. "Nothing to do with anything. Just popped into my head."

She looked as if she wanted to literally pop me in the head. Had she done exactly that to Evie and Candace? I wondered.

"What do you want to know?" Muriel sounded icily calm. "I am very much out of the loop around here. I was sleeping when Ritaestelle took off the other night in, of all things, her bathrobe."

"You almost sound embarrassed," I said. "Did the shoplifting and the drug taking embarrass you, too?"

"I suppose so," Muriel said, "though I never would have said a word to anyone had there not been a murder. I suspected Ritaestelle was taking some sort of mind-altering substance. She started slurring her words and staggering around the house, you see. But if she'd turned into a thief, which seems to be the case, well . . . I can imagine she needed something to make her forget what she'd done."

"You believed she actually stole things she hardly needed?" I tried to keep my voice even, not sound like this was ridiculous.

"I believe it because there's proof. When you talk to Justine, ask her. She'll tell you," she said.

"I will. But why do you think she would do such a thing?" I asked.

"I believed Ritaestelle was troubled and this caused her to do certain things that were entirely out of character." Muriel examined her French manicure, picking off a strip of clear polish and rolling it between her fingers.

"Troubled by what?" I asked, catching Tom's slight smile out of the corner of my eye. Maybe I wasn't as bad at this job as I thought I would be.

"We all come to moments in our life when the past shows us the future. She let opportunities slip by and she was filled with regret. She never married when she had so many suitors. She never knew the joy of sharing a life with a man." Muriel nodded, as if she were convincing herself of this.

"What about Desmond?" I said. "He seems to have brought her joy." Though that had come to a screeching halt now that she'd learned that he'd carried on with Augusta. But if Muriel didn't know this, I wasn't about to tell her.

Muriel laughed, and it was such a sweet, pleasant laugh that I almost forgot that this woman seemed to have no problem telling tales about her benefactor.

"Ah, Desmond," she said. "In and out of Ritaestelle's life. He will leave her again, of that much I am sure. Remember what I said about the past showing us the future?" She turned to Tom then. "And here I thought you were the detective. Yet Miss Jillian is asking all the questions. Why is that?"

"You're saying you want *me* to ask the questions?"

Tom said this in a tone that I had never heard before. He sounded harsh—almost cruel.

Muriel looked back to me, and I noticed a small twitch by her right eye. "What else can I help you with, Miss Jillian?"

She was trying to keep her composure. Perhaps now was the time to rattle her a little more. "I understand your engagement ring went missing." This time the look I caught from Tom was less than approving. He closed his eyes and shook his head slightly. Had I just screwed up? Given away something that Mike Baca wanted to remain a secret for now?

"Yes, but how did you know?" Muriel said.

"I'm not sure I should get into that. Let's move on. Now—"

"I *knew* she took it—and apparently Ritaestelle had the gall to tell you what she'd done. She was always jealous of my marriage, and this is how she pays me back after all I've done for her. By stealing from me." Muriel's lips tightened in anger. But she didn't flush like she had earlier. "Did she give it to you as a gift because you are her new best friend?"

Now I was flustered. How could I get this on track? Throw it right back at her, I decided. "Did you tell the police she took your ring?"

"No. That's family business—or so I thought. Perhaps I jumped to conclusions thinking she gave the ring to you. I suppose she admitted her theft to the police officers and that's how you found out." She looked at Tom. "Would you be so kind as to pour me a glass of water?"

He did so and handed it across the table.

She took it with a shaky hand.

"Am I making you nervous? Because that's not my intent." I was beginning to feel sorry for her, something I suppose a cop would never allow herself to do. But I wasn't a cop and I couldn't help myself, so I added, "Ritaestelle did not give me your ring."

"I am so sorry if you took offense. I'm the one at fault. It's the blood sugar problem," she said. "We get so few visitors since Ritaestelle began to act strange, and I find that rather stressful—which causes big highs and big lows in the blood sugar. And poor Evie losing her life doesn't help.

Then I discovered that my ring had disappeared. No, stress is not good for a diabetic." She took a long sip of water.

Her world revolved around Ritaestelle, hers and everyone's who lived here, no doubt. That seemed so sad. "We've bothered you enough. Your insights have been helpful."

Before she left, Tom asked her about her whereabouts last night. She gave the same answer as her sister and was on her way, tottering out of the dining room on her high heels as fast as she was able.

# Twenty-eight

Once Muriel was gone, I reached for a pimento-cheese sandwich and said, "I messed up about the ring. Sorry."

"She would have found out anyway. I didn't mean to throw you off your game." He plucked several grapes off their stems.

"I don't much care for those cousins, and I feel guilty about that. I should have sympathy for them because they're pretty darn pitiful," I said. The pimento cheese was homemade and yummy. I grabbed another one. "Muriel talked about Ritaestelle wasting her opportunities, and yet what have they done with their lives? Both of them have never stepped out of Ritaestelle's shadow."

"What was the most important thing you learned from them?" Tom asked. He dipped a baby carrot in the dressing and, cupping his hand beneath to catch drips, brought it to his mouth.

"Probably the tranquilizers," I said. "Guess that will be my first question for Ritaestelle when we get back home."

I stood and put a slice of strudel on my napkin. "We should change chairs. Your turn to sit in the top spot."

"Good idea," Tom said, around a mouthful of sandwich.

"You didn't press them too hard about their alibis for last night. Is that because you don't think either of them hurt Candace?" I said.

"Interrogation 101. You get people locked into a story. Then you ask them again later and see if you get the same answer. In this case, Mike will be asking them again and I'll give him what we've got. Then we'll see if they're consistent."

"Makes sense to me," I said. "This is quite an education."

Justine Longworth arrived next, after I'd had only one bite of pastry. But oh my god, what a bite it was. The flaky strudel, rich with cinnamon and butter and apples, practically melted in my mouth.

I tapped at my chin with a new napkin and smiled at Justine, who carried what looked like a black dress in a dry cleaner's bag.

Tom stood, introduced himself and thanked her for coming to talk to us.

She took the chair next to his after draping the dress over a different seat back. Now that I was close to her, and despite her makeup, I could tell she'd indeed had cosmetic surgery. Her mouth was pulled tight by what was probably a recent facelift. A face as thin as hers didn't look normal with the bee-sting look to her lips and the collagen-enhanced cheeks. I had no argument with her hair, though. Layered, then highlighted and low-lighted in shades of brownish red and dark blond, the style and colors suited her complexion.

Her khaki sleeveless dress had that Ann Taylor look. Whatever funds Ritaestelle allotted her relatives, none of them seemed to be wanting.

"You were married to Ritaestelle's brother, I understand," Tom said.

"Yes," she said.

She sounded curt and seemed none too happy to be talking to the likes of us.

"How is your relationship with Ritaestelle?" he asked.

"That's not the kind of information the police were interested in," Justine said. She seemed composed, but again, definitely not happy.

"We're not the police. We were hired by your sister-in-law to find out the truth about past events." Tom offered his best sarcastic smile. "You know, the kind of stuff that made her run to a stranger for help."

"I don't know what you're talking about. Be specific," she said.

Not intimidated, I thought. Maybe this woman had more backbone than anyone else who lived here.

"Is that alcohol I smell on your breath, Ms. Longworth?" Tom said.

Whoa. Good thing we'd changed chairs and he picked up on that. Since Tom's mother was a recovering alcoholic, he probably had Justine figured out the minute she sat down.

"I enjoy a glass of wine every now and then. What does that have to do with anything?" she said.

But that alabaster skin was growing blotchy at her throat. He'd found her weakness instantly and confronted her. I could never have been so blunt.

"Maybe your drinking has nothing to do with anything, but it's—what?" Tom checked his watch. "Two o'clock? A little early, don't you think?"

"Get on with your questions." Her eyes bored into Tom's.

"I already asked one and you didn't answer. Got something to hide?" he said.

"Oh, all right. I get along fine with Ritaestelle. We stay out of each other's way. She prefers socializing, inviting this one and that one here. Has her dinner parties. Me? I like to be alone." She raised her sculpted brows and tried to smile.

"Alone with your friend Chivas? Bet your drink of choice is expensive," Tom said.

He was baiting her, and I had no idea why. But I trusted he knew what he was doing.

"What I do in the privacy of my upstairs rooms is no one's business," Justine said coldly. "It certainly has kept me out of this embarrassment Ritaestelle has created. My husband is turning over in his grave, I'm sure."

"She's a disgrace? Is that what you're saying?" Tom said.

"She's apparently a thief and a liar." Justine turned her head away from Tom, but the facade was beginning to crumble. She was blinking hard.

Softly Tom said, "I can see you don't want to believe that. And who's the real disgrace, Justine?"

Her head snapped back in his direction, and she glared at him, but tears glistened in her eyes. A tense few seconds passed before she said, "I thought she was the sane one. I thought I could depend on her. Obviously that's not the case."

"Who's the real disgrace?" Tom repeated.

She whispered, "I am." Tears slipped from her lids and down her cheeks.

I grabbed a napkin and passed it across to her. My heart had sped up. Were we about to get a confession?

"Thank you," she said to me, then dabbed at her wet face. She made eye contact with Tom again, but this time the hostility was gone. "Ritaestelle is the rock in this family. Always there for everyone. Her leaving us like this, well, you see how selfish I can sound. But in truth, her departure has made me realize how poorly I've treated her and how much I owe her."

"Sounds nice," Tom said, "but that means you didn't always feel that way. What's your main beef with Ritaestelle?"

"The way she treats my son. Like he's a moron. He deserved—" She stopped herself. "No. That's the story I tell myself when I open a bottle of wine at noon. You want to know the real issue?"

Tom leaned toward her, arms resting on the table. "That's why we're here."

"My husband left all the Longworth money not to us, but to Ritaestelle. There. I've said it. My own husband thought I'd fritter it away. Trouble is, he was probably right. I'm not good at anything but leeching off my sister-in-law. And Farley is the same. We depend on Ritaestelle for everything— and that is both a curse and a blessing."

Tom nodded and smiled. "Thanks for being straight. Most refreshing thing that's happened in, oh, the last hour."

Justine bit the side of her mouth. "I don't know anything. That's the truth."

"Maybe you know more than you think." Tom gripped the chair's arms and settled back. "Muriel said that you would know what the police found yesterday when they executed the search warrant. What was she talking about?"

"Oh, that." Justine twisted the makeup-stained napkin. "Some of my jewelry was found behind Ritaestelle's armoire—hidden in a brown paper sack. Items that my late husband bought me."

*Muriel's ring and now Justine's jewelry. Wow.* Those were a step up from a bag of rubber bands.

"You believe Ritaestelle took them?" Tom asked.

Justine shook her head. "I simply cannot picture Ritaestelle sneaking around, grabbing up things that aren't hers and hiding them away. The woman can buy anything she wants."

"Who *can* you picture doing something like that?" Tom said.

"I suppose Muriel or Augusta. Out of spite. They have their own issues concerning the family fortune—or didn't you make them cry and spill their guts, Mr. Stewart?" Her turn for sarcasm. But this time she almost managed a real smile.

Tom laughed. "We saved the best for you, Justine. You've been very helpful."

She reached to her right and rested a hand on the black dress. "Mrs. Hart, would you mind taking this for Rita-estelle to wear this evening? Evie's visitation is tonight, and I'm sure she won't want to miss it."

"No problem. Do you have a time and place?" I said.

"I'll have George write everything down. You'll find a shoebox on the hall table holding the other things she might need."

"One more question," Tom said. "Where were you last night?"

"In my room visiting with my friend Jim Beam. See, I don't go for the expensive stuff. I go for what suits someone like me—someone cheap."

She left the room, shoulders hunched, head down—something no amount of cosmetic surgery could ever fix.

"She's right about the visitation," I said. "Ritaestelle will definitely want to go."

"That's not exactly how I wanted to spend my evening," Tom said.

"I can take her," I said.

"No, *we* will take her. After what happened to Candace, I'm not taking any chances." His turn for a strudel break before the last family member arrived. "The question remains, who did that to Candace and why?"

I said, "I have a hard time even thinking about anyone hurting her. But I guess you're right about being careful."

"I know I'm right," he said.

"Guess what I forgot. To ask about Isis. Someone put that cat outside and—"

"No one will admit to it. We'll find out eventually," he said.

"Why are you so sure?" I said.

"One of these people—my guess for now is Justine—

will crack. The pressure of a police search yesterday, us coming here today and all of them seeing a dead woman tonight will be too much." He rested a hand on mine. "We'll get the truth."

I smiled at Tom but then felt another's presence before I looked toward the entrance to the dining room and saw him.

Farley Longworth was leaning on the doorframe. "Isn't that sweet. I see you've already found a replacement, *Mrs. Hart.*"

# Twenty-nine

He said my name with such contempt, I felt the blood drain from my face.

Tom glanced at me and then at Farley. "What's that supposed to mean, Longworth?"

He sauntered into the room, a small balding man with skin as pale as his mother's. "Why don't you ask her?"

Tom stood. "I'm here to ask *you* questions—because your aunt hired me to do that."

Farley was wearing navy pleated Bermuda shorts and a white polo. All that was missing was a cardigan tied around his shoulders. He took a glass from the table and poured himself some tea before sitting down. "How is Aunt Rita? And how much is she offering you to set up her family to look like criminals?"

It felt like a fist had tightened in my gut. Hearing his voice brought back that awful call he'd made and his terrible accusation that I'd killed John. I swallowed hard and put my hands in my lap. If they began to tremble, I didn't want this man to see. I didn't want him to know how he'd hurt me.

I felt Tom's foot press mine, and that small gesture was enough to settle me.

He said, "Where were you last night?" Tom started off the interview where he'd finished with everyone else.

I wondered why for a second, but it was a direct and almost accusatory question. Yes. That was the right way to go after this guy.

"Did you know my father was a lawyer? He would suggest I have an attorney present to answer questions from even you. What are you? A failed cop?" Farley's smile was smug.

"Oh, I don't think you want to go there, Longworth," Tom said. "I've got a failure list from your aunt that has your name written all over it. Where were you last night?"

Farley rolled his eyes and sighed. "If Aunt Rita thinks this is the way to get her out of trouble, I'll go along. I actually like the old woman. I was at the movie theater. Summer blockbuster time, you know."

"Alone?" Tom asked. "No. Dumb question. You're probably alone most of time."

Farley's tongue flicked around his lips, and he picked up his glass. Then he looked at me. "Where were you? With your boyfriend here? Is he the reason you—"

"You don't know anything about me," I said, keeping my tone even. But I felt ready to erupt. I couldn't let this twerp get to me. "We're here because your aunt is afraid of her own family. Why is that, *Farley*?"

Tom's eyebrows rose in surprise, and I knew the surprise was directed my way because of my harsh tone. I still hadn't told him what Farley had said to me.

Farley stared at me and I stared right back. We were facing off like Syrah and Isis had done the other day.

"Can't answer that one, Longworth?" Tom said with a laugh. "Too tough a question, huh? Yeah, well, I'll bet you could screw up a two-car funeral. That's about how smart you are."

"I don't have to sit here and be insulted." He started to get up.

Tom tapped his temple. "Think money, Longworth. Think about all the comforts of home you'll miss out on when your aunt kicks your ass to the curb because you wouldn't cooperate."

Farley sat back down. "I've told the police everything I know. I didn't hear my aunt leave that night. I was here the whole time. I—"

"What about Evie? Was she here? I heard you liked Evie," Tom said.

"She went home, said she'd work from there even though she wasn't done. But she did call for the password list. I gave it to her," he said.

He'd gone sullen now—like the spoiled brat he probably had always been.

"Password list?" Tom asked.

"I told that cop. The hot one, not the guy," he said. "Ask her."

I wasn't about to make the mistake of giving away the fact that Candace couldn't remember most of what went on here yesterday, so I said, "The Mercy police as well as your aunt want you to cooperate. What is this password list?"

"We all have computers and bank accounts that Evie manages." He paused and in a quiet voice said, "*Managed.* Anyway, we all have passwords, but she keeps a list so she can transfer money into our accounts and I guess so she can check up on what we're doing on our computers."

"Each of you has two passwords and Evie knew them?" Tom asked.

"Didn't I just say that?" he said impatiently.

"You're getting testy, Longworth," Tom said, obviously very interested in this arrangement. "Why would Evie Preston need the password to everyone's computer? Why not just to the bank accounts on a main server in the house?"

"She watched the money, okay?" Farley's face was flushed, his eyes darting everywhere to avoid meeting Tom's.

Tom leaned back with a smile. "Let me guess. Online porn? Or online gambling? Which one was Evie keeping an eye on at your aunt's request?"

"Gambling," Farley muttered. He looked up. "Happy now? And just so you know, she watched what everyone was doing. Like how much dear mummy was ordering from the liquor store every week. Where Augusta was shopping online. How much jewelry Muriel ordered from that stupid QVC television station."

Oh boy. Had that been Ritaestelle's idea? Or Evie's? Is that what got her killed? But I remembered then that he said he'd answered the phone that night. That made me want to ask a question that had bothered me from the start.

"Do you always answer the phone?" I said.

"No one else will, so yeah, I play servant most days." He refused to look at me.

Was he anticipating my question? "Did you talk to

Shawn Cuddahee when he called about Ritaestelle's missing cat?"

"What if I did?" he said. "The man wouldn't be straight with me about what he wanted, so why should I be straight with him?"

"You knew who he was?" I said.

"I know how to use Google. What does that have to do with anything?" But something in Farley's expression and that evasiveness said it did have something to do with *everything.*

"You never passed the message on to Ritaestelle or Evie?" I asked.

"Why should I?" he answered.

Farley Longworth might be the most immature forty-year-old I'd ever met. "Because your aunt loved her cat. You had to know that Shawn calling her more than once was probably about Isis."

I could almost see his brain working to find an angle to put this in a good light. And he found it. "See, that's just it. Do I want my aunt, who's obviously physically and mentally ill, to become more disturbed by the news that her cat was found dead?"

"Come on, Longworth," Tom said. "A rescue shelter wouldn't be calling with that news. The county animal control officer would do that job if Isis had been found dead."

"I didn't know why he was phoning. You know why? Because he was a smart-ass and wouldn't say. I blew it off. So what?"

Smart-ass? I guess Shawn could come across that way. And any conversation between *this* man and Shawn would have gone downhill pretty fast.

"Anyone ever tell you that you're a jerk?" Tom said.

"I think I'm done. Good luck." He rose and turned to leave, but then turned back. "Oh. Tell Aunt Rita I love her, would you?"

Once he left, I took a deep breath, let it out and began shoving strudel into my face. There is nothing as comforting as dessert.

Tom stared at me for several seconds, eyes narrowed. "That guy did more than accuse you of extortion when he called the other day."

I pointed at my mouth, indicating I couldn't answer.

Tom waited, never taking his eyes off me.

After I'd swallowed and paid close attention to cleaning off my hands and around my mouth, I smiled. "Just Hildie to go. Better check what time that visitation is so we can pace our last interview."

"Jillian, what did Longworth say that hurt you so much that you couldn't tell me?"

My turn to avoid a stare. "We've been so involved in these interviews, I haven't checked on my cats since we arrived—not to mention Ritaestelle and Kara." I pulled my phone from my pocket and pulled up the cat-cam feed.

Tom placed his hand over the screen. "Jilly," he said quietly. "Trust me."

Another deep breath needed. Why did this still bother me so much? "Guess you won't quit until I tell you."

"That's me. Persistent," he said.

"And perceptive. That's probably what made you a good cop and makes you a great PI." I sighed. "When Farley called, he said people have been talking, saying that I probably murdered my husband for the house and the money."

"What?" Tom said, incredulous.

"I knew then what Ritaestelle must feel like—what she was going through with all the whispers and stares she must have been getting recently. I wanted more than ever to help her. Because it hurts to think that—"

"No one thinks you did anything to hurt your husband." He slid the phone away and took my hand. "You are one of the most well-liked people to have ever moved into town. Excuse the cliché, but people in these parts don't take kindly to strangers. But you? No one has an unkind word to say."

"You're only saying that—"

"Because it's true," he said. "Besides, that lunkhead is full of hot air. He's a middle-aged bully. Bullies attack other people because they don't want people to look at them and see that they're empty inside."

I laughed. "Lunkhead?"

"One of my mom's favorite words," he said with a smile. "You better?"

"I am fine. Let's see the strudel maker. I might just kiss her."

George Robertson arrived as I was cleaning strudel remains from the table and Tom was pouring himself more iced coffee.

"Please, Mrs. Hart," Mr. Robertson said. "I'll take care of clearing the table. Would you like to take some strudel to Miss Ritaestelle? I'm sure she's missing Hildie's sweets."

"Great idea," I said.

"I'll help you take the dress, her shoes and the dessert to the car when you're ready to leave." He began gathering empty glasses and dirtied napkins. One, I realized, was covered in Justine's makeup. I felt awful for her. She was one miserable woman.

Once Mr. Robertson had most everything on one tray, he said, "Follow me. Hildie's in the kitchen, and there is no way I could get her to come up here and talk to you."

That was how we found ourselves on two of the half dozen stools that surrounded a large stainless-steel preparation area in the center of a gigantic kitchen. To my left was an entry that led to a narrow winding staircase and the elevator that apparently got plenty of use. Across from us were the sinks—four of them—and three windows that looked out on the back driveway leading to the four garages. To the right was a huge refrigerator, gas stove, stacked ovens and a three-tiered rack where fresh fruits and vegetables waited for Hildie to work her magic.

Hildie herself might as well have been an appliance in the kitchen. The chubby, graying woman with the round, ruddy face had said nothing when Mr. Robertson introduced us. She was busy peeling mangoes.

"Hildie—or would you rather I call you by your last name?" I said. "Trouble is I don't know what it is."

"Hildie is fine," she said. "Everyone call me Hildie."

She had an accent—I recalled Ritaestelle saying she was from Germany—but she'd been in this country long enough that her English was probably fine.

"Good. And please, we're Jillian and Tom. Nothing formal down here, right?" The kitchen was about a half dozen steps lower than the rest of the house.

"No. Nothing formal," she answered, focused on her work.

"Thank you for the great food," Tom said. "Bet you keep the folks here well-fed."

"Is my job," Hildie said.

"Yes, but Ritaestelle thinks you are wonderful," I said.

Finally she looked at me. "How is my lady? She okay?"

"She is looking forward to coming home. You can help her with that. We need to know what happened to Miss Preston and why. We need to know who might have been trying to hurt Ritaestelle's reputation."

"Miss Preston is bossy young woman. They didn't like her much." She put her paring knife down, made a mound of the mango peelings and pushed them aside.

"Who didn't like her?" Tom said.

"The family," she said.

Okay, I thought. This might be like pulling teeth, and we had to get home and get ready for a funeral visitation. "But Ritaestelle liked her?"

"My lady is foolish. She likes everyone," Hildie said.

"Was it foolish to like Miss Preston, then?" Tom asked.

"She was cold like a fish." Hildie began to cube the mangoes. "But my lady thought the family needed a person like her. They were always taking advantage. My lady is very generous. Too generous."

"Did you like Miss Preston?" I said.

Hildie stopped cutting and looked at me. "What does this matter?"

*Good question*, I thought. "I suppose it doesn't. Was there any one person in the family who disliked her enough to kill her?"

She considered this for a few seconds. "If love and hate are close, then I would say Mr. Farley. I could tell about him. How he wanted her. But she didn't like him. Not at all."

"He had a thing for her?" Tom said.

Hildie smiled for the first time. "Yes. A thing. She had no thing for him. Who would?"

I was beginning to like Hildie. "The night Ritaestelle left here, did you see or hear anything?"

"I was in my room." She pointed at the ceiling with her knife. "Way up on the top. I hear nothing."

"Did it surprise you that Ritaestelle left like that, so late?" Tom said. "And not exactly dressed to go visiting?"

Hildie smiled at him again. "You're a funny man. Not exactly dressed. I like that. Was I surprised? I think yes. But she was worried. She was sick. I would run away myself if someone was hurting me that way."

"Do you have any clue who might have been hurting your lady?" I said.

"I don't know much. I stay here most of the time. But I know why she came to you." She scooped up her cubed mangoes and tossed them into a stainless bowl. Then she went to the sink and returned with a colander filled with strawberries and blueberries. She added them to the bowl.

"Why did she come to me?" I said.

Hildie walked over to the rack and returned with two limes and a squeeze bottle of honey. She rolled a lime on the counter. "What I see about you now? Or what I knew then?" she said.

"What you knew then," I said, watching her quickly cut the lime in half and squeeze the juice on top of the other fruit.

"She knew you could help her find the black cat." Hildie shook her head disapprovingly as she drizzled honey over the fruit. "Black cats are supposed to be good luck in some countries. Here, I think they are bad luck."

It all came back to Isis.

Tom, his eyes intent on that luscious-looking bowl of fruit, said, "What do you see about Jillian now?"

Hildie looked into my eyes for the first time. "That you have much kindness in you. That my lady did the right thing."

I felt embarrassment heat my cheeks. "Back to Isis. Do you know how she got out?"

"Of course I know." Hildie took a spatula from the drawer in front of her and gently mixed the fruit.

"You know and you never told anyone?" Tom said.

She kept working. "No one ever ask."

I almost laughed. This was a woman who only wanted to work, not be bothered by questions. "How did the cat get out?"

"I saw Mr. Farley take her away, wrapped in a towel so she wouldn't scratch him with her back claws. That Isis, she is good with what she has left. That black cat has what you Americans call an *attitude*."

I could see Farley doing that. Yes, indeed.

# Thirty

We arrived home thirty minutes later after I made a convincing speech to Tom that he should not beat Farley Longworth senseless after the revelations about how that spoiled man had hurt me and tried to kill a cat. Knowledge is power, and we had plenty of that after our visit. Giving Farley some of that knowledge would not be a good idea, and Tom was well aware of that—after he'd calmed down.

When we came in through the back door, I saw Ritaestelle and Kara sitting in the living room. They were listening to a classical music station on a digital TV cable station. My cats hurried into the kitchen to greet us—probably hoping for a treat as well as some petting. I usually gave them treats when I came home after being away for hours. My guilt issues definitely extended to my fur friends.

"There's a visitation for Evie tonight," I called out over the music.

Kara picked up the remote and muted the TV. She stood, and soon Ritaestelle rose as well. Just took her a little longer.

"Oh my," Ritaestelle said. "How will I—"

I held up the dress. "Justine sent clothes, and Mr. Robertson gave me all the information."

"Thank goodness." Ritaestelle's hand went to her heart. "I could not stop thinking about that poor girl today."

Kara took the dress and the shoebox. "Pay attention to your babies. They have been vocalizing their unhappiness about your absence every chance they got—well, Syrah and Merlot have. Chablis just clung to me like a toddler missing her mommy."

I smiled.

Tom set the sack with the strudel on the counter. "I've got to get home, check my messages and change. Meet you at the funeral home?"

I nodded, and he brushed my lips with his before leaving.

"I'll take these to the guest room," Kara said, draping the dress over her arm. She hurried out of the kitchen, her bare feet slapping on the floor.

After I doled out a pile of crunchy tuna treats to my cats, I grabbed a paper napkin and the strudel. Ritaestelle was still standing, Isis in her arms.

"I have something especially for you." I held up the bag. "From Hildie."

Ritaestelle put her cat down, and Isis raced into the kitchen. She'd bully Chablis out of her share of the treats, but I'd given Chablis a few extra anticipating this.

Kara returned and soon the three of us sat down in the breakfast nook to enjoy the strudel. The lake sparkled beneath the low-slung sun, but we'd heard on the radio that storms were moving in from the east. I would need an extra umbrella for Ritaestelle tonight.

I summarized our visit to the Longworth Estate, leaving out many details even though Kara tried to squeeze them from me. Tom and I had to talk to Mike Baca before Kara could print any of what we learned, anything that might prove newsworthy, that is. Plus, Ritaestelle didn't need to know just how nasty her nephew was—though she probably knew more than I gave her credit for.

"That is the best apple anything I have ever tasted," Kara said. "Maybe the paper can do some of Hildie's recipes in a Wednesday edition."

"She would be honored, I am sure," Ritaestelle said.

Kara stood. "I want to make this visitation, too, so I have to get back to my apartment. My kittens have probably shredded an entire roll of toilet paper in my absence. And I have to figure out what to wear. By the way, Candace was released from the hospital. She's at her mother's. She called here when she couldn't reach you."

"Oops. I had my phone on silent while we were at Ritaestelle's house." I pulled it from my pocket. Sure enough, the message icon showed the missed call. I would have seen it if Tom hadn't covered up my phone so quickly when I took it out at the Longworth house.

"Do you mind if I call her now?" I said to Ritaestelle.

"You go right ahead. I need to bathe and dress, perhaps pray on what to say to poor Evie's mother before we meet with the family," Ritaestelle said.

I watched Ritaestelle head for her room, Isis beside her. The limp was almost nonexistent now. Maybe on the ride to the funeral home I would ask her about those tranquilizers. Perhaps she didn't even know what they were. Some of what we'd learned today was certainly puzzling, and those pills were part of it.

I speed-dialed Candace, and she answered after a half ring. "Kara said you went to the big house today. Why? What's going on?"

"Remember how Ritaestelle hired Tom to investigate the case and that she asked me to help him? We went over your notes together this morning," I said.

"Right," she said, sounding like she didn't recall this at all. "This morning seems like a hundred years ago. What did you find out?"

"You should be resting, not thinking about the case. Your brain needs a time-out. Your notes matched up with what we learned." *Your very brief notes,* I said to myself. I wasn't about to add that I now knew a secret about my friend Candace—she relied heavily on her memory when she wrote up her reports, because her notes didn't even begin to give the full picture.

"Nothing new?" she said.

"Nothing that can't wait until you're feeling better," I said.

"Come on, Jillian. Don't freeze me out." She lowered her voice to a whisper. "I am already going insane here with my mother—and I've only been home a few hours."

"Here's a nugget. There's a visitation for Evie Preston this evening," I said. "I'm taking Ritaestelle. I'll call you and tell you all about it the minute I get home. How's that?"

I heard the cat button game commencing in the hallway and smiled to myself. No matter what awful things I'd learned today, no matter what sadness came around, my cats would always find time to play.

"You promise to call me?" Candace said.

"I promise. Now, lie down and get well so you can find this killer."

"You're the best, Jillian. Thank you for caring. Thank you for understanding that I need to know what's going on."

"You bet I understand. And we'll always have each other's back," I said.

After I disconnected, I ventured to the foyer and peeked down the hallway. Syrah was going crazy over one particular button. Must be made of metal because it sure didn't sound like plastic or wood. Chablis, meanwhile, was lying down, front paws tucked, watching Syrah swatting and tossing the thing in the air. That activity was a little too vigorous for her.

I heard the guest bathroom water running and decided I needed a shower myself. I felt a little dirty after my visit to that house today. On the surface, everything at the Longworth Estate was pristine, but it was what we'd uncovered about the people who lived there that had me feeling grimy right now.

When I passed the cats on the way to my room, Syrah stopped, pushing the small shiny button toward me. Guess shiny was better, and there was a scrap of blue fabric attached. How my cats loved fabric, even in minute amounts.

"Sorry, buddy. We'll play tomorrow. I promise."

Ritaestelle and I arrived at Griggs Funeral Home at seven sharp that evening. The small parking lot had only one spot left.

I took Ritaestelle's arm and helped her. The footing wasn't good, even for me.

"I have prayed on this and know coming tonight is the right thing to do," Ritaestelle said. "But I am worried others might not see it that way."

"You said in the car that Evie's mother was very nice on the phone the other day. Maybe that's all that counts," I said.

I heard the crunch of gravel behind us. I turned, worried we might be the next two to be smacked on the head. But it was Desmond Holloway. He came up to Ritaestelle on her other side, and she was so surprised she stopped dead.

"Um, Desmond," I said. "Do you think this is a good time?" I gripped the two umbrellas I held in my left hand a little tighter. This wasn't what the poor woman needed right now.

He ignored me, saying, "Ritaestelle, I am truly sorry for our misunderstanding about Augusta. Please forgive me?"

"Misunderstanding?" Ritaestelle said. "I did *not* misunderstand. What I have done is choose to close my eyes to your flaws. That has now come to an end. If you will please be so kind as to leave me be. I am here to mourn the loss of a young woman who met a tragic and untimely death."

Desmond stepped back and buttoned the top gold button on his nautical-looking blazer. Jeez. We were headed to a funeral visitation, not an outing on a yacht.

He couldn't hide the desperation in his eyes and apparently wasn't about to be dismissed so easily. He grasped Ritaestelle's elbow. "Please talk to me, my precious. Let me make this up to you—"

"Leave her alone," came the strong, firm voice of Nancy Shelton.

When had she arrived on the scene? But I was relieved to see her.

Desmond dropped his hand, and I was grateful. I could tell Ritaestelle was, too.

Clouds had hidden what was left of the sun, and thunder rumbled in the distance. A light rain began to fall.

Shelton said, "You two go inside. Desmond, you stay. I want a word with you."

We left, leaving them behind. I glanced back and saw Shelton's face close to Desmond's, but whatever she was saying, the words didn't carry. But her body language said she wasn't happy with him at all.

I heard the organ music before we even opened the door to the old building. There was only one funeral home within twenty miles of both Mercy and Woodcrest. The Griggs brothers had been in business for more than fifty years, but now Anna Griggs, daughter of one of the brothers, managed the place. She greeted us when we walked in.

If she was surprised to see Ritaestelle, her face didn't show it. She smiled and gestured at the guest book on the table behind her. Two vases of lilies framed the book. She never said a word, just stepped back after we signed and pointed to our left with another smile and a nod. I left the umbrellas in the stand by the door where others had left theirs and helped Ritaestelle down the short hall.

The organ music faded after we left the lobby, and I heard the quiet murmur of voices as we approached. But before we reached the room where Evie's casket was, Ritaestelle stopped. "May I have a moment?"

"Sure," I said.

She closed her eyes and took a deep breath. She then clasped her hands together and bowed her head briefly. When she was finished, she raised her head, and I saw her chin quiver. "I need strength."

"You've got plenty of that," I said.

We walked into the room, and at once all eyes were on Ritaestelle. The entire Longworth family was clustered together, all except for Farley. Tom, Mike and several officers in uniform from both police departments stood in a far corner. The people I assumed were Evie's family stood stoically near her white coffin.

The smell of death lingered beneath the scent of the baskets and sprays of flowers that lined the room. In a building this old, with its seventies-style paneled walls, that awful odor could not be masked even by a million flowers.

Ritaestelle left my side and made a beeline for a woman who looked to be around fifty. Words were exchanged, and the two embraced. Evie's mother, no doubt.

Nancy Shelton appeared next to me. "I told Desmond to leave," she said out of the side of her mouth. "He only came to see Ritaestelle. He cares nothing about the poor Preston family."

"Ritaestelle is not too happy with him right now, so I'm sure she's appreciative," I said. I was stalling. I didn't want to greet the mourners. What would I say? *Hi. Your daughter died in my backyard. Nice to meet you.*

"I heard that your friend Tom dug up plenty on Desmond," Shelton said. "As far as I'm concerned, he did Ritaestelle a favor. Now, would you like me to introduce you to Evie's mother and brothers?"

I inhaled, trying hard to only breathe through my mouth. The smell was making me a little sick. "Wait a minute," I said. "I'll be right back."

I stepped back into the hall, took my phone from the

pocket of my black dress pants and made sure it was silenced. I'd left my purse in the car since I needed to carry the umbrellas and help Ritaestelle, but the phone was my comfort line. I pulled up the cat cam, saw four cats sleeping in various spots and sighed. There. That felt better.

Making sure the phone was silenced, I put it in my back pocket. I tugged at my jacket and pressed my lips together to spread my lipstick. More stalling by worrying over ridiculous things. Truth was, I didn't want to look at that poor dead woman's face.

Shelton stuck her head out the door. She whispered, "Is something wrong?"

"No. Sorry." I walked into the room and followed her lead to where Evie Preston's family stood.

Ritaestelle was kneeling in front of Evie's casket, head bowed. Augusta, Muriel and Justine had moved closer to her, I noted. I wondered what the conversation would be like when they finally got to talk to Ritaestelle.

Nancy introduced me to Loretta Preston, as well as to Evie's brothers, Jeb and Carl. They were big, burly men—so different from their petite sister.

Loretta had dark circles under her red-rimmed eyes, and every line on her face seemed to stand out. The words *ravaged by grief* came to mind. I appreciated the way her sons stood on either side of her, ready to catch her if she fell—because she sure looked ready to collapse.

Loretta Preston grabbed both my hands in hers. "I understand you tried to save my baby girl. That you were heroic in your efforts to bring her back to life. I will be forever grateful that someone showed mercy and kindness at the end of her life."

Shelton leaned close and said, "I'll be over there with the other officers."

"I—I didn't do enough," I said. *Mercy. Such a powerful word.* I recalled feeling like a failure that night, and not much had changed over the last several days. I added, "I'm only sorry no one could save her."

"I take comfort knowing that she's in a better place," Loretta said.

Ritaestelle seemed to be having trouble getting up, and I reached out to help her.

She smiled sadly once she was on her feet. "I am sure you want to say a few words to poor Evie."

*Not exactly.* If having trouble breathing is part of a panic attack, I had newfound sympathy for those who'd experienced one. My chest was tight, and I felt lightheaded. But though I would have preferred to run out the door as I had done at the Longworth house the other day, I took my place on the kneeling bench. I did, however, avoid so much as a glance at Evie. When I bowed my head, I realized this panic had an origin. This was my first funeral visitation since John's death.

The hushed conversations, the flowers and that hovering unpleasant scent were all painful reminders of what I'd gone through not so long ago—after John died. Tears filled my eyes, and I had to bite my lower lip to avoid releasing the sob caught in my throat.

Tom, perceptive as always, arrived at my side and rested a hand on my shoulder. He leaned over and whispered, "This must be hard. Come on." He took my elbow and helped me up.

To get my mind off the past, I immediately looked for Ritaestelle. She was seated in a folding chair along the wall to my left with her relatives huddled around her. Justine was kneeling by her, holding her hand, but the cousins remained standing. I gave Ritaestelle a look that said, "You need any help?"

She shook her head almost imperceptibly.

Meanwhile, people I didn't know were streaming in to pay their respects to Evie. Tom took my hand, and we walked over to the police gathered in the corner. As I joined them, the two paramedics, Jake and Marcy, who'd worked on Evie the night of the murder, arrived, and the uniformed officers went to greet them. That left Tom, Nancy, Mike and me.

Keeping his voice low, Tom said, "I was telling Mike about our visit to the Longworth house today."

Mike said, "I wish the family hadn't said anything to you about the tranquilizers we discovered during the search."

"Why?" I said.

"Because that means they probably told anyone who would listen. Problem was, we had to call them in to Miss

Longworth's room to identify items, and Candace was just bagging the pill bottle."

"That news is all over town, so you're right," Shelton said. "Augusta called me up the minute you left. But what about these passwords you mentioned earlier, Stewart? What's the significance? Seems like that was in Evie's job description."

"I'll let Mike give you a complete report. One thing we did learn for certain is that Farley carried the poor cat out the back door. I don't think he was taking her for her regular veterinary checkup."

Shelton shook her head in disgust. "Farley Longworth is one sorry bastard—excuse my French. You notice he's not here. We should sweat him. Bet he has a lot to tell."

"Agreed," Mike said. "The family's phone records and financials we subpoenaed should come in tomorrow, and that'll show the extent of his gambling problem. But as for those pills we confiscated? I've already spent the day working on that. Those tranquilizers were ordered over the Internet. They had Miss Longworth's name on them, but we can't be sure she did the ordering. The woman doesn't even use a cell phone. Would she have the skills to order drugs online? I doubt it. Good news is, Candace got a decent latent off the pill bottle."

I'd forgotten to ask Ritaestelle about the pills, and now I wished I had. She might have a clue as to who did order them. Could have been Evie for all we knew.

"Prints," Tom said. "Good old Candace printed everyone, I hear."

"Yeah, but Candace can't remember where she put the print cards," Mike said. "She can't remember much of anything, and it's driving her crazy."

"They weren't in her evidence kit?" I asked. The night of the murder I'd seen her put Ritaestelle's card in there after she'd taken her fingerprints.

"No, we looked," Mike said. "But I haven't had a chance to check her vehicle. She might have stuck them in the glove compartment. You didn't happen to see an envelope when you got her notes?"

I should have known he was aware we took the notes. It's not like Mercy officers don't share information. But I still felt like I'd done something wrong. "Candace told us to get them once I reminded her—and I did have to remind her—that Tom was hired to help with the investigation."

Mike said, "I've got no problem with you working for Miss Longworth. Any other PI? Maybe. Not you." He slapped Tom on the back and smiled. Mike and Tom went back a long way, and I was relieved Mike wasn't angry about our involvement.

As they continued to talk, I thought about those fingerprints. When there was a break in the conversation, I said, "Could one of the family members have been worried about those prints and knocked Candace out to steal those cards?"

Mike rubbed his chin with tented fingers. "You may be on to something, but if one of them took the cards, he or she had to know we could print them again." He nodded in the direction of the Longworths. "And we can't rule out that one of them, or maybe Farley, told Candy something incriminating and that someone decided she had to go down. But whatever that information was, it's now erased forever by that blow to her skull. I talked to the doc, and he says she probably won't ever remember much detail from that day."

"At least she's okay," I said softly. I was uncomfortable talking about the case with Ritaestelle's family only six feet away. Was the killer in the room, or was Farley, or even Desmond, the culprit? *Desmond.* The ladies' man. What if he'd made a move on Evie and she threatened to tell Ritaestelle?

Tom pulled me from my thoughts, saying, "Jillian, did you hear me?"

"Sorry. Lost in thought," I said.

"Mike and I want to check Candace's car one more time for those print cards," he said. "Will you be okay here?"

I could read the worry on his face. I'd had a little meltdown on that kneeling bench, and he knew it. "Sure," I said. "Kara was supposed to be here—gosh, where is she?—and she'll probably follow us home."

"I'm glad to play security detail again," Shelton said.

"Thanks, but— Oh, there she is," I said.

And Liam Brennan was with her.

"What's he doing here?" Shelton said.

"Could be he is gathering information about the

family—and Evie's family, too. Were they . . . you know . . . eliminated as suspects?" I asked.

"Rock-solid alibis." Shelton watched Tom and Mike, who had paused to say hello to Kara before they left. "I checked up on Evie's family and told Mike, but he hasn't been sharing everything he knew."

"What do you mean?" I said as Brennan went toward the family and Kara walked over to join Shelton and me. She'd caught admiring looks from several police officers. Her short-sleeved brown linen dress showed off her figure, and with her dark hair clipped back and tumbling down her back, I swore she could have done a photo shoot for *Vanity Fair* right at that moment.

Shelton cleared her throat. "We don't need to get into that right now." She smiled at Kara. "Good evening, Miss Hart."

Kara nodded at her and rubbed circles on my back, saying, "You okay? You look pale."

"I'm fine. Funerals are—well, you know," I said.

She nodded solemnly. "Oh, I know all right." She looked at Shelton. "I haven't met Evie Preston's family, but I'd like to do a human interest story for the paper. What can you tell me about them?"

Shelton, who'd been uncharacteristically pleasant until now, reverted to her normal cranky self in a flash. "Those people are from my town, and I don't want you bothering them. They're grieving."

"But—" Kara started.

"Would you hush?" Shelton said. "The poor girl's body is right over there." She tossed her head in the direction of the casket. The twisting motion strained her navy jacket— did she ever wear anything else?—and a button popped off.

I bent and picked it up. The button looked similar to the one Syrah had been playing with today. As I handed it to her, I said, "Did you lose a button like this before?"

She flushed. "I've gained a few pounds in the last month. I suppose I could have lost one at your place."

"I'll steal the button back from my cat and return it. I was a textile arts major, even did some dress designing before I fell in love with quilting. Are your suits custom-made by—"

"Can you *please* give me insight into the family?" Kara said impatiently.

Shelton turned to Kara, looking equally impatient. "Like I said, you'll upset those people. I can't have that."

"Do you even *want* to solve Evie's murder?" Kara said. But at least she did whisper.

"That's a ridiculous question," Shelton said. Tiny beads of sweat dotted her upper lip. It was warm in the room, and I was sure wearing that suit made it that much warmer.

"Please," I said. "This gathering is for Evie." I looked at Kara. "Can you wait until after the visitation has ended to approach the family?"

"I suppose." She glared at Shelton. "But for now, I think I'll introduce myself." She walked over to them.

"Don't take this the wrong way," Shelton said. "But we're not used to your stepdaughter's aggressive, big-city type of reporting here."

"A human interest story is aggressive?" I said.

She raked a hand through her tight gray curls. "Maybe not, but did you see her headline about Deputy Carson? 'Officer Attacked'? That seemed like someone was shouting at us. We aren't fearmongers in these parts."

"I wouldn't think that a genteel approach to murder and assault would be effective in helping the police convey information to the community or to generate tips," I said.

"I see you've been brainwashed by your stepdaughter," she said. "But I suppose that's part of trying to be a mother."

*Trying?* Maybe there was a grain of truth to that—I was trying—but why did she have to bite back at me? My guess? Nancy Shelton, no matter how hard she tried, couldn't hide the fact that she was bitter. Did she even have a family, or did the Woodcrest Police fill that void for her?

I caught Ritaestelle's eye, and she looked almost pleading now, unlike before. I should have been paying closer attention to what was going on over there. "If you'll excuse me, Ritaestelle looks like she's had enough. She might want to go home."

"You know her that well, huh? Have you asked her if she might want to go to her real home?" Shelton said.

"Ritaestelle was drugged," I said. "What's to stop whoever did it from doing it again?"

"I have been her friend for years. I will protect her," she said.

Guess this mingling of people from Mercy and people from Woodcrest had her feeling territorial. "You're right," I said. "Why don't we ask her?" But I knew what Ritaestelle would say.

We walked over to the circle of women surrounding Ritaestelle.

"Why, Mrs. Hart," Augusta said. "Glad you could take time to say hello to us." She nodded at Shelton. "Hello, Nancy."

Justine said, "We've been trying to convince our Rita-estelle to return home. We miss her and Isis."

Her breath smelled so strongly of alcohol, I was wondering if poor Ritaestelle might be getting intoxicated being so close to her.

"Yes. You need to come home, something I was saying to Mrs. Hart moments ago," Shelton said. "What do you say, Ritaestelle? We'll let the Mercy police do their job and bring this killer to justice while I watch over you."

Muriel cleared her throat. "I don't think it's a good idea at all." She focused on the linoleum floor, her hands gripping her small black handbag tightly.

"Why is *that*, Muriel?" Shelton said sharply.

"Because I have this feeling in the pit of my stomach that it's not safe—not yet," Muriel said. "I mean, look what happened to that police officer. Why don't you take care of *us*, Nancy? We could use some looking after."

"You're afraid?" Shelton said. "What are you afraid of?"

"Indeed, what are you afraid of, Muriel?" Ritaestelle said. She sounded very curious, and I felt the same way.

She smiled at her cousin. "It's a feeling, is all."

"Intuition is important," Ritaestelle said. "I'm taking your advice, Muriel. If Jillian will have me, I would like to remain with her for a few more days. I have the utmost faith that Jillian and Mr. Stewart will get to the bottom of this." Ritaestelle smiled up at me.

Shelton wasn't smiling. "You don't trust me?"

"Of course I do," Ritaestelle said. "But you have always wanted to do things your way, when sometimes, you need a little help. You are working with all the officers, are you not?"

"Yes," she said. "I have the same information they do. But who just helped you fend off Desmond?"

"You did. And that reminded me how close you are to all of us. Even to Desmond at one time. I believe one needs a little distance to see things clearly." Ritaestelle made a gesture that encompassed all the women. "We are all so close to the problem—that problem being who is perpetrating these crimes—that perhaps we cannot see the forest for the trees."

Oh boy. The Nancy Shelton I'd come to know in the last week would surely bristle at that assessment.

But she surprised me by smiling at Ritaestelle. "You're right. It's hard for me to let go and allow other people do what I consider to be my job. If you're more comfortable at Mrs. Hart's house, then I will follow you there and make sure you arrive safely."

Justine, Muriel and Augusta all murmured their agreement. But did any of these women truly agree? Or was it simply in their best interest to go along with the woman who held the purse strings? How deep did the jealousy run? Because it existed. I'd felt it earlier today. I'd been feeling it all along, but on a subconscious level. Seeing them all here together, with everyone being so kind and polite, seeing Ritaestelle exert her will in her soft-spoken yet insistent way—well, I saw how life must have been in the Longworth house. Probably for a very long time. The jealousy might be what Ritaestelle feared. Those undercurrents of ill will would pull her down if she went back there. She was smart enough to know it, too.

"Are you ready to head back to my house?" I asked Ritaestelle.

She started to rise, and everyone wanted to be the one to help her up. But Muriel got to her first. She said, "Before you go, Ritaestelle, I want to tell you how sorry I am."

"Sorry for what?" Ritaestelle said.

Muriel seemed flustered. "For everything. For me taking advantage of you. For—"

Shelton said, "She'll be back home soon enough, and you can sit down together. But Ritaestelle looks too tired to chat right now." Shelton looked at me. "You ready?"

I glanced over and saw that Kara and Brennan were still talking to the Prestons. Kara would get her story, no matter what Nancy Shelton said or did.

"Let me say good-bye to Kara," I said.

After I did and she told me she would call me tomorrow, we left. Muriel, Justine and Augusta had already gone by the time we went out the door. I told Shelton there was no need to follow us, that we'd be fine, but she insisted. Being on the sidelines of this investigation was getting to her, and I couldn't blame her.

The umbrellas had been a good idea, because rain had started to fall. Nancy Shelton kept a firm grip on Rita-estelle's elbow, while I managed to keep us dry during the walk to the car.

Once Ritaestelle and I were driving home, I decided to ask her about the tranquilizers. When I told her about the discovery, she seemed dumbfounded.

"Someone could have ordered drugs with my name on the bottle? Prescription drugs?" she said.

"If they knew enough about you, I think so. The police may be able to see which computer was used to place the order. It's all just more gaslighting," I said.

"Who could be that vindictive?" She shook her head. "I truly do not understand this."

"I believe that Evie found out, and that's why she was murdered," I said. "She did have access to all the computers."

"Our Evie was quite knowledgeable about the computers, of that much I am certain," she said. "Seems a computer can be used to do great harm even though it can also be used to make life easier. She did learn about Farley's problems through monitoring his computer—at my request."

Ah. I'd been right about that. "Could Farley be angry enough with Evie to kill her?" I said.

"I believe that Farley is a coward at heart," Ritaestelle said. "He is far different from his father. I can see him involved in petty crimes, yes. He was already in debt—or would have been had I not been foolish enough to take care of what he owed. But a serious crime like murder? He is not brave enough to kill someone."

"I tend to agree with you," I said, thinking about him as Tom had described him—as a bully.

We fell silent, and I pulled into my driveway ten minutes later. Nancy Shelton pulled up behind me seconds later and got out of her car.

We walked to the front door together, Shelton behind us.

"Thank you so much, Nancy," Ritaestelle said. "You have been most helpful."

She said, "Jillian has a button that might belong to me. I'd like to retrieve it."

"Sure," I said. "Might take me a minute to find it."

We entered the house, and the button she'd come for was right at the junction of the hall and foyer. I picked it up, and my stomach lurched. There was indeed fabric clinging to the button—but more than I'd thought. The navy blue fabric of Nancy Shelton's suits. This button had not fallen off—it had been ripped off. This was what Syrah had been digging for in the pine needles. And he'd carried it back inside the house the night Evie was murdered.

Shelton said, "I see you understand. I won't be needing that button now." Her voice was as hard as granite, her gray eyes cold.

And then she pulled a gun from beneath her jacket.

# Thirty-one

"Both of you, into the living room," Shelton said. Ritaestelle didn't budge. "Nancy, whatever has come over you?"

"You. You came over me a long, long time ago." She pushed Ritaestelle's shoulder with her free hand. "Get into the living room."

I took Ritaestelle's arm and tugged. "Come on. Let's do as she says."

The poor woman's expression was a mixture of fear and confusion. "Certainly. Most certainly."

Shelton followed us into the living room, where four cats were all on their feet *and* on alert. They sensed the danger, probably the minute they'd heard Shelton's voice.

"Why did you kill her?" I said. "Did she find out what you were up to?"

Shelton smiled contemptuously. "What *was* I up to?"

"Gaslighting Ritaestelle. But why?" I said.

"It's none of your business. It was never any of your business," Shelton said. "Turn around."

Goose bumps rose on my arms. "If you plan to kill me, at least explain why."

"I don't owe you any explanation." She swung the gun in the direction of Merlot, whose coat was puffed out so much he looked like a lion. "If you don't turn around, I'm taking out one of your precious cats."

I immediately did as she commanded.

Ritaestelle sounded surprisingly calm as she said, "You

do not want to do this, Nancy. I have harmed you in some serious fashion, so shoot me, not Jillian."

"Shut up," Shelton said. "Just stay where I can see you. And you, cat woman, put your hands behind your back."

Seconds later I felt the cold metal on my wrists, heard the clink as the cuffs snapped closed.

"Get over to the couch and sit. Now." Shelton's voice sounded stressed, and all the anger she'd obviously held in check was pouring out in her words and actions.

I did as I was told, my heart pounding. Was I about to watch her kill Ritaestelle? I would be helpless to stop her, and the thought made my stomach roil.

Using one hand, Shelton lifted her jacket and removed her thin black belt. She turned to Ritaestelle and said, "If you move one inch, I will kill her. Understand?"

Ritaestelle nodded. "I understand. But we can work this out, Nancy. We have been friends for so many years and—"

"You were *never* my friend. You stole from me. You ruined the best thing that ever happened in my life." Shelton knelt at my feet and bound my ankles together with the belt.

Though the temptation to kick her or knee her in the face was strong, that could be a huge mistake. She might manage to hold on to the gun and kill Ritaestelle or one of my cats if I did hurt her. I glanced around and noted that the cats had the sense to have slinked out of the room—or at least out of sight.

When Shelton was finished binding me, she rose and pointed her gun at Ritaestelle again. "Where's your cat?"

"She ran away. She is frightened. I am frightened, Nancy." But Ritaestelle sounded so composed. How did she do that?

"Good. You should be scared. Let's find that cat. Now."

They started looking, with Shelton holding the gun in the small of Ritaestelle's back.

Why did she want Isis? I didn't understand any of this. What was this *best thing that ever happened* that she'd mentioned?

Oh, but I had an idea.

I recalled Ritaestelle talking about the past, how Desmond had once been involved with Nancy Shelton. Had he dumped her for Ritaestelle? Good possibility. And the gaslighting had begun about two months ago—when Desmond came back into Ritaestelle's life.

Would asking questions about this do any good? No. Shelton was too angry. And she obviously had a plan. The fact that she hadn't yet used her weapon was encouraging. We might be able to talk her out of whatever she wanted to do.

But when the two returned and Shelton held Chablis, not Isis, all rational thought left me. "What are you doing?" I said, hoping to conceal the panic welling up inside.

"Couldn't find Isis. But any cat will do." She waved the gun in the direction of the door. "You're driving, Ritaestelle. And if you don't follow my directions, I will kill this cat."

I closed my eyes, wanted to scream *no,* but I kept quiet. This woman was on the edge. She'd been pushed there by something she'd heard tonight. Maybe the encounter in the parking lot with Desmond? The two had spoken after Ritaestelle and I went into the funeral home. Right now, whatever they'd said to each other didn't matter. What mattered was the safety of Ritaestelle and Chablis.

But before I could think of something, anything, to do, Shelton, Ritaestelle and my Chablis left.

I took a deep breath, trying to contain the terror I felt. I had to get out of these cuffs. I had to free my feet.

But how?

Slowly, tentatively, three cats ventured back into the living room. A few tears escaped when I saw them. Merlot jumped up on the couch and began to sniff me.

Syrah leaped onto the coffee table and stared at me as if to say, "What's wrong? Get up."

Isis joined him and they sat there together looking at me.

Syrah may have been able to open doors, but handcuffs were a different story. This was my problem.

Maybe I could get to the security alarm or the landline. I could still use my fingers, even if they were behind me. But just as I was about to get up and hop to the kitchen, I felt my phone in my back pocket.

I tried to visualize the face of the phone and remembered the phone icon was at the bottom left-hand corner. I moved my hands to the right-hand pocket, ready to at least press that icon, then visualize exactly where each number might be, but before I could do this, just moving made the phone redial the last person I'd spoken to. Pocket dialing. This had happened before with my very sensitive touch-screen phone. I never thought in a million years I would be so glad to accidentally call someone.

I heard the phone ring once, twice and then heard the faint sound of Candace's voice.

"Hey, Jillian, how was the visitation?" I could barely hear her say. Her voice was distant and muffled by my clothing.

I shouted, "Candace, can you hear me?"

"Jillian?" she called louder. "What's going on?"

Merlot bent his head against my hip and rubbed against me. Then he began a loud, throaty, insistent meow.

"Merlot?" I could hear Candace say.

At the top of my lungs, I yelled, "Help me."

"Jillian? What's wrong?" This time Candace was shouting, too.

"Come to my house. My *house*," I yelled.

"Your house?"

"Yes." I choked down a sob and hollered, "Yes," louder.

"I'm on my way. Don't hang up," she shouted.

Hang up? I couldn't hang up if I tried.

But I decided that trying to dial 911 was still a good idea. I stood and hopped toward the landline on the kitchen counter. I turned around and tried to pick up the receiver. And dropped it on the tile floor. I heard it break apart, and plastic pieces slid in front of me.

All three cats had followed me and now surrounded me, and Syrah pawed at the broken phone. He then looked up at me and added his own meows to Merlot's—because Merlot had not quit.

The alarm was connected to the Mercy police station, and though I managed to get the pantry door open where the control panel was, the panic button—in fact the entire control panel—was too high for me to reach. It was about three inches too high for me to touch, even with my nose.

I needed a chair, but as I was using my knees and thighs to slowly, painstakingly push a chair toward the pantry, Candace burst through the front door, her weapon drawn.

She wore her pajamas.

"Shelton's taken Ritaestelle and Chablis," I said. "I don't know where they—"

"They're at the mansion," Candace said as she grabbed a kitchen knife to pick the handcuffs open. "When I called Mike, he said as many officers as possible are on the way over there, that Shelton was holding everyone at gunpoint."

"They're still alive?" I said as she freed me.

"Far as I know," Candace said. "I called Tom. He should be here any minute."

I bent and removed the belt from my ankles. "We have to go there. Now."

# Thirty-two

The scene on the circular drive outside Ritaestelle's mansion was pure chaos. We'd been stopped at a roadblock at the entrance to the long driveway, but when the deputy saw Candace in Tom's car, he'd waived us through. I couldn't count the number of police cars in front of the house, their whirling lights blurred by the steady rain.

Tom had arrived at my place only seconds after I'd removed the belt from my ankles. We made it to the Longworth estate in less than fifteen minutes. After I'd explained that Shelton had simply snapped and I wasn't sure why, we'd said nothing else during the drive. We were all too worried about what we would find when we arrived.

Mike Baca stood on the front porch talking on his cell phone. He waved us to him when he saw us get out of Tom's car.

"Shelton's asking for us to bring Desmond Holloway here, but I'm not sure that's what she really wants," Mike said.

"Why?" I asked.

"Because," he said, "I'm talking to George Robertson on his cell phone. He says Shelton and Ritaestelle are in the study. Shelton has given Ritaestelle a gun and told her to either shoot her or Shelton will shoot your cat. Ritaestelle is trying to talk her out of this." He spoke into the receiver then. "What's going on, George?" He listened and then said, "Okay, good. Tell them to come out with their hands raised."

Relief washed over me. "They're coming out?"

"The family members, not Shelton or Ritaestelle," he said.

My heart sank.

"You come, too, George," Mike said. "We'll take it from here." Another pause. "No. You need to get out of there. A hostage negotiator is on the way."

Just then the front door opened, and Justine, Hildie, Muriel and Augusta all filed out, hands in the air. "Where's Farley?" I said.

"Took off with a suitcase full of stuff earlier today," Mike said. "We'll find out later what, if anything, he had to do with this mess."

Uniformed Woodcrest officers grabbed the women as they came out and pulled them off the porch.

My heart was pounding, and I probably would have run into that house if not for Tom's grip on my shoulders.

Only a second later, a gunshot sounded.

Not only could we hear it through the open door, but it sounded through Mike's phone as well.

"Talk to me, George," Mike shouted. And then Mike took off, yelling, "Go, go, go," to the officers waiting with their weapons ready. Mike pointed at Candace. "See where that stupid ambulance is. It was supposed to be here ten minutes ago."

But Tom said, "I've got this, Candace. You two get away from the house." He pulled out his phone. But before he completed the call, the ambulance came roaring down the drive.

I wasn't moving. I wanted to get in there. I *had* to get in there.

Candace said, "Come on. We need to give them room to do their jobs."

Reluctantly I followed Tom and Candace back to Tom's Prius.

I was so stunned by the sound of that shot that I felt numb. "Do you think Ritaestelle's dead? Did Shelton kill Chablis? What is—"

Tom pulled me to him and pushed my wet hair away from my face. "We'll know soon. Let's get out of this rain."

Candace wore my raincoat and had the sense to open an umbrella so as not to allow her stitches to get wet. As for me, I no longer even felt the rain.

She climbed in, and Tom and I sat in the front seats, but we all left our doors open.

Why did someone else have to die? I thought. *Why?*

The wait seemed endless. Finally, paramedics pushed a stretcher out the front door. I immediately jumped out of the car to see who was on the stretcher, to see if the body's face was covered because someone had died.

As they pulled the stretcher to the back of the ambulance, I had my answer. It was Nancy Shelton. She was alive, her body strapped tightly down. Her head was moving from side to side, and she was shouting, "No," over and over.

One shot. One shot. Unless something else happened that we hadn't heard, Ritaestelle and Chablis were okay. They had to be okay.

Mike Baca emerged through those giant front doors and waved us to him.

I had never run so fast in my life. I even beat Tom to the door.

As we joined Mike, he pointed at Jerry Raymond. "The redheaded woman. Cuff her and bring her inside." He turned to us. "And by the way, what are you doing here, Candy?"

"Long story, Chief," she said.

"My fault," I said. "Are they all right?"

Mike nodded. "Miss Longworth is asking for the two of you." Mike looked at both Tom and me. "Go in, but stay away from that room on the right. We have to process the scene in there."

We entered the house.

Meanwhile, Mike turned his attention to Candace, who stopped in the foyer. "I can't have my best officer sick for any longer than necessary. You shouldn't have come here." He looked at her quizzically. "Are you wearing your pj's?"

"I'd say I wore the appropriate outfit," Candace said.

"You should rest that great brain of yours," Mike said.

I glanced back to see Deputy Jerry Raymond leading Muriel inside. She was crying crocodile tears. George Robertson stood in the hallway up ahead talking to a uniformed Woodcrest officer. He smiled when he spotted us.

Mike had a grip on Candace's elbow. "George, this one needs to sit down, lie down or—

"I'm fine, Chief," Candace said. "You can't shut me out of this one."

Mike inhaled and let it out in a huff. "All right, but you sit, you stay quiet, you—"

"I promise," Candace said.

Then Mike led us to the dining room.

Ritaestelle was sitting at the table talking to a Woodcrest officer, my cat held close to her chest. Her face was ashen.

When she saw me, she said, "I am so very sorry, Miss Jillian. But your precious Chablis is fine. She is a little afraid, but she's fine."

We all sat down, and Mike said to the Woodcrest officer, "Thanks for letting us talk in here, Deputy Franklin."

"Miss Longworth has quite the tale to tell," Franklin said. "You up to starting over?"

Ritaestelle smiled wanly. "I most certainly am, Malcolm." She scanned all our faces. "I remember when Malcolm was just a baby. I was at his baptism."

Candace said, "What happened, Miss Longworth?"

"Let us ask the questions, Candy—I mean Candace," Mike said. "We can handle this. You've been—"

"I am fine. Do go on, Miss Longworth," Candace said.

"First," Ritaestelle said, looking down at Chablis. "I expect someone wants to be in familiar arms."

She held my cat out, and I took Chablis from her and held her close. She began to purr—and shed clumps of hair that stuck to my wet blouse. When cats are afraid some of them do shed like this.

I sat down, and Ritaestelle began to speak. "This all began many years ago, when Nancy and I were very young and matters of the heart left both of us scarred. We both hid our scars well—but they were always there."

"This was about Desmond Holloway, wasn't it?" I said.

"Yes, but about so much more. I thought I was being a kind person, a generous person, but I was wrong. I have hurt others. As Mr. Stewart so aptly put it"—she smiled at Tom—"I have lived my life wearing blinders."

She went on to talk about Desmond, how he told her when they first became romantically involved decades ago that he was done with Shelton—and all the others. "I never knew how hurt Nancy was when he chose me. Of course, he only chose me because I had money. When he returned to Woodcrest two months ago, Nancy informed me tonight that he did not even recognize her. She had to tell him who she was. You can imagine how upset that made her."

Tom nodded. "I'd substitute 'enraged' for 'upset.' That rage is what started everything."

"Yes," Ritaestelle said. "When she reminded him who she was, he compounded the problem by telling her that he'd come back to be with me."

George entered the room with a blanket over his arm and carrying a tray. I flashed back to earlier in the day. So much had happened since.

Once he'd set down coffee and sweet rolls and home-made chocolate chip cookies, he stopped by Ritaestelle's chair at the head of the table. "I am so happy to have my lady home." Then he took the blanket to Candace, helped her remove the raincoat and draped the blanket around her shoulders.

Ritaestelle smiled at him—such a sweet, gentle smile—before he turned and left.

"We pushed Shelton tonight," Mike said. "We gave her enough information about the case—that we had a print on the medicine bottle, one in the car, that the financials were coming in tomorrow, that Miss Longworth probably didn't order the tranquilizers, and—"

"But Shelton wasn't in this house day and night," I said. "How could she drug Ritaestelle, hide stolen items and—" I stopped, picturing Muriel in handcuffs. "Oh. She had help."

"Yes," Ritaestelle said. "The way Muriel acted at the funeral home, the way she was apologizing? Nancy told me she knew Muriel would . . . what was the word she used? Fold. Yes. She said that Muriel would fold."

"Okay, I get all this," Candace said. "But what happened in here? What happened tonight? I don't get any of that."

Ritaestelle closed her eyes briefly. "Yes. That was quite terrifying. Chief Baca, would you mind pouring me a cup of coffee? And if anyone would care for something stronger?" She raised her eyebrows. "George would be happy to bring you anything you would like. Brandy? A cocktail? Wine?"

Even though wine sounded wonderfully medicinal, I opted for coffee. We all did. I even poured half-and-half from the little china pitcher into a saucer for Chablis. I held the saucer so she could lap up the treat.

"This coffee is great," Candace said, nodding. Then she winced and touched the back of her head. "Remind me not to nod. Nancy Shelton sure knows how to take someone down. But why me?"

"You printed everyone yesterday," I said. "I think she stole your print cards because she knew Muriel might have left print evidence somewhere it shouldn't have been—like in the Caddy. But deep down she knew this was all coming to an end." I looked at Mike. "Right, Chief?"

"Yup. Things were spinning out of control, and tonight she decided to make one last headline by making a splash. She wanted to humiliate you, Miss Longworth. Make sure people in town talked about you for a long time."

"I sort of remember taking the fingerprints," Candace murmured. She still wasn't my normal Candace. "Sorry. What happened when she brought you here?"

Ritaestelle looked at me. "I am so grateful she did not harm you." Then she stared at the wall straight ahead. "When Nancy brought me inside at gunpoint, she threatened to kill anyone who came near us or anyone who tried to leave. She told George to line everyone up in the hallway and that she would know if anyone tried to leave. Then we went into the study. Of course George called the police immediately, though I did not know that at the time."

"This is the confusing part. What did she want?" I asked.

"Like Chief Baca said," Ritaestelle replied, "she wanted to make an exit that would forever link us. She wanted me to kill her."

"*What?*" I said. "Shoot her?"

"Yes. I ended up doing so, too. But only because she was about to . . . to harm your precious cat. I could not have that. As soon as we sat down in the study, she held your poor cat so tightly, and then she produced another gun, one she had strapped to her ankle."

"Even bad cops don't go anywhere without their backup weapons, I guess," Tom said.

"She set the gun on the table between us and told me that I was going to kill her. That was to be my legacy, she said—that I had killed a crazy woman in my fancy house. And if I did not pick up the gun and shoot her, then she would kill poor Chablis and then shoot herself. Whatever scenario I chose, the damage would be done."

Ritaestelle released a tremulous breath, the first time I'd seen her less than calm. "But first, she wanted me to know about all the harm I'd done. How I had driven Justine to drink, spoiled Farley, supported my freeloading cousins. Then she told me how she had enlisted Muriel to help her make me look like a fool to everyone—and that Muriel was happy to help. Ruining my reputation, she said, was the best revenge for stealing the only man she had ever cared about and for acting like I was running Woodcrest—even though being in charge was her job as police chief. She said she truly enjoyed every minute of listening to people talk about me when the shoplifting became known. Everyone was whispering and shaking their heads in confusion and contempt at what Nancy called my fall from grace."

"What about Evie?" I said softly. "Why did she kill her?"

Ritaestelle lifted her coffee cup to her lips with shaky hands and sipped. "That is the saddest part of all this. Nancy told me that she was simply in the way. Evie came here the night I left to seek your help, Jillian, though I had no idea. When I drove out of the garage and away from the house, I never even saw Evie's car parked near the front door."

"Why was she here?" Tom asked. "Was it something she learned from the family computers?"

"Yes. She had called here about the passwords the night she died. Through these passwords, she had discovered that Muriel ordered those drugs using my credit card. She confronted her. But when Evie heard me leave, she took off after me. Unfortunately, Muriel immediately phoned Nancy." Ritaestelle hung her head. "This is all my fault. I was so unaware of what was going on around me."

"Shelton caught up with Evie at Jillian's house," Tom said. "They argued, Evie ran off or Shelton ordered her down to the lake, and we know the rest."

Ritaestelle said, "Nancy did not offer details except to say that Evie was about to make a serious mistake, that she had to stop her." She gazed down at her hands. "I have never even held a gun before tonight, never wanted to since my dear brother died in that hunting accident. I am only grateful that I hit what I aimed for. Her shoulder. My wonderful George rushed in and took care of me as he has done for so many years."

"Envy," I said quietly, stroking my sleeping cat. "I understand now why it's considered one of the deadly sins."

# Thirty-three

A week later, my cats had finally settled back into their normal routine. Isis, according to Ritaestelle, was happy to be home, but she was considering adopting a kitten as her playmate. Farley still hadn't turned up, but Ritaestelle said that when he ran out of money, she expected he'd return. And she promised that she would not take him in, that she would tell him to get a job.

Meanwhile, I'd managed to collect almost all those buttons. The one that belonged to Nancy Shelton, however, was in an evidence envelope somewhere. If Shelton hadn't popped another button, if she hadn't feared that I'd find the one she lost in her struggle with Evie, things might have turned out differently. Yes, my cats had once again helped me figure things out—and Merlot, Candace told me, was good at sounding the call for help.

"Merlot's never talked to me on the phone before, never made those sounds I was hearing that night," Candace said. She and Kara and I were sitting in the kitchen nook. "I knew something was wrong when I heard him so clearly and Jillian sounded so far away."

My wonderful hero, Merlot. He and Chablis were both asleep on the window seat, and I smiled at how peaceful they looked. Syrah was probably on the hunt for buttons I hoped he wouldn't find—at least for a while.

"So Merlot is why you knew Jillian was in trouble when she managed to do a redial that night?" Kara asked before sipping her sweet tea.

"Yes," Candace said. "He might as well have been talking." I looked past them out at the dark blue lake, thinking about a young woman who didn't have to die.

"You're sure quiet," Candace said.

I turned to her. "Sorry. It all seems so senseless. If those people would have talked out their problems, if they would have been straight with Ritaestelle, and she with them. If—"

"There are always what-ifs when it comes to murder," Candace said. "Here's one for you. What if you hadn't decided Ritaestelle was truly in need of help? If you hadn't followed your heart, Nancy Shelton might have gotten away with murder."

"I doubt that," I said. "The evidence you and Mike collected would have pointed to her eventually."

"But she might have killed Ritaestelle or herself before that happened," Kara said. She tore off a piece of the apple strudel we'd been enjoying, one of two that Ritaestelle had George deliver to me this morning.

"You sure showed up late to get your story when everything imploded at the estate last week," I said to Kara.

"Yeah," she said around a mouthful of pastry. "I was kinda busy, had my scanner turned off."

"You know, I don't think that was your shirt you were wearing when I saw you outside the Longworth house once we finally came out. Looked like, oh, maybe something a *lawyer* would wear." I smiled at her.

"Yup. Maybe an *Irish* lawyer," Candace added.

We all laughed, but Kara wasn't about to give away anything about her and Liam Brennan. Not yet, anyway.

"Shawn called me this morning," I said. "He got some great news."

"So tell us," Candace said, eyeing the strudel.

"A big anonymous donation. He said he can buy enough food and cat litter for years," I said.

"Bet I know where that came from," Kara said.

"We all do. But I liked the card that came with it." My turn to take another bite of Ritaestelle's gift. Pure heaven.

"What did the card say?" Candace asked.

"'Thank you for helping cats in trouble,'" I said, just as

Syrah leaped into my lap to have a sniff at what was on the table.

I rested a hand on his warm back—he'd been sunbathing somewhere—feeling so grateful that all of us, cats included, were safe.

Also available from

# Leann Sweeney

## *The Cat, the Professor and the Poison*
## A Cats in Trouble Mystery

Between her kitty quilt-making business and her
three beloved cats, Jill has her hands full. That
doesn't stop her from wanting to solve the
mystery of the milk cow that's gone missing from
her friend's farm.

But imagine her surprise when a stolen cow leads
to the discovery of fifty stray cats and one dead
body—a victim of cold-blooded murder...